Grey Griffins

WITHDRAWN

Grey Griffins

The Clockwork Chronicles | Book 2

THE
RELIC
HUNTERS

DEREK BENZ & J.S. LEWIS

LITTLE, BROWN AND COMPANY
New York Boston

Copyright © 2011 by Grey Griffin Industries, LLC

www.greygriffins.com

Little, Brown and Company

Hachette Book Group
237 Park Avenue, New York, NY 10017
Visit our website at www.lb-kids.com

Little, Brown and Company is a division of Hachette Book Group, Inc.
The Little, Brown name and logo are trademarks of Hachette Book Group, Inc.

First Paperback Edition: April 2012
Originally published in hardcover in May 2011 by Little, Brown and Company

Library of Congress Cataloging-in-Publication Data

Benz, Derek.
    The relic hunters / Derek Benz & J. S. Lewis. — 1st ed.
    p. cm. — (Grey Griffins. The clockwork chronicles ; bk. 2)
    Summary: Tragedy brings distance to the Grey Griffins, but their united quest to capture Von Strife continues, pitting them against killer clockworks, spiderlike beasts, and an army of animated dead as they work together to prevent the building of the Paragon Engine.
ISBN 978-0-316-04519-3 (hc) / ISBN 978-0-316-04520-9 (pb)
    [1. Friendship — Fiction. 2. Magic — Fiction. 3. Schools — Fiction.
4. Robots — Fiction. 5. Adventure and adventurers — Fiction. 6. Good and evil — Fiction. 7. Fairies — Fiction.] I. Lewis, J. S. (Jon S.) II. Title.
    PZ7.B44795Rel 2011
    [Fic] — dc22

                                                                    2010041553

10 9 8 7 6 5 4 3 2 1

RRD-C

Printed in the United States of America

DEDICATION

Derek:

For Ioulia and Noah, my inspiration. And for my Columbia University friends who stood in the trenches with me for the last two years. You are the best.

Jon:

For Chewbacca, who is more than a sidekick. Without you, the *Millennium Falcon* would have never made the Kessel Run in less than twelve parsecs.

THE GREY

THE LEADER: Max Sumner

After his grandfather's mysterious death, Max learned that his billionaire family was a part of the secret Templar society. He became the Guardian of the *Codex Spiritus*, an enchanted book that holds monsters, evil faeries, and other dangerous creatures captive within its magical pages. The *Codex* can change shapes, from a book to a ring to a gauntlet capable of channeling Max's family power: Skyfire!

THE INVENTOR: Harley Davidson Eisenstein

Built like a linebacker and incredibly smart, Harley is a technological prodigy who designs gadgets critical to any successful monster hunt. Unlike Max's wealthy family, Harley and his mother are barely getting by. But he's not bothered; he knows that happiness isn't measured by how much money you have in your bank account.

GRIFFINS

THE SLEUTH: Natalia Romanov

Fearless, fiery, and intensely smart, Natalia uses her keen observational skills and her analytical mind to solve any mystery. As a part of her sleuthing kit, Natalia carries a Phantasmoscope, which allows her to see into the faerie spectrum. Since a close friend betrayed her, Natalia has had a hard time trusting other girls. She feels more at home with the Griffins than with anyone else.

THE CHANGELING: Ernie Tweeny

Ernie became a changeling after a transfusion of faerie blood, which gave him super speed, rapid healing, and enhanced eyesight. But there's a catch: whenever Ernie uses his powers, he becomes more faerie and less human. Despite that risk, he has vowed to fight evil as his superhero alter ego, Agent Thunderbolt.

THE KNIGHTS TEMPLAR

The Knights Templar is an ancient society that has sworn to protect mankind against unseen dangers like monster invasions and zombie uprisings. Recently, the Templar were nearly exterminated by an army of werewolves called the Black Wolf Society. They are slowly rebuilding their strength.

MAX SUMNER STUMBLED THROUGH A TUNNEL OF ice as the voices of the dead echoed all around him. They were telling him that he was going to die here, just like everyone else who had come to this haunted place.

Soon, the tunnel emptied into a circular chamber that was pulsating with blue light. People were trapped like statues inside the frozen walls. Most victims were probably around twelve years old—Max's age—when they died. Some were older and at least one was younger, but they had all suffered the same fate—their eyes were lifeless and their faces were locked in terror.

The voices grew louder. Max raised his hands to his ears, but they couldn't block out the ghastly sounds. He could feel his sanity slipping away. Then, just before he lost all sense of time and place, one voice cried out over the others.

"It's not too late...."

Max willed himself to walk to the far end of the room, where the voice was coming from. There he saw a familiar face under the ice. It was Robert Hernandez, the boy who had been murdered by a former teacher at their school.

Max reached out to Robert, but the moment his hand scraped against the ice, the ground started to shake. Fissures shot through the surface of the ice. Max jammed his fingers into the cracks and pulled away chunks of ice and rock that crumbled as they hit the floor.

Before long, Max's chest was heaving, and sweat was pouring down his forehead. As Max paused to catch his breath, he was distracted by a journal lying in the rubble. He picked it up, thumbing through the pages until he came to a sketch labeled THE PARAGON ENGINE.

The object in the sketch was covered with gears and steam-driven pistons, but the bulk of the machine was a ring. The phrase GATEWAY TO THE SHADOWLANDS AND BEYOND was written in looping script at the bottom of the page.

The room began to spin. Max nearly lost his footing. Then, in a flash, the icy crypt was gone, and Max was standing in the shadows of the Paragon Engine. It was real. Gears spun with rhythmic precision. Energy shimmered in the center of the ring like the surface of the sea, and the silhouette of a boy gradually emerged. Max pounded against the energy, but he couldn't break through. Tendrils of frozen light leaped out and grabbed him by the arm.

Max was about to scream. Then he saw the face of the boy on the other side. His voice failed. Max was looking at himself!

Frost crept over his boots, then up his legs. Max tried

to break free. He was too weak. It climbed into his mouth, down his throat, and into his lungs. Breathing became impossible.

Max sat up in his bed with wild eyes, gasping for air. His chest was heaving and his skin was covered in goose bumps. It was as if he'd burst out of freezing water to gasp for air. Another nightmare. Another premonition?

Max reached for his dream journal. He was still in a haze as he struggled to pick up the pen. Not that it mattered. By the time he was ready to record an entry, the dream had slipped from his memory.

PART ONE

DIVIDED

MONSTER HUNTERS

Strange things had been happening in Avalon, Minnesota.

Once known for ice-cream socials and its quaint Main Street, the tiny town in the middle of nowhere had been overrun by the bizarre. Last night, a Tundra Troll destroyed a fishing shack that sat on the icy surface of the lake. Witnesses thought it might have been some kind of bear, but it was dark and they didn't get a good look. Besides, bears don't have horns coming out of the sides of their heads or tusks jutting up from their jaws.

"It's a good thing nobody was here," Max Sumner said as he walked through what was left of the fishing shack. Even though he was only twelve years old, Max was the leader of the Grey Griffins, a team of young monster hunters tasked with saving the world from the creatures that go bump in the night.

Natalia Romanov pulled a clump of white fur out of a splintered board and inspected it with her Phantasmoscope, a multi-lens magnifying glass that allowed her to see into the faerie spectrum. "It was definitely a Tundra Troll."

"The tracks are heading out to the island," Harley Eisenstein said, kneeling in the snow. He was a head taller than the other two, and his shoulders were nearly twice as broad.

"It's weird being here without Ernie," Natalia said as she sealed the fur specimen in a plastic bag.

Ernie Tweeny was the fourth member of the Grey Griffins. A transfusion of faerie blood had turned Ernie into a changeling and given him superpowers. Now he could run faster than the eye could see. The adjustment hadn't been difficult until his friend Robert Hernandez, another changeling, was murdered. Ernie was convinced that the Grey Griffins could have saved Robert, which was why he hadn't spent any time with them over their winter break.

"I thought changelings couldn't get sick," Harley said.

"They can't," Natalia said. "The faerie blood enhances their immune system. They even heal faster than we do."

"He's not sick," Max said. "He's avoiding us."

"That's ridiculous," Natalia said.

4

"What if he's right?" Max asked. "I mean, maybe we could have saved Robert."

"Robert is dead because a lunatic ripped his soul out of his body," Natalia said. "We didn't have anything to do with that."

Max sighed. "I guess."

"We better get going," Harley said. "These tracks are pretty old. We don't want that thing showing up at your grandma's back door."

Harley was a virtuoso when it came to anything with a motor, and he had retrofitted the Griffins' snowmobiles with steam-powered propulsion units.

Snow spit out from the treads of their snowmobiles as the three friends tore across the surface of the lake in pursuit of the Tundra Troll. When Harley's skis hit the steep shoreline of the island, he pressed a button. Silver flames erupted from the tailpipes, and the snowmobile shot into the air.

It touched down, sending snow exploding into the air. Then Harley shot toward a narrow path that was cut into the trees.

"Right behind you," Natalia said through her communication link. She'd decided to take a more cautious approach. Her engine groaned as she climbed up the steep embankment.

Once Natalia was a safe distance away, Max activated

his propulsion unit. The momentum sent him flying up the hill. He jumped higher than he'd intended to, and the snowmobile started to pull away. His legs ended up in a full split, and his fingers began slipping from the handlebars.

Max crashed to the ground. His head snapped forward before the momentum nearly threw him off the back of the snowmobile. Somehow he'd managed to hang on, but now he was heading toward the trunk of a maple tree. He thrust the handlebars to the right. The tread skidded as the snowmobile went sideways toward another tree. He twisted back to the left, straightening the snowmobile, and headed down the path after the other two.

The sun was just starting to rise, but it was caught behind a bank of clouds that threatened to unleash another winter storm. Without the headlights on their snowmobiles, it would have been impossible to follow the winding path through the forest.

"Are you picking anything up on the scanner?" Max asked over the roar of his motor. He could see Natalia up ahead. Her auburn braids were flailing behind her helmet as she sped along the trail.

"*Not yet,*" Max heard Harley say through his earpiece. "*Wait. . . . there's something big, and it's heading our way.*"

There was a loud crack before a tree fell across the path, and the impact shook the ground. Harley pulled back on his brakes to avoid the tree, but he was still going too fast. The snowmobile veered to the left, then the right, before smashing into a snowbank.

The snowmobile stopped, but Harley didn't. He flew over the handlebars and into the trees, where he landed on gnarled roots jutting up from the snow. Harley groaned as his breath rushed out of his lungs.

"Harley!" Natalia shouted. She pulled up just as an enormous creature stepped out from the shadows. It stood over ten feet tall and had mangy white fur that hung damp from the snow.

The Tundra Troll threw its head back and roared. The horrible sound echoed through the trees, sending birds leaping from their perches into the sky.

Harley scrambled to his feet, ignoring his aching ribs and sore back. He reached his snowmobile as the Tundra Troll towered over Natalia. The monster looked down at her before tilting its head to the side, saliva dripping from its massive jaw and onto the snow. With nostrils flared, it roared once more.

Natalia cowered, covering her head with her arms. Max tore off his helmet and removed the glove on his right hand. He twisted the enchanted ring on his finger, and the ring shimmered before melting into a liquid that coated his hand, forming a medieval glove. Max flexed his fingers, and streaks of blue energy crackled across the surface.

At the same time, Harley pulled a multishot grenade

launcher from the holster of his snowmobile. He threw the strap over his head before bringing the butt of the launcher to his shoulder.

Max raised the gauntlet. A bolt of blue lightning shot from his palm. It lit up the morning haze and slammed into the troll's shoulder, knocking the monster off balance. Max struck again. The troll shook its head before bellowing. It picked up the fallen tree and threw it at Max, but the beast missed.

Harley pulled the trigger of the grenade launcher. A canister shot from the barrel and burst, shooting out a net. Like Max's gauntlet, the net crackled with blue light as it wrapped around the troll's head and torso. The troll fought to break free, but the energy singed its skin and held back the monster.

Natalia took deep breaths and then closed her eyes as she reached for the oversized revolver that hung from the holster on her hip. Each cartridge was filled with enough tranquilizer serum to knock an elephant out for a week. She took aim with both hands, then squeezed the trigger three times in rapid succession. The first dart struck the monster in the neck. The second hit its shoulder. The third, its stomach.

The Tundra Troll became enraged, ripping the net in two before tossing it aside. The monster looked down at the darts sticking out of its hide and pulled them out in succession. Its eyelids were heavy. It stumbled, but it wasn't done.

The troll lunged for Max, but there was a blur of motion as a white wolf tore out from the shadows and jumped over the fallen tree. The Tundra Troll spun around. The wolf leaped, its jaws wide, and it clamped down on the troll's shoulder. They fell to the ground, and snow rose in a great cloud. When it settled, the wolf was standing on the troll's chest with its muzzle pulled back in a wicked snarl.

The Tundra Troll picked up the wolf by the nape of its neck and threw it into a tree trunk, where the wolf crumpled.

"Sprig!" Max shouted.

The troll tried to stand. It made it to one knee before its eyes started to close. Natalia hit it with another dart, this time in its back. The monster yowled, grabbing at the tranquilizer dart, which was just out of its reach. Harley stood on the fallen tree, looking down at the troll, with the barrel of his grenade launcher pointed at the monster, but he didn't need to pull the trigger.

The troll swayed, then fell. Its breathing was shallow as it lay unconscious. Breathing heavily, Max walked over to join his friends as they looked down at the sedated monster.

"I don't know how long the serum is going to last," Natalia said. She took off her helmet and strapped the tranquilizer gun back in her holster.

"You know, I wonder what kind of pet a Tundra Troll would make," Harley said.

"You're kidding, right?" Natalia said.

"I don't know. Think what would happen if a burglar tried to break into your house and he found one of these babies."

"I'd rather not."

Max raised his palm and released a stream of light from his gauntlet. The blue energy swirled until it formed a crackling sphere of light. The captivity orb hit the troll in the chest, and the blue hue began spreading over its body. Once the Tundra Troll was encased, a bright light flashed, and the orb and the troll disappeared.

"Nice work," Max said to Harley and Natalia. Then he walked into the woods to check on Sprig.

No longer a wolf, the shape-shifting faerie had turned back to her natural form. With large eyes, pointed ears, spiky fur, and a pink nose, she looked almost feline as she lay in the snow.

Spriggans were famous for being mischievous, sometimes ruining crops and spoiling milk. But once they found a human partner, they were the most loyal creatures—at least so far as a faerie could be loyal.

"Are you okay?" Max asked.

Sprig was licking blood off her forepaw. "We are fine," she said, her voice soft. Max could barely hear her above the wind. He reached out to pet her back, but she recoiled under his touch. "It's a bit tender."

"What was that?" Harley asked.

"What?" Natalia said. "I didn't hear anything."

Max stood up.

"There it is again," Harley said. "Did you hear it?"

"What was it?" Max asked.

"I don't know.... It was moving too fast, but it sounded like branches snapping." Harley loaded his grenade launcher and moved off the path.

SURROUNDED

"Was it another Tundra Troll?" Natalia asked as she followed Harley into the forest.

"I don't think so," Harley said. "They can't move that fast."

Overhead, Sprig, who had shifted into a falcon, landed on a branch as Harley scrambled onto the trunk of a fallen tree. He pulled out his binoculars.

"Do you see anything?" Max asked.

"Not yet," Harley said.

"What about you, Natalia?" Max said. "Are you picking anything up in the faerie spectrum?"

Natalia was scanning the area through her Phantasmoscope. Faeries could stay hidden to the naked eye by appearing as mice, butterflies, chipmunks, or any number of other animals. But with the Phantasmoscope, Natalia could see through their disguises. "Something passed through here," she said, "but the trace is so weak that I can hardly detect it."

Max frowned as he walked into a clearing and knelt down.

"What is it?" Harley asked.

"A footprint."

"What kind?"

"Look for yourself."

Harley shook his head. "You have to be kidding me."

The print was shaped like a human foot, but the pattern looked like a tire tread. There was only one person who wore shoes like that.

Natalia cupped her hands around her mouth. "You might as well come out, Ernie!" she called.

All they heard was the wind whistling between the branches.

"Come on!" Harley said. "Stop messing around."

Still nothing.

"The tracks go this way," Harley said.

Max and Natalia followed him on a winding path that zigzagged and wound through the trees before ending at a house in shambles.

It looked like it used to be a grand Victorian structure. There were gabled windows, a turret, and a porch that wrapped around the front. Time had stolen its beauty. Windows were broken, a wall had caved in, the white paint had chipped away, and a portion of the roof was missing.

"Ernie went through a lot of trouble to ditch us," Max said as Sprig landed in the branches overhead. "Maybe we should leave him alone."

"That's not happening." Harley trudged up the steps to the front door.

Natalia shrugged and followed, but Max didn't move.

"Come on, Sumner," Harley said, pushing the door open. "You know how Ernie gets. He just wants attention."

Ernie stepped out from behind a tree. "No, I don't."

Natalia jumped. "You scared me."

Ernie had always been the shortest member of the Grey Griffins, but over the past year he'd grown nearly six inches. Now only Harley was taller, but not by much. Ernie was still thin, though, with a mess of black hair that needed to be cut weekly now that he was a changeling.

Despite the temperature, Ernie had foregone his winter jacket and stocking cap in favor of his Agent Thunderbolt costume. It consisted of a vintage World War I army helmet, aviator goggles, leather gloves, and a shirt with a bolt of lightning stitched across the chest.

"What are you guys doing here?" he asked.

"We're hunting a Tundra Troll," Harley said when he caught Ernie looking at his grenade launcher.

"I called you three times," Max said. "Where have you been?"

"I've been busy, I guess."

"Doing what?" Natalia asked. "Aren't you supposed to be bedridden with a debilitating cold?"

Ernie's eyes narrowed. "What does it matter?"

There was a clatter in the trees. Sprig had spotted a mouse scampering across the snow and swooped down from her perch to grab it with her talons. She returned to the branches to eat her meager meal.

"So what is this place?" Max asked.

Ernie walked up to the house and then turned back to Max. He wouldn't look him in the eye. "It's just a place I like to come to think."

"When did you find it?"

"A few days ago," Ernie said. "Look, it's no big deal. Besides, I was getting ready to go back home. Maybe I'll catch up with you later."

"You're hiding something," Natalia said. "I can tell by the way your eyes keep shifting."

"No, I'm not."

"See the way you're fidgeting? It's a classic tell. Why won't you look me in the eyes?"

"Fine," Ernie said. He looked her in the eyes. "I'm not hiding anything."

"Then you won't mind if I go inside and take a look," Harley said. He took a step toward the doorway, but Ernie got in front of him.

"I thought you weren't hiding anything," Harley said.

"Come on," Max said. "Let's leave him alone."

"I'm not going anywhere until Ernie tells us what he's doing out here," Natalia said.

"You're the detective," Ernie said. "Why don't you tell me?"

"You're infuriating, do you know that?"

"Look, we're trying to have a meeting, okay?" Ernie said.

"We?" Harley asked.

Ernie's eyes shot wide as if he wasn't supposed to say that.

"Who else is out here with you?"

"Nobody."

"It's okay," a soft voice spoke.

Max recognized the changeling who emerged from the doorway. Her name was Hale, and from the looks of things, her transformation from human to faerie had accelerated over the winter break. Her antennae had grown, her eyes were red, and her wet skin looked like it belonged to a tree frog.

"What's going on?" Natalia asked.

A dozen more changelings emerged from hiding places, each a unique combination of human and faerie.

"Think of it as our clubhouse," Hale said as she put her hand on Ernie's shoulder, which Max found odd.

"It looks like it should be condemned," Natalia said.

"Not everybody has a billionaire friend to buy them a

16

fancy place to hang out," Hale said. She was looking at Max. "People like us are stuck with whatever we can find."

There was an uncomfortable silence. Max averted his eyes and kicked at the snow. He didn't like it when people judged him for his parents' money. It wasn't his fault they were rich.

"So what's with the guns?" Hale asked.

"We were hunting," Harley said.

"For what? A dragon?"

The changelings laughed.

"Close enough," Max said. "It was a Tundra Troll."

"And you bagged it without a scratch? I'm impressed," Hale said. Max blushed from the compliment. "Those things are nasty."

"What happened to your inhibitors?" Harley asked. The dean of the changeling program at Iron Bridge Academy made all the changelings wear devices that restrained their powers. The inhibitors also carried tracking devices, which allowed Dean Nipkin to know where those students were at all times.

"Oh, we still have them," Hale said, turning so Harley could see that hers was lodged behind her ear. "We just found a way to circumvent them."

"How?" Harley asked.

"Tell him, Annie," Hale said.

A slender girl who didn't look old enough to attend Iron Bridge stepped forward. Her hands were locked behind her back, her eyes focused on the ground. "I reprogrammed them."

"You reprogrammed the inhibitors? I didn't think that was possible," Harley said.

"I can kind of control machines," Annie said.

"We still show up on the grid," Hale said. "But no matter where we go, Dean Nipkin thinks we're back at school. And now we have our full powers."

"Why didn't you do that before?" Natalia said.

"Nobody asked me," Annie said.

"Why aren't you with your families instead of hanging out here?" Natalia asked. "I mean, this is supposed to be our winter break."

"We're too dangerous," Denton said. He looked like an anthropomorphic lion, complete with intimidating fangs, a tail, and a mane that had grown thick over the last few weeks. "Nipkin convinced our parents that it was better to keep us locked up so we didn't hurt anybody."

"Ernie was able to go home," Natalia said.

Ernie turned away.

"That's because he's one of you," Denton said.

"What's that supposed to mean?" Natalia asked.

"It means he's a Grey Griffin," Hale said. "Everyone knows you get special privileges."

"No, we don't."

"Whatever," Hale said. "Look, this is as close to Christmas vacation as we're going to get, so we'd appreciate it if you wouldn't blab to Nipkin. Otherwise she's going to lock us up and throw away the key."

"How did you find out about this place?" Max asked, hoping to cut the tension. "I've lived here my whole life, and I've never seen it before."

"It used to be part of the school," Hale said. "There's an elevator that leads to one of the subway stations. It's only a few stops away from Iron Bridge."

"Raven found it," Ernie said. He held up a key that was fastened to a chain around his neck. "You need this to activate the portal inside the elevator."

"Where is she?" Natalia asked. Raven Lugosi was a changeling who had the ability to draw memories from inanimate objects. If there were secret passages, Raven could certainly find them.

"Back in Sendak Hall," Denton said. "She thinks we're reckless."

"Aren't you worried about...?"

"Smoke?" Hale asked, referring to the changeling who had kidnapped Robert. "We have a few surprises if he decides to show his face."

The other changelings murmured in agreement.

Sprig flew down from her perch. The moment she landed, she shifted into a white wolf. Her fur standing on end, she snarled, revealing a set of teeth that rivaled Denton's. "Max should leave this place."

The changelings stopped laughing. Max watched as Denton's eyes narrowed. A girl named Nadya who had been sitting in a second-story window leaped down, landing nimbly on the snow. A spray of crystals erupted from her palm to form a club of ice.

"Easy, Sprig," Max said. He reached out to scratch behind her ear. "Ernie's friends are our friends, too."

"Look, unlike the Grey Griffins, we have Ernie's back," Yi Lu said. He was flipping a fireball in his hand.

"What's that supposed to mean?" Natalia asked.

"Changelings look out for each other."

Natalia spun to face Ernie. "What did you tell them?"

Ernie turned away.

"If we had been there, Robert would still be alive," Yi said. Then flames erupted in both hands. "Unfortunately, you were there instead."

"Is that supposed to scare us?" Harley said, taking a step toward Yi. He was a head taller than the changeling, but Yi didn't back down. Sparks jumped from Yi's skin. Then his hair turned into a blaze of fire, and flames burst from his eyes.

"You tell me," Yi said. "You're the one who walked in here with a grenade launcher."

The other changelings closed ranks, circling the Grey Griffins like a pack of hungry wolves. Sprig growled before snapping at the girl holding the ice club.

Max didn't want to fight, but it didn't look like he was going to have a choice. He twisted the *Codex* ring on his finger, and the gauntlet reappeared. Blue energy sparked as Max flexed his hand.

20

Ernie stepped between Yi and Harley. "Stop it!"

Yi's chest was heaving. Harley's eyes were narrowed.

"I can't believe you told them that Robert's death was our fault," Natalia said, her fists clenched. Her body was shaking. Ernie tried to look her in the eyes, but he couldn't. "Robert is dead because Otto Von Strife tore his soul out of his body. We didn't have anything to do with that."

"We could have fixed him," Ernie said. He was mumbling. His voice was barely a whisper.

"I hope you don't honestly believe that," Natalia said. "We did what we did to save your life, and this is how you thank us? I know you're upset because your friend is dead, Ernie, but this is pathetic."

"Forget it, Natalia," Max said. The gauntlet disappeared, turning back into the *Codex* ring. "Let's just go."

Natalia started to say something else, but she closed her mouth. Then she stomped through the woods back to the snowmobiles. Harley, Max, and Sprig followed, leaving Ernie alone with the other changelings.

THE INVITATION

Ernie wasn't the only member of the Grey Griffins who'd chosen to hang out with new friends. Even though Natalia was upset, she decided to keep her plans with Brooke Lundgren, whose father was the director of Iron Bridge Academy. In the past, Natalia had been jealous of Brooke, but over the last few months the two had become fast friends.

While the girls went shopping in Bloomington, Harley headed into New Victoria with Monti McGuiness, a Templar inventor who had become something of a mentor to Harley. None of them extended an invitation to Max, so he sat alone at his kitchen table with a plate of chocolate chip cookies and a mug filled with milk.

Max lived in an enormous house on the shores of Lake Avalon. His family had more money than they could spend, but Max would have traded it all to bring them back together. His parents' divorce had been devastating, and Max just wanted things to go back to the way they used to be.

Of course that would have been impossible. It was widely believed that his father was dead, the victim of an ancient dragon by the name of Malice Striker. Max missed his dad, but he was also angry. After all, his father had betrayed the Templar by joining a band of werewolves called the Black Wolf Society. Then he manipulated Max to help in his scheme to destroy the world.

Max sighed.

"What's with the long face?" A man with short hair that blended into the stubble on his beard walked into the kitchen. He was wearing a pair of faded jeans and a tight-fitting sweater with a distressed griffin on the front. "Didn't you catch the troll?" He tossed a paper sack onto the countertop and reached over to pluck a cookie off Max's plate.

"Oh, hi, Logan," Max said. "Yeah, we got it."

"Then what's wrong?" Logan said, his Scottish accent curling his words.

Logan was his bodyguard, but Max considered him family. He was also everything Max wanted to become. The Scotsman could hold his breath for over six minutes and punch through a brick wall, and he used to race

Ferraris in Europe. However, what Max admired most was Logan's confidence. The world could be crumbling down around him, and Logan wouldn't flinch. Max wished he could be like that.

"Come on, then," Logan said. "Give us the story, will you?"

Max sighed. "Well, Ernie blew us off again."

"Is that so?"

"He told us he was too sick to go hunting, but he was actually hanging out with some of the changelings."

"I suppose it makes sense," Logan said. "They're all running scared, so they're probably relying on one another for support. I can't blame them for that."

"It's just that...I don't know. The Grey Griffins are supposed to support him. Besides, Ernie doesn't seem like the same person anymore."

"He's not," Logan said. "Change is a part of life."

"Maybe you're right."

"I'm always right," Logan said with a wry smile. "What about your other cohorts?"

"Natalia went shopping with Brooke, and Harley is somewhere in New Victoria with Monti."

"Let me get this straight," Logan said. "You're upset because your friends are having fun without you."

"When you put it like that, it sounds ridiculous."

The Sumners' plump housekeeper walked into the kitchen with an envelope in her hands. She stepped in front of Logan, ignoring the Scotsman, and handed it to Max. "I believe this is for you."

"Thanks, Rosa."

Max slipped his finger under the flap of the envelope. Then he pulled out a single piece of parchment with the Iron Bridge Academy coat of arms printed at the top.

Iron Bridge was a private military school run by the Knights Templar. Its students were trained to save the world from unseen dangers such as six-armed ogres, poltergeists, and savage werewolves.

"Very official," Logan said. "What is it?"

"Apparently, I'm being transferred into a class called Archaeological Reconnaissance and Excavation."

"Who's the teacher?"

"It doesn't say." Max tossed the paper across the table. "With my luck, it'll be Nipkin."

"Maybe this will cheer you up," Logan said. He grabbed the paper sack from the countertop and tossed it to Max.

"What is it?"

The bag crinkled and crunched as Max reached in to pull out a few packs of trading cards.

"Aren't you getting a little old for that game?" Rosa said as she started preparing dinner.

"You're never too old for Round Table," Max said.

"I'd have to agree with the boy," Logan said.

The trading-card game had originally been developed

to teach children in the Templar community how to fight monsters and faeries without risk of injury. Over the centuries, children continued to play well into adulthood. Before long, games once played in the back of pubs became global tournaments.

Max opened the paper bag to dump the rest of the contents on the table. Each pack was wrapped in shiny foil. "Have they even announced the Clockwork Chaos expansion series?"

"I have a mate who works in the game-design department," Logan said. "He agreed to give me a few packs in exchange for a bit of a favor."

"Like what?"

"Don't worry about it," Logan said. "You need to learn how to take clockwork soldiers down. It starts with the cards, and then we'll start training in the SIM Chamber. After that, we'll see about a field test."

"But we've already gone up against clockworks."

"Trust me, Max. It's only just begun."

NEW VICTORIA

The usual drizzle that blanketed New Victoria had turned into a full-blown storm. Lightning flashed, thunder echoed, and Monti McGuiness pulled out what looked like a pocket watch. With the click of a button, the lid snapped open. He spun a small dial attached to the face, and a metal bar sprouted from his backpack, unfolding an umbrella over his head.

"That's better," Monti said. He removed his goggles and wiped them with a handkerchief.

"I don't suppose you have another one of those, do you?" Harley asked.

"Sorry."

"I should have remembered to bring an umbrella."
Monti looked up at the clock tower. "It's too late
tonight, but maybe we can rig one of these up for you
next week."

With cobblestone streets enveloped by fog and a sky-
line filled with smoke billowing from chimneys, New
Victoria could have been the backdrop of a Sherlock
Holmes story. It was on an island in the middle of Lake
Avalon, but few from the town of Avalon knew it
existed.

The strange city was caught between the world the
people of Avalon knew and the Shadowlands, a land of
wild magic ruled by an overlord named Oberon and his
bride, Titania. Because of that, New Victoria was invisible except to those who had access to the right portals.

"By the way," Harley said, "how's everything going
with those clockworks back at your workshop? Have you
been able to rebuild them yet?"

"I'm afraid not," Monti said between coughs. "I knew
Von Strife was a genius, but they're more complex than
I'd imagined. He was a century ahead of his time, maybe
more. I mean, I've been working around the clock, and I
haven't got a single machine to fire up yet."

"That's probably why you're getting sick," Harley
said. "People need to sleep."

Monti shrugged. "That and the weather, but I don't
have much choice. I'm shorthanded, and I don't see that
changing anytime soon."

"I could come by after school to help out."

Monti stroked his chin. "You know what?" he finally said. "As long as your mom is okay with it, that might work out."

"Really?"

"We'll have to find a way around the liability issues. It won't go over well in the press if you lose a hand in one of the machines."

Harley shrugged. "You could always build me a new one. You know, with interchangeable parts. There could be a grappling hook...a claw...maybe even a grenade launcher."

"You're starting to sound like Doc Trimble," Monti said, referring to the school physician, who had a prosthetic arm.

"Did you hear that?" Harley asked as they passed the graveyard behind the Cathedral of St. Peter.

Monti shook his head. "I didn't hear anything."

"There it is again," Harley said. He stopped to look through the tall iron fence, which was topped with barbs.

Monti cocked his head to the side. Then his eyes opened wide. "Moaning?"

"Yeah."

"You don't think it's...forget it."

"Zombies?"

"Impossible. Right?"

A loud gong sounded, and Monti jumped. The church bells were announcing that it was six o'clock. The sun

29

was long gone, and a thick cluster of clouds was blotting out the moon. The only source of light in the entire city was the meager gas lamps that lined the streets, and that wasn't much.

Then they heard the echo of footfalls. A man in a long coat, a scarf, and a top hat crossed their path. His brow was furrowed and his nose was sharp. Monti looked over his shoulder to make sure the stranger didn't double back. When he turned around, he could see another figure standing not half a block away.

"Who's that?" Monti asked.

"I can't tell."

The figure started walking toward them. At first he was nothing more than a silhouette against the grey sky, but soon enough Harley could see that he was dressed in an overcoat and a driving cap. He was small, but that didn't mean he wasn't dangerous. There were plenty of urbanized goblins living in New Victoria, and they could be wicked.

"Stop right there," Monti said. He flicked his wrist. A spring-loaded mechanism inside his sleeve released a small plasma pistol into his hand.

"Take it easy," the stranger said. He held his arms wide to show that he wasn't holding a weapon. As the stranger walked beneath the light of a gas lamp, Harley narrowed his eyes as his lip curled back into a snarl.

"What's wrong?" Monti asked when he saw Harley's reaction.

"That's Aidan Thorne," Harley said through his clenched jaws.

"Wait," Monti said. "You mean the changeling who took Robert?"

"We call him Smoke, but yeah," Harley said. Smoke took off the cap to reveal blond hair that was twisted into spikes, and he had a pair of aviator goggles pulled over his blue eyes.

His changeling ability allowed Smoke to teleport anywhere in the world if he'd been there before, or if the spot was in his line of sight. Smoke had been a student at Iron Bridge, but he'd turned on the Templar and helped Otto Von Strife abduct Robert Hernandez. No one had seen him since Robert's death. Until now.

"Did you miss me?" Smoke asked.

"Not especially," Harley said. "What do you want?"

"I came to deliver a message to Agent Thunderbolt."

"As you can see, he's not here."

"Yeah, I heard he's hanging out with the other changelings." Smoke turned his attention to Monti, who was still holding the plasma gun. A cloud of vapors swirled around Smoke, and he disappeared, emerging on the sidewalk with his hand wrapped around Monti's wrist. "I'll take that," he said before he vanished again. A moment later he was back where he had been.

"I don't need a plasma gun to take you out," Harley said.

"That's probably true," Smoke said. "Of course you'd

31

have to catch me first, and even if you could, you wouldn't be able to hold on."

Something moaned inside the cemetery. It was closer than before. Then more voices joined the strange choir.

Smoke smiled. He popped in front of Harley with a large envelope in his hand. "You're sure that you won't give this to Ernie?"

"What's wrong? Doesn't Von Strife pay you enough to cover the postage?" Harley asked.

"I really think the two of us could have been friends," Smoke said.

"I doubt it," Harley said.

Smoke looked down at the envelope and then at Harley. "Tell Ernie that I'm looking for him...and that I have something I think he'd be interested in."

"Ernie wasn't your biggest fan to begin with, and now that Robert's dead because of you, I'm pretty sure he's not going to want to talk to you."

"You see, that's where you're wrong," Smoke said.

Harley raised an eyebrow.

"I helped liberate Robert."

"Tell that to his parents."

"Maybe you really are as dumb as you look," Smoke said. The moaning grew louder. Smoke turned to look at the cemetery and smiled again. "Sorry, but I have work to do. See you around, Eisenstein." Smoke vanished.

"What do you think that was all about?" Monti asked.

"I don't know," Harley said. He was squinting, wondering if those silhouettes inside the cemetery were zombies or if his eyes were playing tricks. Then he turned back to Monti. "How would you stop someone who can teleport like that?"

"I'm not sure," Monti said, scratching his head. "The best you could hope to do is sedate him so he can't use his power."

"That's what I figured."

A clap of thunder shook the ground before a massive bolt of lightning flashed through the sky. Then hail started to fall, bouncing off the ground and battering the steam-powered cars parked in the street.

"We'd better get out of here," Monti said. "Besides, the subway will be here any minute."

THE AGENTS OF JUSTICE

Ernie walked briskly down the foggy street in a section of New Victoria called Bludgeon Town. He kept in the shadows, avoiding the gas lamps. He didn't want to be spotted. Not yet.

His boots clicked on the cobblestones as he crossed the street. A steam-driven car approached. Ernie side-stepped to avoid getting drenched as its tires splashed through a puddle. Then he stopped to watch the driver. It was a clockwork dressed in a coat and tie. In the back-seat sat a man in a top hat with a white scarf wrapped tightly around his neck. A beautiful woman sat beside him.

Ernie pulled the collar of his coat up around his neck and crossed over to the street corner, where a stray dog pawed at a trash can outside a butcher shop. The dog stopped to look at Ernie and growled. Ernie ignored it.

He was running late. According to the clock tower, it was nearing midnight. Ernie hoped his parents were still asleep. He didn't want them to worry, not that they needed to. One of his superpowers was being able to heal at an incredible rate.

He heard a shuffling sound behind him. Ernie walked faster down Wellington Row. Though it was Sunday, the pubs were filled with unsavory patrons. Night mongrels, they were called. Thieves, charlatans, and even murderers were among their number. They were the lords of Bludgeon Town, but Ernie wasn't here for them. He was looking for slavers—men and women who made their living by abducting people and selling them to the highest bidder.

His heart started to race, and his hands began to sweat. Ernie closed his eyes as his breathing grew shallow. "You'll be fine," he whispered. The words didn't seep past his ears. He turned down an alley.

It was dark. The fog was thick. Ernie could hear two tomcats fighting, followed by the sound of glass breaking. The footsteps still echoed behind him. Ernie smiled, but there was no joy in the expression. It was his nerves. He was frightened, yet he had never felt more alive.

Ernie looked up when he heard two people arguing

through an open window, but he couldn't stop. He was on a mission. Lives were at stake.

The scuff of shoes padding along behind him continued. Ernie risked a glance over his shoulder, but all he could see was a silhouette. The man was large, with broad shoulders and a wide belly. His hands were in his pockets, and his strides were long.

As the man passed under a gas lamp, Ernie caught a brief glimpse. His head was covered in stubble and so was his chin. There was a scar that kept his lip in a permanent snarl, and a tattoo stretched across his neck. It was a black widow, the symbol of the slavers guild.

"I got you," Ernie whispered. He'd seen the man before, or at least his picture.

Tom Glover was his name. Annie, the changeling who could control machines, had accessed the chief constable's database using her DE Tablet, a portable computing device designed by Charles Babbage. She'd pulled the records of all known slavers, and Tom was at the top of the list.

Ernie passed a wall of wooden barrels behind a pub. Ahead was a brick wall. It was a dead end, and Ernie was almost there. He clenched his jaw when the first bell sounded, announcing that it was turning midnight. Just a few more paces, Ernie thought. He started counting down, just like he had practiced.

Ten... nine... eight...

Ernie could still hear Tom following him.

Seven...six...five...

He slowed down. He needed Tom to think he was an easy target.

Four...three...two...

The echo of Tom's steps grew closer.

One.

Ernie stopped. He could feel his heart in his throat, and his lungs had trouble holding air. His skin itched, and the hairs on the back of his neck were standing up. The shuffling stopped. Ernie turned to face his hunter.

"Ho there, laddie. Are you lost?" Tom asked. He kept his hands in his pockets.

Ernie looked to the right and then the left. He didn't have to pretend to be nervous. It came naturally.

"What's wrong? You ain't one of them dumb urchins, is you?" Tom asked.

A deep breath, followed by another. "No, sir," Ernie said. He removed his cap, wringing it in his hands like a wet towel. His eyes were focused on his boots as though he were speaking to royalty.

"Well, then," Tom said. "What brings you to old Bludgeon Town? Them boots is too fancy for a street urchin. I'm guessing you're one of them changelings come to rid the world of the likes of me. That about right?"

Ernie raised his head. He threw his shoulders back and his chest out. Then he smiled. Those nerves had given way to a deep rage. He was ready to enact justice that was, in his mind, long overdue. "Something like that."

As the twelfth bell sounded, a wooden barrel tipped over. The lid fell away before a thick black liquid spread across the alley. Tom spun around in time to see Yi emerge from the shadows. His hands were cupped and filled with flames. The glow, reflected in his amber goggles, was eerie against his face. His smile was sinister.

"What's this? Two of you, is it?" Tom asked. "Well, this must be my lucky day."

Yi brought the fire to his lips and then blew. The fire streamed from his hands toward the tar before exploding into an inferno. Tom was trapped behind a wall of flames. So was Ernie, but he wasn't alone.

A bat fluttered down from the dark sky before swooping around Tom's head. He swatted at the bat with meaty hands, but it was too quick. It taunted the slaver, and then it bit the back of his neck.

Tom slapped at his neck, but the bat was already out of reach. "Them things have rabies," he said. His eyes filled with worry.

"You never know," Ernie said. "It might have been a vampire."

"There ain't no such thing," Tom said, though his face looked nervous.

The bat shimmered as though it were out of focus before it disappeared. Then, with a pop, a girl with green skin and red eyes took its place. It was Hale, the shape-shifter.

"What is this?" Tom asked. He rubbed his eyes as though what he had seen wasn't possible. Yi walked through the blaze to join them. Sparks leaped from behind his goggles as fire burned in his hands. He threw flames at Tom's feet. Tom jumped out of the way, but Yi was relentless. He laughed as Tom danced a jig.

"I'll not be mocked by the likes of you!" he shouted.

Tom leaped at Yi, who stumbled back before falling to the ground. A rope weighted down by iron balls at each end flew out of one of the windows above and latched around Tom's ankles, tying him up. Yi rolled away as Tom tore at the bonds, but he couldn't break free.

"I'll kill you!" he shouted. "Every last one of you."

Denton jumped down from the window. His tail swished as he walked over to the slaver. Then he snarled, revealing his curved incisors, and held out a pair of handcuffs for Tom to see.

"You get close enough and I'll break your neck, boy," Tom said.

"I doubt it," Denton said. He grabbed Tom's wrist, and the slaver tried to pull away. He swung at Denton with his free hand. Denton dodged before wrenching Tom's arm behind his back. Then he latched on the handcuffs.

"Where's Tejan?" Denton asked between heavy breaths.

Tejan Chandra, a small boy with dark skin and raven hair, walked out from behind the wall of barrels. His eyes kept darting from Tom to the door of the pub.

"It's okay," Ernie said as he placed his hand on Tejan's

39

shoulder. "We'll protect you. All you need to do is make this guy forget his past...forget that he was ever a slaver...and forget our faces." Then Ernie reached into his pocket. He pulled out a mask and covered his face. So did Hale and Yi. Ernie tossed a mask to Denton. He hesitated before he put it on.

"Are you ready?" Ernie asked.

Tejan nodded. He walked over to Tom, who was trembling in fear.

"Please," he said. "I promise I won't bother you no more. Old Tom will change his ways. I've seen the light. Please!"

Tejan placed his fingertips on Tom's temples and took a deep breath. Then he turned back to Ernie. Ernie nodded. Tejan closed his eyes.

When it was over and Tom's memories of slaving had been wiped, Denton hoisted Tom over his shoulder and carried the slaver's unconscious body to the street, where he tied Tom to a gas lamp with a thick piece of rope. Denton left a note pinned to Tom's shirt.

We will not live in fear.

It was signed *The Agents of Justice*.

INFAMOUS

It was the first morning back to class after winter break, and Natalia was already dreading the subway ride to school. Natalia and the *Zephyr*, the enchanted subway that connected New Victoria to her hometown, had gotten off on the wrong foot last semester when Natalia commented on how old the *Zephyr* was. Unbeknownst to Natalia and thanks to MERLIN Tech, a special technology created by the Templar, the *Zephyr* had a personality. And could hold a grudge.

The moment Natalia sat down in the subway car, her bench lurched. Natalia flew out of her seat before toppling to the floor.

"I've had just about enough," she said as she scrambled to pick her things off the floor. Her face was bright red. The students seated nearby were laughing. "How many times do I have to apologize before this bucket of bolts will leave me alone?"

"We tried to warn you," Todd Toad said. "The *Zephyr* doesn't like it when people make fun of her."

"Subway trains aren't living creatures," Natalia said. She reached for a tube of lip gloss that had slid beneath Todd's bench.

"When you mix magic and technology, strange things can happen," Todd's brother, Ross, said. "That's the beauty of MERLIN Tech."

The Toad brothers looked nothing alike. Ross was the pudgier of the two. He had a thick shock of auburn hair that looked like an overgrown hedge. Todd was unusually thin, with square glasses and rabbit teeth. They had one thing in common, though. Natalia thought they were both annoying.

Natalia rolled her eyes and stood up. Then she grabbed one of the leather straps that hung from the ceiling. "Did anyone see Ernie this morning? I think he missed the train."

"I didn't," Harley said.

"Me neither," Max said as he stroked Sprig's back while she slept next to him in her natural form.

"We saw him," Todd said. "He's sitting a few cars back with Kenji Sato."

"The kid with the Bounder drake?" Max asked.

"I guess," Todd said with a shrug. "He's the only Kenji I know."

"That's weird," Max said. "Ernie's scared to death of that thing."

"Not anymore," Ross said. "It was perched on his head."

"Thanks for the update," Natalia said. "Now if you don't mind, we have official Grey Griffins business."

"We don't mind," Ross said.

"Yeah," Todd said. "Go right ahead."

Natalia stared at them until they got the hint.

"Oh, sorry," Todd said. They put on headphones that were both plugged into the same portable music player.

"I doubt they even turned it on," Natalia said. She lowered her voice as she leaned toward Max and Harley. "Anyway, I think I know why we didn't see much of Agent Thunderbolt over the break."

"Why?" Max asked.

Natalia pulled out a folded newspaper from her purse and tossed it to Harley. Sprig opened an eye warily, but then she went back to sleep. "Take a look at the story on the bottom of the front page."

"'Evil Spirits Banned from Ice-Cream Parlor'?"

"Try the other one."

"'Vigilante Crime Fighters Strike Again,'" Max read aloud.

"So?" Harley asked before he yawned.

"Keep reading," Natalia said.

Max sighed. He wasn't in the mood to read the newspaper, but he didn't feel like arguing.

A masked vigilante group calling itself the Agents of Justice continues its fight against alleged members of a human-trafficking cartel. This marks the third time in less than two weeks that suspected kidnappers have been found tied to gas lamps in an area that locals refer to as Bludgeon Town.

There are some who believe these vigilantes are students from the changeling program at Iron Bridge Academy lashing out in response to the disappearance of two classmates, Becca Paulson and Robert Hernandez, both presumed dead.

"It's preposterous," Connie Nipkin, dean of the changeling program at Iron Bridge Academy, said. "The changelings are carefully monitored for their own safety, and I can assure you that none of our students have been wandering around the streets alone."

When Max finished reading, he folded the paper, handed it to Natalia, and then sat back against the bench.

"There's no way Ernie could pull off something like that," Harley said. "I mean, come on. We're talking about the same kid who refuses to water-ski because he thinks a giant snapping turtle is going to swallow him."

"Who else would dress up in a costume to fight crime?" Natalia asked.

"Look, I know that's Ernie's fantasy," Harley said, "but I'm telling you, there is no way he's wandering around New Victoria looking for a fight. Did you see the picture of the guy they caught? He had a tattoo on his neck, and it looked like he could bench-press a car."

"I'm more worried about Smoke," Natalia said. "What's going to happen when Ernie bumps into him?"

"Yeah, well, Smoke is definitely looking for him," Harley said.

Natalia frowned.

"Monti and I saw him in New Victoria last night. He wanted us to give Ernie a message."

"What?"

"I'm not sure," Harley said. "I told him to bug off."

Natalia bit her lower lip. "What are we going to do?"

"I wouldn't worry too much," Max said. "Ernie's fast enough that he should be able to get away from just about anything."

"Not if he's asleep," Natalia said.

"The Templar placed nullifiers around his house," Max said. "Smoke can't get in or out—at least not when he's using his power. He'll have to walk in like everyone else, and since it's under twenty-four-hour surveillance, I doubt he'll show up anytime soon."

"All it takes is one mistake, and we could lose him forever," Natalia said.

Max sighed. "Why didn't he come to us?"

Before anyone could answer, the students heard the brakes screech. The passenger car lurched, and sparks flew outside the window as the lights flickered overhead. Moments later the *Zephyr* came to a stop.

Ross fell from his seat and tumbled down the aisle. The flap of his backpack flew open, spilling the contents across the floor of the subway car.

"What are these?" Natalia asked, reaching down to pick up a mask and a black driving cap from under a stack of comic books.

Ross regained his balance and snatched the mask out of Natalia's hand. "Those are expensive collectibles, thank you very much."

"You don't even want to know how much they cost," Todd said.

"Try me."

"Never mind," Ross said, placing them back in his bag.

"If they're so expensive, what are you doing carrying them around in your backpack?" Harley asked.

Ross looked like he'd just gotten caught with his hand in the cookie jar.

"Are you two part of that Agents for Justice nonsense?" Natalia asked.

Ross looked to Todd for help, but Todd was watching the commotion outside.

"This isn't good," Todd said over the murmurs of the

46

other students. His head was craned out the open window.

"What?" Natalia asked, forgetting about the mask and the hat.

"I heard the conductor talking about shield failure this morning."

"What?"

"Here's the deal," Todd said. "To move between dimensions, you need a powerful shield, or you get pulled apart like quantum spaghetti."

"That's disgusting," Natalia said.

Max could see small clockworks on wheels through his window. They were heading toward the engine as the tunnel echoed with the sound of air wrenches, welding torches, and clanging metal.

"Assembler bots," Todd said.

"Technically they're Assembler clockworks," Ross said.

"You're right," Todd said. "If they were robots, they'd have wires and silicon chips."

"Let's just hope they can get that shield repaired," Ross said.

"Wait," Natalia said. "They're going to test it first, right?"

"That's a good one," Ross said.

"Then how are they going to know if the shield is working?"

Lightning raced along the underside of the subway train before slamming into one of the clockworks. With a yelp, it flew backward.

The *Zephyr* flared back to life.

"It looks like we're about to find out," Ross said.

THE MASK

"You can open your eyes now," Harley said once the *Zephyr* crossed safely into the Land of Mist. "The shield held."

Natalia lowered her hands and blinked. When she looked out the window, she saw that they were speeding through a glass tunnel beneath the enchanted waters of Lake Avalon. Exotic fish swam through a kelp forest as iridescent crabs the size of small cars crept along the bottom.

"Look at that," Ross said. He was pointing out the window as a shadowy form approached the *Zephyr*.

"What is it?" Natalia asked with a wrinkled nose.

"I have no idea," Ross said.

The creature looked like a science experiment gone wrong. Its head and torso were vaguely human, with spikes protruding from its shoulders and back. However, from its waist down it was a fish.

"We really need to start carrying a camera," Todd said.

"I saw one that I liked at Mad Meriwether's," Ross said. "Maybe we can stop by after school and pick it up."

"Don't forget, we have that..." Ross stopped and looked at Natalia out of the corner of his eye. Then he lowered his voice to a whisper. "You know, the m-e-e-t-i-n-g."

Natalia rolled her eyes.

The Toad brothers settled back into their bench, content to listen to music as the *Zephyr* trundled along its path. Meanwhile, Max shuffled through a stack of his new Round Table cards, trying to memorize the strengths and weaknesses of each clockwork so he'd be ready when Logan quizzed him.

Soon, the *Zephyr* pulled up to the subway stop at Iron Bridge Academy. There was a cloud of steam. The doors slid open, and the students filed onto the platform. Chatter echoed off the brick walls as everyone got in line to take the escalator up to the campus.

Max still wasn't used to the clothing of the Templar

society. Like Harley, he stuck with blue jeans while the rest of the boys dressed in waistcoats and vests, with bow ties, ascots, derbies, and sporting caps. Frock coats were common, as were pocket watches and canes. None of it looked very comfortable as far as Max was concerned.

Natalia, however, loved the fashion. She wore an army green military cap with a high-collared shirt, a matching vest and hose, a camel-colored skirt, and brown boots. There were plenty of girls dressed in ruffled skirts and ankle boots, corsets and camisoles. Wide hats with plumage were the rage, as were gloves and shawls.

The critical accessory worn by everyone was a pair of goggles. The brand, style, and the way a person wore his or her goggles said a lot about the individual. Some wore them over their eyes indoors or out, rain or shine. Others pushed the goggles up to their foreheads. There were ornate riding goggles, gunnery goggles, and aviator goggles from wars long past.

"I don't see Ernie anywhere. Are you sure he didn't miss the train?" Natalia said as she pulled her goggles up over the bill of her cap. Then she followed the Toad brothers onto the escalator.

"Of course we're sure," Todd said.

"He's right there with Catalina," Ross said, pointing back to the crowd below.

Ernie was leaning against a pillar as he talked to Catalina Mendez. Unlike Scuttlebutt, her lumpy Bounder imp, Catalina was actually pretty. She was tall and slender,

51

with dark eyes, long lashes, and black hair that she had pulled back in a ponytail.

"Watch your step, please," a service clockwork wrapped in polished brass said from the top of the escalator.

Max walked out of the depot and into the cold morning air. It was a dreary morning, and the entire campus was shrouded in fog. Like the rest of New Victoria, Iron Bridge Academy didn't appear to belong in the modern world. Some of the buildings looked like warehouses, others like apartments.

The faculty housing had steeply pitched roofs, dormers, and wraparound porches. Buildings such as the menagerie were constructed entirely of steel girders and large panes of glass. At the heart of it all stood a massive structure made of grey brick with white trim. It housed a research facility, dormitories for the few students whose parents didn't relocate to the area, offices, and most of the classrooms.

"I don't know what's worse," Natalia said as she opened her parasol to keep the drizzle from spotting her clothes, "the rain in New Victoria or the snow back in Avalon."

"Should we wait for Ernie?" Max asked as Sprig shifted into a pigeon before flying off to the rooftop of the school.

"Do whatever you want," Harley said. "I have to finish a report on Lord Merlin Silverthorne before home-room starts."

"Wait, do you hear that?" Natalia asked.

Max strained his ears. After a few moments he heard an angry voice carry across the school yard. A thin woman was arguing with someone beneath a gas lamp near the front entry. "Is that Dean Nipkin?" he asked. There was too much fog to be sure, but the rectangular glasses perched on the end of her sharp nose were hard to miss.

"I think so," Natalia said, "but who's she scream-ing at?"

"That's Chief Constable Oxley," Ross said.

"Who?" Harley asked.

"You know, as in the highest-ranking officer of the law in New Victoria?" Todd said.

"I heard he has a clockwork arm, just like Doc Trim-ble," Todd said. "They say his first arm got gnawed off by a horde of Vampire Pixies."

"Give it a rest already," Natalia said.

The chief constable was a large man, with broad shoulders, an ample belly, and a handlebar mustache. His size, however, didn't appear to intimidate Dean Nip-kin in the slightest. He stood quietly with his hands tucked behind his back as she berated him.

"I wonder what they're arguing about," Ross said.

"You know perfectly well what they're arguing about," Natalia said. "If I were you, I'd start talking before it's too late. Then again, I bet the sentence for obstruction of justice is only four or five years, tops."

"Yeah, well...we gotta go," Ross said before running off.

"We'll see you in homeroom," Todd said over his shoulder.

RESCHEDULED

Ernie managed to ignore the other three Grey Griffins for the entire morning, despite sharing three classes together. Max tried to make eye contact with him, but every time he did, Ernie turned the other way.

"Don't forget to save a chair for Ernie," Max said as the Griffins sat down at their usual table in the dining hall.

"Why?" Harley asked. "He's sitting over there with the Toad brothers."

Max turned to see Ernie and the Toad brothers talking, laughing, and eating in the back of the room. He shook his head before slumping into his chair. It hurt to be rejected—especially by one of his best friends.

"I'm telling you," Harley said between mouthfuls of stuffing with cranberries, "you have to let it go."

"He's right," Natalia said. "If Ernie wants to be a jerk, that's his problem. But you can't let it get to you like this."

Max swirled his mashed potatoes with his fork. "I know. It's just that I keep thinking Ernie was right about Robert. Maybe I should have done something."

"Like what?" Harley said. "You were following orders. Period."

"I guess."

"Are you going to eat that?" Harley asked. He was pointing at a dinner roll.

"You can have it," Max said.

"Thanks." Harley ripped it open and slathered it with butter before stuffing half of it into his mouth. He washed it down with an entire glass of milk.

"Do you even taste your food when you eat like that?" Natalia asked.

Harley belched.

"You realize that you're supposed to behave like a gentleman," Natalia said, though it didn't seem to have much effect. Harley continued to inhale his food. When he was finished, he wiped his mouth with the back of his sleeve.

As Natalia sat there looking disgusted, Max found himself smiling for the first time all day. The Griffins were more like siblings than friends. Bickering came as naturally as breathing.

Max did his best not to look at Ernie for the rest of the lunch hour. Instead, he enjoyed his meal and talked about past adventures with Harley and Natalia.

"Are you finished with that, sir?"

Max turned to see a clockwork that looked like a trash can on treaded wheels.

"Yeah, thanks," Max said.

"Very good." The clockwork took his plate. A compartment opened up from its chest, and the clockwork scraped the food off the plate before sliding it into a rack. Then it pulled out what looked like a miniature ruler to scrape the crumbs from the tablecloth.

Max looked over his shoulder to find Ernie deep in conversation with the Toad brothers. It looked like Ernie was holding an invitation to the new class, just like the one Max had received over the weekend.

"Max, did you hear what I just said?" Natalia asked.

He turned back around. "Sorry... what was that?"

"We were thinking about going to the Spider's Web on Wednesday," Natalia said. "Do you want to come?"

"Yeah, sure." It had been a while since they had gone to the comic shop, and it sounded like a good diversion.

The bell rang, announcing that lunch was over. Max was about to reach for his backpack when he found the Toad brothers standing in front of him, smiling.

"What's going on?" Max asked.

"Did you hear the news?" Todd said.

"You know, about the Round Table tournament?" Ross said.

"Not yet." Max stood up and tried to slip past them to head toward the exit.

Todd and Ross followed.

"We were worried that it was going to be canceled, but it's back on," Todd said.

"That's great."

"The tournament is going to pick up right where it left off," Ross said. "Except it's not going to be open to the public."

"Yeah, it's going to be in a secret location," Todd said. "You still have your *Toad Report* on Mendez, right?"

Max shrugged. "It's somewhere."

"Don't worry about it," Ross said. "We can get you another copy."

"You realize how historic this is, right?" Todd said.

"Not really."

Todd and Ross looked at each other with raised eyebrows before turning back to Max.

"This is a really big deal, Max," Ross said. "You could be one of the youngest duelists in the history of the Templar academies."

"Do you know what that's going to mean for our business?" Todd said.

"No, but I have a feeling you're going to tell me," Max said.

"Remember how we made our deal, right?" Todd

said. "We gave you free *Toad Reports* for the entire tournament, and you agreed to be a spokesperson for our brand."

Max closed his eyes and took a deep breath.

"We're ready to expand into the professional tournaments," Ross said. "With your endorsement, Toad Brothers, Incorporated, is going to become the most powerful company in the gaming industry."

"Look, guys, I have a lot on my mind right now."

"We know," Todd said. "That's why we arranged a practice duel for you."

"Let me guess. Xander?" Max asked. After all, Xander Swift was the undisputed amateur Round Table champion in the world, and for some reason, the Toad brothers were dying to turn Max and Xander into rivals.

"Actually, we had someone else in mind," Todd said. He looked at Ross from the corner of his eye.

"Don't get us wrong," Ross said. "We can't wait to see you go head-to-head with Xander, but if you're going to prep for your Round Table duel against Catalina, you need someone who plays like her."

"Yeah, and somebody who looks like her, too," Todd said.

The brothers started laughing, but Max frowned. He wasn't sure he still wanted to play in the tournament after what had happened to Robert Hernandez. The Toad brothers' annoying game of guess-who wasn't helping.

"Are you going to tell me who it is?"

"Don't make us ruin the surprise," Ross said.

"This is stupid," Max said.

"You don't get it," Todd said, "but you will. Round Table is going to put you on the map."

"Yeah," Ross agreed. "So are you going to show up?"

Max sighed before shaking his head. The Toad brothers thought they were applying pressure with their comments, but they weren't. Max didn't care if he was on the map or not. Still, he committed to being in the tournament, and he was going to see it through, even if he was having doubts about continuing. He figured practice would do him some good. Still, Max didn't want the Toad brothers to think that they had won. "I'll think about it," he finally said.

ROLL CALL

Max was already having a tough day when he walked through the door of his Bounder Care class with Sprig. She had taken the form of a white tiger that morning, and she hadn't changed since. Some of the other students were intimidated, and she liked the reaction.

Brooke Lundgren was already seated in her desk. Honeysuckle, her overly protective Bounder pixie, was there, too. Neither looked at Max. In fact, Brooke hadn't spoken to him in months.

Max didn't get it. They'd been neighbors their entire lives, and now everything felt awkward. Everything seemed to fall apart after a murderous creature known as a Reaper attacked Brooke. He wasn't sure if she blamed him for it or what the problem was. Girls were too confusing—especially Brooke. To avoid any drama, Max decided to sit on the opposite side of the room. It was easier that way.

"How's it going?" Kenji asked when Max walked by. His drake, Sparky, was perched on his shoulders, asleep.

"Hey, Kenji."

Sprig growled. She wasn't overly fond of other Bounder Faeries, much less any faerie at all. However, the spriggan appeared to take particular pleasure when it came to annoying Kenji's drake. Max warned her against it, but she ignored him.

The drake opened a single eye before closing it again. Then he yawned. In a flash of light, Sprig changed into an Ice imp. She wasn't much taller than Max's knee, with bandy legs, long arms, and leathery wings. She smiled ruefully as a snowball formed in her hand. Then she threw it at the drake.

"What the…?" Kenji jumped out of his chair as the ice crystals flew down his collar and ran down his back.

"Sprig, don't!" Max said, but it was too late.

The drake screeched as he took flight. He retaliated by belching a ball of flames. The fireball was intended for Sprig, but it hit Brandi Stewart instead. She was stroking the neck of her catterfly when one of her braided pigtails caught on fire. Max couldn't believe what he was seeing.

"I'm so sorry," he said as he ran to the sink in the back of the room to get a pitcher of water.

Catalina's Digger imp got so nervous that he vomited. Then Honeysuckle got in on the act. The pixie tried to douse the flames in Brandi's hair, but she didn't have much luck. At the same time, Sprig started throwing snowballs at the drake, but an errant throw took out a lightbulb, sending a shower of glass falling from the ceiling.

"Sprig, knock it off!" Max couldn't believe what was happening.

Akinyi Butama, the Bounder Care teacher, walked into the room. She had been smiling, but it didn't last. She grabbed Brandi's arm and dragged the frightened girl to the sink, where Max stood with the pitcher. Ms. Butama took it and doused the fire in Brandi's hair. Brandi looked like she was about to cry as her catterfly fluttered in the air next to her.

"What's the meaning of this?" Ms. Butama asked.

All eyes turned to Max.

"Mr. Sumner?"

"Well…I…" He looked at Sprig, who had turned back into a tiger. She was already lying on the floor, snoring next to his desk.

"His spriggan threw a snowball at Sparky," Kenji said.

"Is that true?" Ms. Butama asked.

"Look, I'm really sorry," Max said.

"We'll discuss this later," she said, cutting Max off before he could explain himself. Then she walked over to her desk, where she picked up a phone to call the maintenance crew. A few minutes later, a service clockwork with a mop and a bucket filled with steaming water and a fragrant solution entered the room and started cleaning up the mess.

"You're lucky we didn't get detention," Max said to Sprig after class. She was prowling next to him as the white tiger. "Why do you like teasing that drake?"

"Because it smells of foul sulfur," Sprig said. Then she growled at a boy who was trying to reach for a book at the top of his locker. When he turned to see the tiger, he tried to run, but his feet got crossed up. He dropped his books. Everyone started to laugh. Sprig was smiling.

"You need to stop doing that," Max said to Sprig, helping the boy to his feet. "I'm sorry about that."

The boy was too discombobulated to do anything but pick up his books, shut his locker, and run off to his next class.

"I'm serious," Max said as he walked down the hallway. Sprig was at his side, her head held high as she purred. "You can't do stuff like that anymore."

"Yes, Max," she said. "We will be on our best behavior, we will."

The last class of the day—the new class—was to be held in a small building on the outskirts of the school grounds. To get there, Max walked through a set of double doors that led to a rose garden with a gurgling fountain in the center. Harley was waiting for him.

"Where's Natalia?"

"I haven't seen her since lunch," Harley said.

"Should we wait for her?" Max asked as Sprig shifted into a falcon. Then she took to the air. It was chilly, but the clouds had parted to reveal a sliver of sunshine.

Harley looked at his watch. "We better get going."

"She's never late."

"I guess there's a first time for everything."

With Sprig soaring overhead, the boys cut through the garden, then across a wide lawn. It wasn't long before they came to what looked like a one-room schoolhouse. It was a simple wooden structure with a gabled vestibule and a small bell tower.

A bell chimed as Max opened the door. The cozy room had scuffed wooden floors, two rows of desks that held two students each, and a potbellied stove that sat squarely in the front of the room.

"There's Natalia," Harley said. "Looks like you won't be able to sit by Brooke."

Harley was smiling, but Max wasn't. He watched Natalia and Brooke as they talked and laughed in the front row.

Neither noticed the boys when they walked in. Honeysuckle, however, did. She flew to Brooke's ear and whispered something. Brooke turned around, and Max held her gaze for a moment, but she looked away before opening a book.

"I thought you wanted to meet at the fountain,"

Harley said as he slid into the desk behind the girls. Max hesitated. He wasn't sure he wanted to sit that close to Brooke, but he did anyway. Sprig sat on her haunches next to him.

As Max sat down, Brooke glanced over her shoulder. It was subtle, but Max was sure that she was looking at him. Then, when they made eye contact for the second time, she rolled her eyes and turned back to her book.

Max frowned. His first reaction was anger, but it flared and died down and was replaced by confusion. He wanted to ask her what was wrong, but there was no way that Max was going to do that in front of a bunch of people.

"I guess I forgot," Natalia said. "Sorry."

The bell chimed. Max turned around to see Kenji walk in with Sparky. When Kenji saw Max, he scowled and moved to a desk in the back of the room.

"Don't even think about it," Max said when he saw Sprig's ears perk up.

Catalina and her imp had snuck in as well. The Bounder still looked nauseated. His eyes were drooping and his skin was flushed. Catalina wouldn't even look at Max. She sat across from Kenji as her portly imp struggled to climb into the desk next to her.

"That thing is ugly," Harley said in a whisper. "I wonder if her parents let it in the house."

Max turned to see Ernie walk in with the Toad brothers.

"You don't get it," Ernie said. "Kryptonite isn't the

only thing that can take Superman out. He's susceptible to magic. That's why Captain Marvel could win."

He had been talking so loudly that everyone in the room turned to look at him. Embarrassed, Ernie sat down in the first available seat. Unfortunately, Catalina's Bounder Faerie was already sitting there.

Scuttlebutt yowled, and Ernie shot into the air. His pants were covered in mucus. Ernie reached down to wipe it off, but that only made things worse. The slime was now stuck to his hands, stretching between his fingers.

"That smells disgusting!" Ross exclaimed.

Catalina jumped up and grabbed the imp before running out of the room.

"What am I supposed to do?" Ernie called after her as he wiped his fingers on the front of his shirt.

Everyone in the room was laughing.

Natalia pulled out the front page of the *New Victoria Chronicle* before tossing it to Ernie. "Of course, you can use this as a towel," she said. "You might want to read the cover first. It's about a bunch of juvenile delinquents running around New Victoria. The chief constable thinks that they're changelings from Iron Bridge. Can you believe that?"

Ernie's eyes shot wide open, and his jaw dropped. Then, recovering, he furrowed his thick eyebrows into a frown, pressing against the top of his aviator goggles. "I don't really care what the chief constable thinks," he said.

"Sure you don't," Natalia said. The final bell chimed, and Natalia turned back around before Ernie could say another word.

The door opened, and all eyes turned to the procession of changelings walking into the room. Yi Lu, the pyrokinetic, was first. Kenji's drake hissed at him, and Yi responded by snorting flames. Denton was next. His lion's tail swished behind him as though it had a life of its own. Hale, the girl with the green skin and antennae, was right behind him, followed by Raven. She looked as frustrated as ever, not that anyone could blame her. Dean Nipkin was lurking over her shoulder.

"Take your seats," the dean said.

"We saved you a seat," Natalia said, waving to Raven.

When Natalia learned that Raven could talk to inanimate objects, she decided to enlist her to help solve the mystery of the Clockwork King, Otto Von Strife. The only problem was that Raven had a well-earned reputation for having a prickly personality, so Natalia decided to befriend her first. She figured the old saying was true, that it was easier to catch flies with honey.

It was a disaster at first. Raven had found Natalia to be annoying, but Natalia's persistence not only earned Raven's help, but the two had also somehow become friends, or at least as close to friendship as Raven could get.

Raven hesitated, but she decided to join them.

"Have you met Brooke?" Natalia asked.

Raven shook her head.

"It's nice to meet you," Brooke said.

Raven's eyes went from Brooke to Honeysuckle and then back to Brooke. "Yeah, nice to meet you, too."

The door creaked open one last time. A stout man walked down the aisle before placing his briefcase on the empty desk at the front of the room. He was dressed formally in a brown suit with a gold vest, a white shirt, a bow tie, and a bowler derby. His shoes were polished, his grey beard was trimmed, and his round spectacles glinted in the lamplight.

Then he smiled at the students, revealing a peculiar set of wooden teeth.

THE RELIC HUNTERS

"Obadiah Strange?" Ernie asked with raised eyebrows.

The man removed his hat, then bowed. His bald head looked like it had been buffed and waxed. "In the flesh, Mr. Tweeny," Strange said. Then he took a moment to look around the room. When his eyes fell on Dean Nipkin, he cocked his head to the side. "I didn't expect to see you today, Connie. To what do I owe the pleasure?"

"We have a strict policy regarding changelings," the dean said. "Since you have elected to conduct your class outside of Sendak Hall, I thought it would be prudent to join you. For safety precautions, of course."

Strange broke into a wide smile. "Though I appreciate your offer, I'm afraid that won't be possible."

Dean Nipkin frowned.

"It does my heart good to know that you've taken such an interest in your flock," Strange said, "but we'll be fine. The students will return directly to Sendak Hall. Good day."

There was a collective gasp.

"Excuse me?"

"I'm quite certain that you heard me," Strange said, his tone pleasant. "Your eavesdropping skills are legendary. Now if you don't mind." He waved his hand as though shooing an annoying insect away.

"Well, I…" The dean was so flustered that she was incapable of forming a coherent thought. She grabbed the front of her jacket, straightened it, adjusted her hat, and then turned to leave without another word.

Before she could exit, Catalina Mendez came through the door with her bedraggled imp in her arms. Behind Catalina was a tall boy with mahogany skin and long dreadlocks held in place by a pair of brass goggles pushed up on his forehead.

"I didn't know that Xander Swift was going to be in this class," Todd said as though he'd just spotted a movie star.

Dean Nipkin looked put out. "If you don't mind," she said, before forcing her way between Catalina and Xander.

"Such a charming woman," Strange said as the dean

stomped her way across the lawn. "Oh, and please. Come right in, Mr. Swift. That goes for you as well, Ms. Mendez. We have plenty of seats for everyone."

"How's it going, Sumner?" Xander said after he took the seat behind him.

"Hey, Xander."

"Now where were we?" Strange asked. "Ah, yes. Welcome to Archaeological Reconnaissance and Excavation. Does anyone know what we'll be studying?"

Kenji raised his hand. "A bunch of junk that's stuck in the dirt?"

Everyone laughed, including Strange.

"I suppose that will be a part of it," he said. "Now you may not know this, but Iron Bridge Academy has a long history of graduates who have gone on to do amazing work in the field of archaeology. Given the current state of affairs, we'll need to find a few more who are up to the task. My hope is that you'll fill that void."

"Does that mean we'll get to dig stuff up?" Ross asked.

"That's the plan," Strange said. "You see, even as we speak, there is a race to find important relics that could tip the balance of power in the world."

"Like the Brimstone Key?" Natalia asked.

"Indeed," Strange said. "Does anyone know who possesses the key at the moment?"

Natalia raised her hand, but Strange ignored her. "What about you?" he said, looking at Raven. "Miss Lugosi, is it?"

Raven nodded.

"You wouldn't happen to know who holds the Brimstone Key, would you?"

"Otto Von Strife."

"And why is that important?"

"Because if he opens a gateway to the Shadowlands, a bunch of monsters are going to pour through and destroy Earth."

"So are we going to try to get it back?" Denton asked.

"We'll leave that to more capable hands," Strange said. "However, there is another object of importance that we will try to discover before Von Strife gets his hands on it. In fact, it may be even more important than the Brimstone Key."

"What is it?" Todd asked. He was sitting at the edge of his seat.

"All in due time," Strange said. "Now I want you to know that this is going to be an unusual class. There will be no homework, written tests, or pop quizzes."

There was a smattering of applause. Ross was so happy that he squealed, earning a round of laughter. Strange raised his hand to silence them.

"Don't misunderstand," he said. "This class will push you to the limits of your abilities, but should you survive, you'll join an elite membership as a Relic Hunter."

"Our great-great-grandfather was a Relic Hunter," Todd said. He had raised his hand, but he didn't wait for Strange to call on him.

"Tobias Toad, if I'm not mistaken," Strange said.

"Yeah, how did you know?" Ross asked.

"I met him, though that was a long time ago."

Ross frowned. "How old are you?"

"Older than I look," Strange said. Then he turned to a map hanging on the wall. "Now, the most famous of the Relic Hunters was Aleric Saxon. He undertook a series of legendary expeditions, including the search for the lost city of gold in Mexico and for the doomsday calendar in Sumeria."

"Is he the guy who used vibration frequencies to find stuff?" Todd asked.

"I'm impressed."

"We tried to make one of those machines he used a couple years ago, but we couldn't get it to work."

"What were you hoping to find?" Strange asked.

Todd looked at Ross, who shook his head.

"It's kind of a secret," Todd said.

"Either way," Strange said, "Aleric was the first to discover that objects have unique signatures. For instance, a religious artifact like the Holy Grail will emit a different frequency than faerie gold, which has a different frequency than pirate treasure."

He went on to talk about Saxon's quest to find the crystal skulls in South America. The students were so enraptured by the tale that they lost track of time. When the bell rang, everyone sat there, wanting to hear the end.

"We'll have to continue next time," Strange said to his disappointed audience. "However, before you go I need to collect your accidental death and dismemberment clauses."

"Death and dismemberment?" Todd asked.

"It's a necessary form, I'm afraid," Strange said. "The world is a dangerous place, but those who survive will divide the spoils."

"I didn't get one," Ross said. None of the other students had, either, so Strange grabbed a stack from his briefcase before giving each student a copy to take home.

"Do you have a moment, Mr. Tweeny?" Strange asked after he gave Ernie a form.

"Sure," Ernie said as the last of the other students left the room.

"How was your break?" Strange asked.

Ernie shrugged. "Okay, I guess."

"Did Santa bring you anything special for Christmas?"

"I don't really believe in Santa anymore," Ernie said. "I'm kind of too old for that."

"Of course. How foolish of me."

"It's no big deal."

"I know it's a bit late, but I got you a little something," Strange said. "It's just a souvenir from my travels, but I think it might come in handy." Strange reached into the desk drawer before pulling out a brass mechanism. It had several dials and a single lever on the side.

"What is it?"

"An Interdimensional Phase Adjuster."

Ernie frowned.

"Watch closely." Strange entered a combination on the dial before pulling the switch.

There was a humming sound. Ernie watched as Strange went out of focus. Ernie rubbed his eyes. Strange vanished. Ernie looked around the room, confused. He reached out to where Strange had been sitting, but all he got was a fistful of air.

"Where are you?" Ernie asked.

Strange materialized on the far side of the room. "I never left you, my friend."

"No way," Ernie said. "That thing makes you invisible?"

"Oh, it does much more than that. You see, the IPA is a favorite tool of the THOR agents," Strange said, referring to the Tactical Headquarters for Operations and Research, a Templar Special Forces unit. "I'm surprised that Logan hasn't told you and the Grey Griffins about it. This amazing bit of technology will turn you into a ghost."

"A ghost?"

"Not technically, of course. It vibrates your molecules at a rate that lets you occupy space in two or more dimensions at one time. You'll be invisible to the naked eye. You can scream and nobody will hear you. In fact, you'll even be able to walk through walls."

Ernie looked at the device. "Are you sure I should have one of these?"

"I'm unaware of any laws that would keep you from owning it, if that's what you mean."

"But it had to be really expensive."

"Nonsense," Strange said. "Besides, when you've lived as long as I have, you tend to accumulate more money than you know what to do with."

"It's incredible."

"I'm glad you like it," Strange said. "I was hoping it might come in handy during your adventures in Bludgeon Town."

Ernie's heart started pounding, and his hands began to sweat.

"Relax," Strange said after a wink. "Your secret is safe with me."

"How did you know?"

"For better or worse, there isn't much in this world that goes on without my notice. Besides, you're the talk of the town. You can't walk into a pub or barbershop without hearing about the Agents of Justice."

"Really?" A smile crept across Ernie's lips.

"May I give you a bit of advice?"

"Sure."

"Getting a mention on the front page of the *Chronicle* is impressive," Strange said. "But fame has its disadvantages."

"What do you mean?"

"It's hard to maintain the element of surprise if everyone knows who you are."

"I didn't think about that."

"You've stirred up a hornet's nest," Strange said. "Are you willing to lead the other changelings to war? Because there will be casualties."

"All we want to do is scare the slavers so they leave us alone."

"I'm afraid it doesn't work that way," Strange said. "They'll be out for blood."

Ernie sighed.

"Don't misunderstand," Strange said. "Until changelings are treated equally, you'll never get the protection you deserve. If the Templar aren't going to protect you, as far as I'm concerned, you've a right to protect yourself. Besides, if you're half the leader I know you are, the other changelings will follow you to the Shadowlands and back."

"I don't know."

"I haven't a doubt."

"What am I going to do about the chief constable?"

"Don't worry about him," Strange said. "He's a little slow on the uptake, if you catch my meaning. Besides, if any of them were doing their jobs properly, you wouldn't need to be out there, now would you?"

"Exactly."

"Can you believe that we're going to be Relic Hunters?" Todd asked as some of the archaeology students lingered on the lawn outside their new classroom.

"You guys know that Strange is immortal, right?" Ross asked.

"Whatever," Denton said.

"No, he really is. That's his changeling power. You can even ask Ernie. Those two are tight." Ross turned to look for Ernie, but he wasn't there. "Hey, have you guys seen him?"

"He's still inside," Max said, nodding toward the door. "He's probably getting more of that dragon dung tea."

"That sounds disgusting," Denton said.

Max frowned when he saw Raven talking to Natalia in hushed tones.

"She can't come tonight, but I was thinking that Brooke could join us Wednesday," he heard Natalia say. Raven frowned. "I can still study tonight, though."

Raven narrowed her eyes. "Yeah, I guess," she said.

"Wait a minute," Harley said as he cut into their conversation. "I thought we were going to the Spider's Web Wednesday."

"Oh, no. I forgot," Natalia said.

"Obviously."

"Do you two mind going without me?" she asked.

"I guess," Harley said, shrugging. Max just stood there. It was bad enough that Brooke wasn't talking to him. Now Natalia was blowing him off.

SENDAK HALL

Natalia had been looking forward to the final bell on Wednesday. She had to fight the urge to watch the clock during Strange's Relic Hunting class, and when they were finally dismissed, she jumped out of her chair to pack her things.

Until she transferred to Iron Bridge she had never had a friend who was a girl. Now she had two, and she was hoping they would all get along.

"I'm a little nervous," Natalia said as her heels clicked on the cobbled path that led to Sendak Hall.

"It's strange, but I am, too," Brooke said while Honeysuckle flew ahead. "I hope we don't run into Dean Nipkin."

"That makes three of us," Raven said, "but I wouldn't worry about it. She left for some kind of conference this morning. She's not supposed to be back until Monday."

Sendak Hall was never meant to be a prison, yet to the changelings at Iron Bridge Academy, that's exactly what it had become. There were guards at the front entrance and watchful gargoyles on the rooftops. Changelings weren't allowed to wander the campus without supervision. They weren't even allowed to eat lunch with the other students, although other students could choose to sit with the changelings.

Dean Nipkin insisted the rules were in place to protect the changelings from further attacks. She also wanted to protect the other students from any potential accidents. After all, Iron Bridge Academy was once closed after a changeling lost control of her powers. The explosion was so devastating that most of the campus was destroyed, and it had taken nearly a century to reopen the school.

"I didn't think you were allowed to have visitors," Natalia said as the three girls closed in on Sendak Hall. The trees along the path kept most of the rain from reaching them. Natalia's umbrella handled the rest.

"Technically, we're not, but I took care of it," Raven said. She walked up the front steps and right past the guard. He didn't move. Neither did Natalia and Brooke. "Are you two coming or not?"

"We're not going to get in trouble, are we?" Natalia asked as she eyed the guard.

Honeysuckle looked at Raven before whispering something into Brooke's ear. Brooke whispered something back behind a cupped hand. Honeysuckle didn't look happy, but when Brooke raised her eyebrow, the pixie flew away.

"Sorry," Brooke said before she hurried up the steps.

Natalia followed, though slowly. Her eyes never left the guard. "How did you do that?"

"I didn't," Raven said. Then she pointed to a boy wearing a linen duster jacket with a tweed vest, black pants, boots, and brass goggles pulled on top of his driving cap. He waved to the girls as they walked by.

"Who's that?" Natalia asked. Her voice was barely above a whisper.

"I'm not sure if anybody knows his real name, but we call him Geppetto," Raven said.

"Why?"

"Because if he gets inside your head, he can control you like a puppet."

Natalia and Brooke looked at each other with wide eyes.

"Don't worry," Raven said. "As long as you're with me, he'll leave you alone."

The girls walked past a large room filled with clusters

of sofas and chairs. The walls were covered in floral wall-paper, and paintings hung inside ornate frames. Three boys were playing Round Table. Natalia recognized Tejan from the tournament, but she hadn't seen the other two before.

When they got to Raven's room, it wasn't anything like what Natalia had expected. The space was surprisingly large. Sheer curtains let in what little sunlight there was, her bedspread was covered in a floral pattern, and the walls were a soft yellow. She even had a painting of wildflowers.

"This is amazing," Brooke said as she walked over to the window. "You can see the entire city. Look, there's the Cathedral of St. Peter."

"Yeah, it's great," Raven said. "It reminds me of all the amazing things in the world that I'll never get to be a part of."

"That's not true," Natalia said. "Besides, I thought that Annie found a way to override the inhibitors. You can go anywhere you want."

"It's not the same thing," Raven said. "Why should we have to sneak around? Do you know what Dean Nipkin does if she catches one of us outside Sendak Hall?"

Brooke shook her head. Natalia just stood there.

"We get placed in solitary confinement," Raven said. "It's a room about as big as a broom closet. There aren't any windows, and the only furniture is a toilet."

"That's terrible," Brooke said. "Does my dad know about it?"

Raven shrugged. "Why wouldn't he? He's the director of the school, right?"

It looked as though Brooke was about to defend her father, but she must have thought better of it. Instead, she closed her mouth and turned back to the window.

"That's what I thought," Raven said loud enough for Brooke to hear. Then she walked over to a steamer trunk and opened it. She pulled out something wrapped in cloth and tied with a string. Inside was the mangled cover of a journal. "I'll probably get expelled for showing you this."

"Why?" Natalia asked.

"Because it belonged to Otto Von Strife."

Natalia frowned.

"You know," Raven said, "as in the guy who is kidnapping changelings to steal their souls?"

"Of course," Natalia said, "but how did you get it?"

"Smoke left it in his dorm room," Raven said. "The pages were missing, but I was still able to lift the memories. Von Strife is crazy, but now I understand why Smoke thinks the guy is trying to protect us." Raven paused as she bit the inside of her cheek. "Well, at least his daughter, anyway."

"She had leukemia, right?" Natalia asked.

Raven nodded. "It's probably better if I just show you."

"You can do that?" Natalia asked.

"I've never tried with two people before, but I suppose there's a first time for everything. Are you game?"

"I am," Natalia said, glancing at Brooke.

Brooke looked hesitant, but she nodded.

"Okay," Raven said, leading the girls over to a small sofa. She set the cover of the journal on the table before sitting down in a chair next to the other two. "Now I can only see what an object wants to show me, but this journal doesn't seem to hold much back."

"How does it work?" Natalia asked.

"Just set your hand on top of mine, close your eyes, and if you feel like you have to barf... well, don't."

SHARED MEMORIES

Raven placed both of her hands on the scarred leather cover, and then she closed her eyes. As Natalia and Brooke set their hands on top of Raven's, the world appeared to slip away. They soon found themselves in a stark room with a desk and a metal table, and though the girls knew they weren't there physically, everything seemed so real.

Natalia was overwhelmed by the smell of rubbing alcohol and kerosene as a girl about her age came into focus. She was sitting on the table wearing a nightgown with the right sleeve pushed up. It looked as if the sun hadn't touched her skin for months, and she was frighteningly thin.

A tall man in a white lab coat was standing next to her. His silver hair was pulled back over his forehead, and he was holding a syringe with a long needle.

"That's Von Strife," Natalia said, though she wasn't sure if anyone could hear her.

"Just watch," Raven said.

"All right, Sophia," Von Strife said. "I know you've been stuck with needles more times than you can count, but we need to make sure that everything is progressing as it should be."

"I know," Sophia said. She smiled at her father.

He pushed back her corn-silk hair before kissing her forehead. "Let's get this over with, shall we?"

Sophia nodded. The smile never left her lips, even as he plunged the needle into her flesh. Von Strife waited until the syringe was filled with her blood before pulling it back out. When he went to dab the wound, it had already disappeared.

"You're healing exponentially faster than a normal human," Von Strife said. "It's an extraordinary side effect of the serum that helped us get rid of your cancer."

"When can I go back to school?"

"Hopefully soon," he said before standing to his full height. Von Strife walked over to his desk, where he filled a vial with the blood sample. As he did, his eyes drifted to a picture that hung on the wall. It was Von Strife, with a striking woman holding a much younger Sophia on her lap.

"You have your mother's eyes," he said.

Sophia walked over to her father and placed her hand in his. He looked down at her, his eyes red.

"She was so beautiful," Sophia said.

"As are you, my dear. Now run along so I can finish my notes. If you're feeling up to it, perhaps we'll take a stroll when I finish."

Sophia started toward the door, but Von Strife called her back. "I almost forgot," he said. Then he opened a drawer and pulled out a package wrapped with a golden bow.

"Is that for me?" she asked, her blue eyes wide with excitement.

"As a matter of fact, it is," Von Strife said.

He smiled as Sophia carefully untied the bow. Inside was a wooden box with brass accents and a cherry finish. She looked to her father, who nodded. Then she unhooked the latch and opened the lid. A soft melody started to play as a porcelain ballerina inside the box spun in pirouettes.

"It's amazing," Sophia said.

"I thought you might enjoy it. Now run along, and I'll be with you shortly."

Sophia took her music box and left the room. Von Strife stared at the door long after his daughter was gone. Then he sat down at his desk, slumped over with his head in his hand as he wrote in his medical journal.

"The infusion of changeling blood into the test subject was successful; however, her conversion process from human to faerie continues to accelerate exponentially," he muttered as he wrote. "All tests to stunt the transformation have failed. If I am unable to stabilize her soon, the subject will lose every shred of her humanity within a month."

"Hold on," Raven said. "I'm going to flash forward."

The image went out of focus before it resumed. Von Strife was now standing in front of an iron door that was bolted shut. "Sophia, dear," he said, "I promise I will fix this."

There was a crash on the other side. Then the wailing began. "Father...please. Help me!" Sophia managed amid the snarling.

Von Strife stood with his back against the door. He held the music box in his hands, and the melody played as Sophia battered the door from the other side. "I'm so sorry," he whispered.

The scene shifted once more.

Von Strife was standing in an observatory with a glass ceiling as flashes of lightning tore through the sky. Medical clockworks moved about the room, checking the conduits and readying the condensing rods.

Sophia lay on a gurney, unconscious. Her body was covered in soft green fur that looked like moss. Long feather-like tufts swept over her forehead. It was obvious why Von Strife had to sedate her. Her mouth was a beak, talons had replaced Sophia's feet, and her hands ended in sharp nails that looked like they could cut through rock.

At the end of the gurney, near her feet, stood an iron ring filled with shimmering light. Inside the base, gears turned as the machine hummed.

"I hope you can forgive me, but this is the only way," Von Strife said through trembling lips. "I'll come for you as soon as I can."

He looked over to a table where Sophia's music box sat open as the melody played. Von Strife closed his eyes before breathing deeply. Then he gave the order.

A pair of clockworks pulled on chains to raise lightning catchers that jutted into the angry sky outside. Another clockwork connected the wires from the lightning catchers to the machine at the base of the iron ring. Lightning flashed before shooting down the copper wires. It wound around the coils. The light inside the ring flared before it swirled into a vortex.

Von Strife looked down to realize he was clutching his daughter's hand. Her claws cut into his skin, but he didn't care. Sophia's body began to move toward the ring. Her feet were the first to pass through. Then, as the machine swallowed the rest of her body, she started convulsing.

"What have I done?" Von Strife wailed. He tightened his grip, trying to hold on, but the machine wouldn't let go. His hand slipped, and she was lost. He turned to stare at the porcelain ballerina as it twirled inside Sophia's music box.

Raven removed her hands from the journal, and the girls found themselves back in the dorm room.

"What just happened?" Natalia asked.

"As far as I can tell," Raven said, "Von Strife sent his daughter into the Shadowlands."

"That doesn't make sense," Natalia said. "Von Strife was going to break into the Shadowlands to bring her back. Why would he send her there?"

A Surprise Guest

The dark sky opened, releasing heavy rainfall over the entire campus. Harley and Max had forgotten their umbrellas, so they decided to cut through the school on their way to the subway depot. Sprig had morphed into a white tiger again. She was tormenting the nervous students, who gave her a wide berth.

"What do you suppose they're up to?" Max asked now that the girls were safely out of earshot.

"I doubt they're talking about you, if that's what you mean."

"That's not what I meant."

"Then why were you acting so weird in class?" Harley said.

"Was I that obvious?"

"You weren't exactly smooth."

"It's not what you think."

"Whatever you say."

Max paused as he looked to make sure nobody was listening. "It's just that... w-w-well..."

"When did you get a stuttering problem?"

"Knock it off," Max said as a grin spread across Harley's lips. "Do you think Brooke is mad at me?"

"Why would she be?"

"That's what I'm wondering," Max said. "I mean, she hasn't said a word to me in, I don't know, months. Did I do something wrong?"

"Don't ask me."

Max stopped at the glass door that opened out onto the wet lawn. He felt Sprig lick his hand as a streak of lightning shot across the sky. It didn't look like the rain was going to let up. "If we want to catch the next train to Avalon, we should get going."

"Can you turn into an umbrella?" Harley asked Sprig. She growled her disapproval as Harley pushed the door open and walked out into the storm.

Max followed, grasping the neck of his jacket to keep the water from seeping in. Sprig decided to morph into a mallard. Water beaded on her feathers as she flew across the lawn and into the entryway of the subway depot.

By the time the boys reached her, they looked like they had jumped into a shower with their clothes on. Harley peeled off his sweatshirt and wrung it out as Max shook some of the water from his hair. Then Sprig jumped into his arms, nestling in for warmth as Max stroked the back of her neck.

"I guess it wouldn't bug me if she wasn't hanging out with Natalia all the time," Max said as they went down the escalator.

"Are we talking about Brooke again?" Harley asked.

"She's not talking to me. Neither is Ernie. And when was the last time Natalia blew us off?"

"I don't know."

"Never."

"So what's your point?"

"I don't know.... It kind of feels like the Grey Griffins are falling apart."

"Why?" Harley said. "Because Ernie's acting like a twit and the girls are hanging out together?"

"So you don't think—"

"No, I don't," Harley interrupted.

The boys rode in relative silence as the gears beneath the escalator churned. Sprig snored in Max's arms.

"Hey, is that Logan?" Harley asked, pointing to a man leaning against a brick pillar below.

"What's he doing here?"

"He's your bodyguard, not mine," Harley said.

"Good afternoon, fellas," Logan said as the boys stepped off the escalator.

"Are we in trouble or something?" Max asked, deciding to get to the point.

"What makes you say that?"

"You've never met us here before."

"I was thinking about taking you blokes for a bit of a diversion, but if you don't have the time…"

"We were just going to go to the Spider's Web," Max said, "but I guess we could hang out with you instead."

Harley shrugged.

"Who could pass up enthusiasm like that?" Logan said. He put one hand on Max's shoulder and another on Harley's.

"Can Sprig come?" Max asked.

Logan looked down at the faerie in Max's arms. "It doesn't bother me, but I don't think she'll like it. There'll be iron, and lots of it."

"Did you hear that?" Max asked Sprig.

"Yes, we heard," Sprig said. Like most faeries, spriggans were allergic to iron. She didn't bother to open her eyes.

"So what do you want to do?"

Sprig jumped out of his arms. Then, without a word, she turned back into a white tiger before prowling up the escalator and onto the front lawn.

The ground started to rumble as a stream of light

flared out from the tunnel in the distance. Moments later the *Zephyr* appeared. Its brakes echoed against the brick walls long after it came to a stop.

"Where are we headed?" Max asked as the boys followed Logan into one of the cars.

"If I told you that, it wouldn't be a surprise, now would it?"

A STRANGE THEORY

The *Zephyr* pulled into the Farringdon Street station. Logan led the boys out the door and up the steps into the bustling heart of New Victoria. "Stay close," he said as they wound through foggy streets filled with sounds of clanging steel, whirring motors, and peddlers selling everything from fresh fish to miracle cures.

"Are we going to Monti's lab?" Max asked as they crossed over to Walpole Road.

"It's hard to slip one past you," Logan said.

Monti's lab was in the warehouse district, an older part of the city that sometimes got dangerous after nightfall. The massive lab was made of brick, steel girders, and glass. Clouds of steam poured out of Monti's chimneys as Max, Harley, and Logan walked to the loading dock in the back.

Logan knocked on the door. Moments later, a horizontal slat snapped open to reveal a set of amber eyes that glowed in the murk. "So good of you to come by, sir," a mechanical voice said.

"I brought the munchkins," Logan said.

"The master will be pleased."

The slat shut. It was followed by the sound of bolts being unlocked from the inside. The door swung open to reveal a clockwork that would have almost looked human if it weren't wrapped in brass casing.

"This way, if you please," it said before shuffling across the floor of a room that could have fit three gymnasiums side by side.

An entire wall was covered with a network of pipes, gauges, and wheels. There were hoists and welding machines, cranes, and carts rolling over tracks. Overhead, catwalks crisscrossed beneath a ceiling that was constructed of interlocking steel girders filled with giant panes of glass. They were beaded with raindrops, but Max could still see the silhouettes of zeppelins flying lazily through the dark sky.

A hacking sound bellowed above the noise.

"What was that?" Max asked.

"Monti," Harley said.

As they followed the clockwork around a partition, they found Monti coughing. The clockwork fetched a bottle of water and handed it to Monti, who took a few sips and closed his eyes.

"You still haven't gone to the doctor, have you?" Harley asked.

"I thought I'd be better by now," Monti said. He was wearing a white lab coat covered by a leather apron, with thick boots, his horn-rimmed glasses, and a pair of brass goggles pushed up over his thinning hair.

"You're a bit off-color," Logan said.

"What do you mean?"

"You know, pale as a ghost."

"Ah," Monti said, finally understanding. "I'm not surprised. I haven't been out to see the sun in weeks."

"That's not what I mean," Logan said. "You don't look right."

"I'll be fine," Monti said before taking another swig of water. "By the way, where's Agent Thunderbolt?"

"Probably off with his Agents of Justice," Max said.

"You don't really think he's caught up in that mess, do you?"

"I don't know what to think anymore," Max said.

"It seems our Agent Thunderbolt has taken to spending his time with other changelings," Logan said. "It's a bit of a sore subject."

"I see," Monti said. "Does that go for Natalia as well?"

"She's studying with Brooke and Raven," Harley said.

"Girl power, huh?"

"Something like that."

"I was thinking that you could show the boys your new toy," Logan said.

"The Mark Four armor?"

"That's the one."

"Well, then," Monti said after another coughing fit, "right this way."

Though it was cold outside, it was hot and humid in the lab. Max took off his jacket before tying it around his waist. He was still uncomfortably warm. Clouds of steam rolled across the floor like fog as clockwork servants moved about the space. They were carrying various components that belonged to any number of the dozens of projects that Monti was working on.

Monti led them through a set of double doors and into one of his test facilities. He flipped a series of switches. The lights hummed to life, revealing an iron monster. "I present to you the Mark Four battle armor."

Standing against the wall and covered in scaffolding was an enormous suit of mechanized armor. It looked a bit like a clockwork, but the chest was actually a cockpit. It was covered in thick armor with rivets popping out near the edges of the iron plating. The arms were thick with hydraulics and rotating gears, all lathered in grease.

"Where did you get it?" Harley asked.

"I picked it up at a salvage station," Monti said. "She's the last of her kind, unless you count the model at the Templar Library, but that's just a replica."

"Have you taken it out?"

"Not yet," Monti said. "I still have to run some diagnostics. Why don't you crawl up there and take a look?"

"Seriously?"

"Of course."

Harley scrambled up the ladder before lowering himself into the cockpit. He sat in the seat and placed his feet on two pedals. A set of mechanical arms hung from the ceiling. Harley slid his own arms on top before grabbing what amounted to a joystick.

"Be careful with the firing mechanism," Monti said. "There's live ammo in some of the chambers."

"Live ammo?" Logan asked with a raised eyebrow.

"I wasn't expecting visitors," Monti said.

"What about the other thing?" Logan asked.

"You mean the portal scanner?"

"How's it coming?"

"Slower than I'd like."

"Come on down from there," Logan called up to Harley. "There's more to see."

Harley slipped out of the armor's restraints and climbed down the ladder.

Monti led them back into the lab, past rows of metal shelves full of labeled boxes. Each was filled with a variety of components ranging from gears and pinions to wires and bolts.

"Is that a shooting range?" Max asked.

"Yeah," Monti said. "We're working on developing a freeze ray."

They stopped to watch a clockwork take aim at a mannequin. A spray of what looked like condensed sleet shot out of the barrel of a large gun. It slammed into the mannequin before encasing it in a thick sheet of ice.

"What's that for?" Logan asked.

"Zombies," Monti said. "They don't do well in cold climates. The water in their tissue freezes and they can't move, so I figured a freeze ray would be the best way to stop them."

"What's this about zombies?" Logan asked.

"Obadiah gave me a book about the zombie infestation of 1645," Monti said. "There was some kind of viral outbreak that turned people into the walking dead."

"I see," Logan said.

"There was a report in the *Chronicle* this morning," Max said. "People have been claiming that zombies are walking through the streets."

"It's probably nothing," Monti said. "I mean, it's not like I'm worried about a zombie uprising or anything. I just like those old zombie movies, that's all." Monti walked over to a workbench that was tucked in a corner. He sat on the stool and picked up a small device with wires hanging out of it.

"So that's it, then?" Logan asked.

"I know it doesn't look like much, but yes," Monti said.

"Why would you need a portal scanner?" Max asked.

"That's a good question," Monti said. "Why don't you ask your bodyguard?"

"Because Von Strife is trying to build another portal to reach his daughter," Logan said.

"Wait," Harley said. "Didn't we already blow up the only gateway to the Shadowlands?"

Monti removed his glasses and rubbed the bridge of his nose. "Obadiah thinks that Von Strife is trying to build something called a Paragon Engine."

Monti opened up a notebook to show the boys sketches of a massive iron ring that was attached to its base by steel girders. Max stared at it for a moment, wondering where he had seen those drawings before.

"What's wrong?" Monti asked.

"Oh...nothing," Max said.

"Are you sure?"

"Yeah. I'm fine."

"Anyway," Monti said after another coughing fit, "if Von Strife can pull it off—and I doubt that he can—it would give him the power to create an artificial portal that's not only strong enough to open another gateway into the Shadowlands, but it could give him the ability to travel through time."

"Why don't you think he can do it?" Max asked.

"According to legend, Lord Saxon destroyed the last Paragon Engine decades ago," Monti said. "It would take years just to track down the parts, even if they still existed."

"Not if he had Saxon's maps," Max said.

"We have all of those in Saxon's diary," Monti said. "Don't get me wrong. If anybody can build a Paragon Engine, it's Von Strife. The man is a certifiable genius. I mean, as much as I hate to say it, he's kind of a hero of mine—at least when it comes to his work. But even with an intellect like Von Strife's, the odds are stacked against him."

"So how much longer on the scanner?" Logan asked.

"I was hoping to have it finished tomorrow," Monti said. "I mean, portals are nothing but wormholes stabilized by negative energy, but there are still variances."

"Like what?" Harley asked.

"For one, natural portals give off a different signature than the artificial kind."

"So you're going to try to scan for any artificial portals that would match the signature of a Paragon Engine," Harley said.

"That's the goal," Monti said. "If Von Strife fires one up, we should be able to pinpoint his location. Then we send in the cavalry, arrest him, lock him up, and throw away the key. All I need to do is get this thing working."

"What's wrong with it?" Max asked, suddenly interested. After all, THOR agents had been trying to track Von Strife for months, and they hadn't gotten very far.

"That's a good question," Monti said as he flipped the device over. "The theory is pretty straightforward, but the build has been tricky."

"Is that an Intra-Cellanator?" Harley asked, pointing to one of the components.

Monti opened his mouth to answer, but all that came out was a cough.

"You should go see Doc Trimble," Logan said.

"Yeah," Max said. "That cough sounds terrible."

"I'll be fine. I just need some rest, that's all," Monti said. Then he turned back to Harley. "By the way, how do you know about Intra-Cellanators?"

"I'm not sure. I must have read about it somewhere." Harley shrugged. "Have you thought about using a copper coil instead?"

"Well," Monti said, mulling it over, "it's a bit unorthodox, but I think you might be on to something." He walked to a box on a nearby shelf, rummaged inside, and pulled out a sheathed copper coil. He returned to his workbench and handed Harley the coil. "You do it."

"I don't want to mess it up."

"Right now, it's nothing but a worthless piece of junk," Monti said.

"Before the two of you get sidetracked," Logan said, "I was hoping you could show me the Jaguar."

"We just finished the conversion this morning."

"What conversion?" Max asked. "Did you add a nitrous system to it or something?"

"It's a bit more than that," Logan said. "Have you ever ridden in a flying car?"

THE AEROCAR

"You're serious?" Max asked.

"A man should never joke about his car," Logan said.

"I've got to see this," Max said as a clockwork with a square body and a tiny head zipped by on belted wheels. It was carrying what looked like a submachine gun.

"What was that?" Harley asked.

"An energy weapon," Monti said. "That particular model fires plasma bolts, but it's been jamming up. Maybe you could take a look at it later."

Harley lit up. "Okay."

"Only if I can help test them," Max said.

"I can arrange that," Monti said.

A piercing whistle came out of a pipe, followed by a cloud of steam.

"It's wicked hot in this place," Logan said as he took out a handkerchief to wipe the sweat from his brow. "You can make a car fly, but you can't install a decent air-conditioning system?"

"I'm afraid the steam is an occupational hazard, but you get used to it," Monti said.

He entered a code into the keypad next to an over-sized garage door, and it opened to reveal a sweeping view of the garage below. It was nearly as big as the workshop, with brick walls and a forest of steel beams that held up the vaulted ceiling.

There was a tank hoisted on hydraulic lifts where clockwork repairmen worked on the undercarriages, while others worked on cars and motorcycles. Monti led everyone to a vehicle sitting on four stilts. It was covered by a tarp that fell away after a quick yank.

"You're looking at what used to be a 1948 Jaguar XK120," he said. "It was a beautiful car, but now it's special."

The sleek roadster had been retrofitted with wings mounted to the body. The doors had been welded shut, and what used to be a convertible top was now a glass and chrome canopy. It looked like something out of the past, but with a nod to the future.

"So is she ready to fly?" Logan asked.

"I had one of my clockwork test pilots take it out this morning."

Logan snatched the keys from Monti's hand. He pressed a button on the remote, and the hatch opened. A clockwork pushed a set of portable steps over to the driver's side.

"I only have room for one passenger at a time," Logan said as he climbed into the cockpit. "So who's first?"

"Go ahead," Harley said, looking at Max.

"Are you sure?" Max asked.

"Yeah. I want to take a look at that plasma gun."

The clockwork pushed a second set of steps to the passenger side. Max scrambled up and sat next to Logan. There was a steering wheel in front of Logan and a throttle between the seats.

"Put this on," Logan said, handing Max a wireless headset. Then he placed the key in the ignition, and the instrument panel lit up. "Everybody clear out there?"

"You're good to go!" Monti shouted.

"What about you?" Logan said as the hatch closed.

Max gave him a thumbs-up as the garage door on the exterior wall opened. Rain and wind swept across as clouds swirled overhead.

"Hold on." Logan turned the ignition. Silver flames leaped from the exhaust pipes as the aerocar started to shake. When he pushed on the throttle, the Jaguar shot out the door and into the open air. The thrust from the takeoff was so powerful that it pinned Max to the back of his seat.

Logan pulled back on the steering wheel, and the

nose of the Jaguar lifted. He accelerated and the aerocar burst forward, rising into the sky as rain pelted the windshield. Logan flicked a switch, turning on the wipers. Then he sent the Jaguar into a roll. It spun like a corkscrew as it continued to climb. Max felt his stomach flip, just like it did whenever he rode a roller coaster.

"Not bad," Logan said as the aerocar shot into a bank of clouds, where there was no visibility. When they broke free of the clouds, Logan leveled out.

"What happens if we crash?" Max asked. They were going so fast that everything outside was a blur.

Logan laughed. He pulled back on the steering wheel. The aerocar rose higher, spinning again. Max closed his eyes as he felt his lunch climb up his throat. Then Logan banked hard to the left. The Jaguar rolled. If it weren't for the seat belt, Max would have been thrown into the hatch.

"You look a little green," Logan said. Then he smiled.

Max kept his eyes straight ahead.

"What do you say we head back into the city for a bit?" Logan said. "I told the chief constable that we'd help him with patrols until he can get a lead or two."

"Do you really think it's changelings from our school?"

"It's hard to say," Logan said as he turned the aerocar back toward New Victoria. "They'd have to get past Nipkin first, and we both know that's no easy task."

"It might be easier than you think."

"Is there something you're not telling me?"

110

Max wouldn't look Logan in the eyes. Of course, thanks to Natalia, he knew that one of the tells of being guilty was the avoidance of eye contact, so he concentrated on his shoes and didn't say anything.

"Listen to me," Logan said with furrowed brows. "If those kids are wandering the streets of Bludgeon Town looking for trouble, they'll find all they want and more. They're either going to end up in a slaver's net or dead. Do you want that on your head?"

The last thing that Max wanted was to get Ernie angrier with him, but it was better than Ernie getting kidnapped, or worse. Max sighed and his shoulders slumped, but he still didn't look at Logan. "They found a way to turn their inhibitors off," he finally said.

Logan clenched his jaws before he pushed the throttle to maximum speed. The engine roared as they tore through the rain, heading straight to Bludgeon Town.

PART TWO

HUNTED

PATROL DUTY

"Are you going to tell Nipkin?" Max asked.

"What do you think?"

"We don't have any proof."

"What about common sense?" Logan said. "Ernie is upset. He rallied the changelings to make a preemptive strike before any more changelings get kidnapped. Sound about right?"

"If you say something, he's going to hate me."

Logan took a deep breath.

"Please," Max said.

"I'm not making any promises," Logan said. He could see that Max was torn between keeping his friend's secret and possibly saving him from danger. "Look, why don't you take the controls for a bit?"

Max looked out the window. The world was a blur.

"I don't know."

"It's either that or we crash," Logan said. As the dash unfolded, revealing a second steering wheel, he folded his hands behind his head.

"What are you doing?" Max asked before grabbing the steering wheel. The nose dipped. All Max could see through the windshield was water.

"You might want to pull back a touch," Logan said.

Max overcompensated. This time the nose shot straight up. His stomach lurched.

"Take a deep breath," Logan said. "Then level her out nice and slow. She'll do whatever you tell her. And you might want to open your eyes. We're closing in on the docks."

Max could see an armada of boats moored in the bay. Wooden buildings dotted the shoreline beyond. Overhead, a zeppelin was anchored to a loading tower. Moments later the aerocar buzzed over a cluster of streets where peddlers were selling their wares to sailors and fishermen.

"Head toward those chimneys," Logan said.

Max nudged the steering wheel to the left.

"You might want to steer clear of that bell tower," Logan said.

This time, Max jerked the controls to the right, sending the aerocar into a corkscrew. The wing clipped a brick wall, and the aerocar ricocheted.

Logan grabbed his steering wheel before pulling them out of the roll.

"Thanks," Max said. His heart was pounding, and his palms itched.

Logan gave the controls back to Max, who managed to avoid a network of clotheslines loaded with dingy laundry. Then he maneuvered around smokestacks and a seagull.

"I don't see any activity down there. Maybe we should head back so Harley can have a turn," Max said.

"Hold on," Logan said. He took out a pair of binoculars.

"What's wrong?"

"I think we found the Agents of Justice."

Logan grabbed the steering wheel before pushing the throttle forward. The engine roared as the aerocar shot toward Bludgeon Town. Max took the binoculars. He could see a man in a skullcap surrounded by six children in masks.

"Can you see Tweeny?"

"I don't think so," Max said. He adjusted the settings to get a wider view. There was movement in a window. Someone was holding a rifle. Max pushed the binoculars at Logan.

"What's wrong?" Logan asked through clenched teeth.

"A sniper."

"You're going to have to bring us in," Logan said. He

let go of the steering wheel before reaching back to grab a duffel bag.

"What?"

The aerocar dipped to the right. Max grabbed the steering wheel, and they leveled off. Logan pulled out a dart gun. He attached the barrel before loading the chamber. Then he flipped another switch, and the hatch opened up. Wind tore through the cab, blowing Max's hair like a wheat field in a storm.

"Time to go to sleep," Logan said as he looked through the scope. He squeezed the trigger. With a pop, a tranquilizer dart shot from the barrel. It hit the man in the window.

Twenty slavers rushed out from the shadows and into the alley. One pulled out a net. It spun through the air before latching around one of the masked vigilantes.

More nets flew. One of the children raised a hand. Blue liquid sprayed from her palm. It encased one of the nets in ice, stopping the net in midair before it fell to the ground and shattered.

"We have to help them!" Max yelled as the slavers closed in.

"Listen to me," Logan said. "I'm going down there, and you're heading back to the lab."

Max watched as two of the children were trying to free a third who had been caught in a net.

Logan grabbed Max by the arm. "Did you hear me?"

Max nodded.

"Look out!"

They were headed toward an apartment building when Max pulled back on the steering wheel, narrowly dodging it. Silver flames shot out from the exhaust as they broke into the open sky. Max could feel his heart pounding. His palms were sweating, and he worried about holding on to the steering wheel.

"Head back around," Logan said.

Max pulled back on the throttle to cut their speed and then banked hard to the left.

"Lower," Logan said.

Max pushed forward on the steering wheel. The aerocar dropped below the roofline and into a patch of fog. The only light was from the gas lamps. Logan put his dart gun behind the seat and removed his seat belt before standing up.

"What are you doing?" Max asked. His eyes were wide.

"Keep her steady."

"Logan!"

The aerocar passed over the slavers. Logan jumped with his arms and legs stretched wide. He landed on one of the slavers and knocked him unconscious.

As Max brought the aerocar out of the streets and into the sky, he could hear Logan breathing heavily through the communication link. The hatch clicked shut.

"*Head back to Monti's,*" Logan said.

Max was already heading back to the street. "But—"

"It's not open for discussion."

Max looked for a radio to call for backup, but he couldn't find one. There were too many controls, and he couldn't focus long enough without risking a wreck. Then something crashed down from above. A clockwork landed on the wing, and the aerocar dipped to the right. There was another thud. The nose dipped. A second clockwork was standing on the hood.

Max pulled back on the steering wheel before he slammed the throttle to full, but the aerocar flew in reverse. It slammed into a wall, shuddering as loose bricks fell across the trunk. Both clockworks lost their balance and fell over the side.

"Get out of here before more of those things show up," Logan said through the headset.

"How do you go forward?"

"Green switch on the left."

Max flipped it. He pushed the throttle while pulling back on the steering wheel and shot into the sky. "Sorry," Max said, "but I'm not leaving you down there."

Max turned around, and the quick motion made his stomach jump into his throat. He headed back to the alley.

"Let's see what else this thing can do," he muttered as he randomly flipped switches and pressed buttons.

A monitor lowered from the ceiling. It gave Max a view of the two clockworks that were chasing him on a flying hybrid of a motorcycle and a snowmobile. Bolts of energy exploded from guns mounted to the vehicles.

Max banked hard right, then left. He wove through chimneys and skirted past steeples. So did the clockworks. They opened fire, peppering the aerocar with plasma bolts. One hit the left wing. Max could see smoke billowing from the engine.

He jammed the throttle forward. The streets below blurred. He was closing in on an abandoned warehouse, but Max didn't change course. He could feel his sweat dripping down his cheeks.

"This better work."

He closed his eyes. Then, at the last possible moment, he pulled back on the throttle. At the same time, he yanked the steering wheel until the nose of the aerocar pointed straight up. Max pushed the throttle to full thrust. The aerocar shot into the sky. He could feel the hull scrape against brick. Sparks flew, and the aerocar rattled.

Max glanced at the screen. The clockworks couldn't pull away, and they crashed into the wall. There was an explosion. Fire. Metal. Brick. Max headed back to the alley. By the time he got there, constables were swarming everywhere. Some held slavers in handcuffs. Others searched behind trash bins.

"*I thought I told you to head back*," Logan said through his headset.

"I ran into some trouble."

"I can see that."

"Do you want a ride?"

Max could hear Logan sighing. *"That was a nice bit of flying."*

"Thanks."

"You know, I'm starting to think you don't need me."

"Yeah, right."

"That day is coming sooner than you think."

THE PRICE OF FAME

After the incident, Max had to endure two hours of monotonous questioning from Chief Constable Oxley. When it was over, Max wasn't sure if he was a suspect or if he was going to get the key to the city. Either way, it was better than what he had to deal with the next morning. A picture of Max flying the aerocar had made the front page of the *Chronicle*.

From the moment he stepped foot into the subway depot, Max was the center of attention. He was peppered with an endless string of questions, most notably from the Toad brothers.

At school, people pointed and whispered as he walked

down the halls. Then, in class, a boy named Winston Ainsworth asked Max for an autograph.

"Go on," Harley said. "You're a celebrity now."

"You don't have to make it out to anybody," Winston said, holding out a piece of paper. "Just sign your name."

Max was blushing as he signed his name. Then Winston went back to his desk and folded it carefully before sliding the autograph into a protective sheet of plastic.

When Max went to grab his DE Tablet from under his desk, he caught Ernie glowering at him. They locked eyes for a moment, but Max turned away, wondering what he'd done this time.

Max felt anger starting to rise in him. He wanted to ask Ernie what his problem was. After all, Max thought, he'd risked his life to help save Ernie's friends. He didn't ask for the attention. If anything, Max hated it.

By lunch, Max had signed more than twenty autographs. One of the maintenance clockworks had even asked for a signature, so Max decided to eat lunch in the courtyard to avoid further embarrassment.

"Where do you think you're going?" Harley said as Max walked down the hallway with his tray. Sprig was padding next to him as a white tiger.

"Out."

"If you want to be a hero, you're going to have to get used to the fans."

"I never wanted to be a hero."

"Stop being so sensitive," Harley said.

Sprig growled as they walked out the door and into the courtyard.

"Save it," Harley said.

"Why aren't you sitting with Natalia?" Max asked.

Harley shrugged. "A bunch of girls took over our table."

"Was Brooke there?"

"Does it matter?"

"I guess not."

"Yes."

"Yes, what?"

"Brooke was there."

"I figured."

Harley sat down on the ledge of a fountain filled with sparkling fish. Max took the stone bench across from him. The seat was damp from the morning rain. It was chilly out, but the sky had cleared up enough to make it tolerable.

"So Logan isn't going to tell Nipkin about the inhibitors?" Harley asked before taking a bite of his turkey sandwich.

"Not yet."

"Did you recognize any of the kids in the masks?"

"I don't think so."

"What did you tell Oxley?"

"He had a book filled with pictures of all the changelings, but I couldn't identify anybody. I told him they were all wearing masks."

"Do you think he believed you?"

"It's hard to say," Max said as he poked at the noodles in his chicken soup.

"The article in the *Chronicle* mentioned they'd caught seven of the slavers, but none of them are talking. They wouldn't even tell the constables their names."

"They're probably scared of Von Strife."

"I can't blame 'em," Harley said. "By the way, we fixed the jam in that plasma gun. Monti let me shoot a few rounds. You should see what it did to that mannequin."

"I bet," Max said, not hiding his sullen tone.

"What's wrong?" Harley said. "You just saved the lives of six changelings. You should be on top of the world."

"Tell that to Ernie."

"You can't do anything about the way he's acting, so you might as well get over it."

"I guess." Max slurped down a few spoonfuls of soup before pushing his tray aside. The wind picked up, shaking the shrubs as spray from the fountain splashed against his cheek.

Natalia and Brooke were already at their desk by the time Max walked into Obadiah Strange's class with Sprig in tow. They didn't notice Max as he slid into his desk, but Honeysuckle did. She had been tending to a plant that hung next to the window. When she saw Max, she zipped down to whisper something in Brooke's ear.

"When did you get here?" Natalia asked.

"A couple of minutes ago."

"Are you okay?"

"Yeah, I guess."

"We missed you at lunch."

Max felt his eyes roam to Brooke before turning back to Natalia. "I ate in the courtyard."

"In this weather?"

Max shrugged. "It wasn't that bad."

Water was dripping from Harley's long bangs as he took a seat next to Max. Then Ernie and the Toad brothers walked in, but Obadiah Strange and the other changelings were nowhere to be found.

"I don't know if it's such a good idea," Todd said.

"Yeah, you guys really messed up."

Ernie shot his hand over Ross's mouth. "Not here," Ernie said as his eyes darted across the room.

"Are you three talking about the Agents of Justice?" Natalia asked.

"No," Ernie said.

"Oh, really, then what were you talking about?"

"That's confidential," Todd said.

"Yeah," Ross said. "Confidential."

"It's kind of hard to keep a secret when you're on the front page every morning."

"I wouldn't know," Ernie said. "Maybe you should talk to Max about that. Or has he been too busy signing autographs?"

"Why are you acting like such a brat?" Natalia asked.

Obadiah Strange walked through the door with three of the missing changelings.

"Sorry we're late," he said. "We had a little matter to clear up."

Hale, Yi, and Raven took their seats as Strange placed his briefcase on his desk.

"Where were you?" Natalia asked Raven.

"Dean Nipkin wouldn't let us go to class, so Strange came to get us."

"What did Nipkin do?"

Raven shrugged. "What could she do?"

"Before we begin today," Strange said before turning to Max, "it appears as though congratulations are in order."

"Oh...um, thanks." Max could feel his ears turning red as he lowered his eyes.

"You're far too modest," Strange said. "In fact, I hear the mayor has decided to give you the key to the city. That's quite an accomplishment for someone your age."

"Nice work, Sumner," Xander said.

"Wow, the key to the city?" Todd said.

"That's like..." Ross said, trying to think of an appropriate phrase. "I don't know, it's—"

"Impressive?" Kenji said as his drake eyed a mouse skittering across the floor.

"Yeah, it's impressive," Ross said.

"All right," Strange said. "I think we've embarrassed the young man enough. Now I've put this off long enough, but it's time to collect your accidental death and dismemberment clauses. Would you mind gathering them for me, Miss Lugosi?"

Raven didn't move. It was as though she was locked in a staring contest with Strange, but just when it was about to get uncomfortable, she got out of her desk to collect the forms.

"Thank you," Strange said before walking over to open one of his desk drawers, where he pulled out a small metal box connected to a wand by a spiraling cord. "Now, who can tell me what this is?"

"That's the scanner Saxon used to find all his treasures," Todd said.

"Yeah," Ross said. "A Vibration Frequency Detector, right?"

"Very good," Strange said. He spent the rest of the class talking about the first expedition he went on with Lord Saxon.

Strange and Lord Saxon had traveled to Jerusalem to find the Seal of Solomon, a signet ring that was thought to give the wearer control over demons and genies called Djinns. When he got to the part of the story where they had fallen down what they thought was a bottomless pit, the bell rang. Nobody moved.

"You're going to finish the story, right?" Ernie asked. "I mean, you can't just leave us hanging like that again."

The rest of the students murmured in agreement.

"I'm afraid we're out of time," Strange said. "Now

over the next few days, we'll be going through some exercises in the simulation chamber."

"Are you sure that's a good idea?" Ross said. He was looking at Yi.

"Yeah, somebody almost blew that place up last semester," Todd said.

"That wasn't my fault," Yi said.

"Well, it wasn't a band of leprechauns," Ross said.

Yi stood up. His fingertips started to spark, and his hands burst into flames.

OUT IN THE OPEN

Sensing a threat, Sprig popped up to see what was happening. When she spotted Yi, she pinned her ears back and lowered her head, growling as she bared her teeth.

"See what I mean?" Ross said. "The guy is a maniac."

Strange walked over and placed his hands on Yi's shoulder. "That's enough, Mr. Lu. We must defeat ignorance with education, not with might."

The entire class watched as Yi struggled to calm down.

"Relax," Max said as he reached out to stroke Sprig. Her eyes didn't leave Yi, but she stopped growling.

"Breathe slowly," Strange said as he guided Yi back to his desk. "Now take your seat."

"Think what would have happened if you weren't here," Todd said. "He probably would have—"

"That's enough," Strange said. His voice was calm, but his eyes were filled with anger. "These poor students are already dealing with the irrational fears of the people who should be protecting them. I will not tolerate bigotry in my classroom. Is that understood?"

Todd and Ross nodded.

"That will be all," Strange said, dismissing the class.

"Nice one," Ernie said as he put his DE Tablet in his backpack.

"I didn't know that stating facts was a crime," Ross said.

"That's not the point."

As Yi stormed down the aisle, Todd caught him by the arm. "Look, we're sorry."

"Save it," Yi said. His hand was glowing like an ember as he grabbed Todd's wrist.

"Let go!" Todd said. "That really burns."

"Knock it off," Ernie said.

Yi let go. Todd's wrist had turned bright red, and blisters had begun to form.

"Come on," Hale said. She placed her hand on Yi's shoulder. "He's not worth it."

"What's that supposed to mean?" Ross asked.

"Let it go," Todd said as he watched the two changelings walk out the door.

"He just burned you with his powers," Ross said. "A real superhero wouldn't do that."

"Do you know how hard it was to get the other changelings to accept you two?" Ernie asked. "They don't trust anyone, and to tell you the truth, neither do I."

"You can trust us," Ross said.

"Not if you make comments like that."

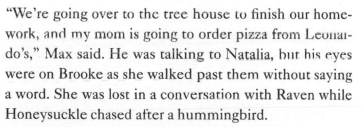

"We're going over to the tree house to finish our homework, and my mom is going to order pizza from Leonardo's," Max said. He was talking to Natalia, but his eyes were on Brooke as she walked past them without saying a word. She was lost in a conversation with Raven while Honeysuckle chased after a hummingbird.

"I can't," Natalia said. "Maybe tomorrow?"

"When have you ever had plans?" Harley asked.

"I'm studying with Brooke and Raven," Natalia said. Then she turned to Max, who was kicking at a clump of grass. "Are you okay?"

"Yeah, I'm fine."

Natalia hesitated as she looked at him. "Okay," she finally said. "I have to get going."

Max turned to walk to the subway depot with Harley as Natalia went to catch up with the girls.

"Hey! Wait up!" Max heard someone call. He turned

around to see the Toad brothers struggling to catch their breaths. Their faces were red, and sweat was pouring down their cheeks.

"Look, we don't have a lot of time," Ross said once they caught up, "but if you have plans tomorrow night, break them."

"Do I even want to know why?"

"Round Table practice," Todd said.

"I don't know," Max said. "I'm thinking about dropping out."

"Sorry," Todd said. "You're contractually obligated."

"What are you talking about?"

"It's part of our contract. You know, the one where we gave you free *Toad Reports*," Ross said. "You need to read the fine print."

"Don't look at me," Harley said after Max gave him a pleading look.

Max turned back to the Toad brothers. "Who am I supposed to practice against?"

"We don't want to ruin the surprise," Todd said.

"Can you at least tell me where we're supposed to meet?"

Todd and Ross looked at each other. "You know that house where you found all the changelings? Be there at seven o'clock."

"You want me to play Round Table outside in the middle of winter?" Max asked. "It's going to be ten below."

"Don't worry," Ross said. "We took care of everything."

Friday was remarkably quiet. People had stopped asking Max for his autograph, and there were no more Agents of Justice sightings. By the time night rolled around, Max was actually looking forward to playing Round Table, even if it was outside in the dead of winter. If nothing else, it was going to give him a chance to break in some of his new clockwork cards.

"You're sure you want to do this?" Harley asked as they headed toward the house.

"I could use the practice," Max said. Wisps of vapor escaped from his mouth each time he exhaled, and his footfalls crunched through the snow as he walked. Sprig pranced next to them as an arctic fox.

"You realize we're being watched, right?" Harley asked.

"I saw the one in the upstairs window."

"There're two more in the trees, and another one behind the thicket on the side of the house."

"Do you think this is a setup?" Max asked as Sprig bounded up the steps.

"I guess we're going to find out," Harley said. He was about to knock on the door when it swung open.

"You made it," Ross said.

There was a fire burning in the hearth inside. Ernie was there, locked in a Round Table duel with Yi in the front room. A small crowd had gathered to watch them, and from the sound of things, Ernie was ahead.

"We have everything set up," Todd said, leading them into the house.

"It's actually warm in here," Harley said as he pulled off his ski mask.

"Everything's been sealed up tight," Todd said. "We brought in some generators, got the fireplaces cleaned out, and we even have some portable gas stoves that we bought at a sporting goods store in Bloomington. You want some hot chocolate or something?"

"Maybe later," Max said as he removed his gloves.

There were candles everywhere, from the mantle to the stairs and just about anywhere there was a flat surface. The wooden floors had been swept clean of debris, and sheets of plywood now covered the broken windows.

"We tried to get Catalina to come tonight, but she wouldn't do it," Todd said. "I guess I can't blame her. I mean, you guys don't want to give away all your secrets before the big match, right?"

"I suppose," Max said.

"So we got the next best thing," Todd said. "Now look, I don't want you to be intimidated just because she beat Xander."

"I thought he was undefeated," Max said.

"When it comes to sanctioned duels, he is," Todd said. "She beat him in a street match. Twice."

"Who is she?"

"Hale," Todd said, in a tone that suggested Max should have already known that.

136

There was a group of at least a dozen changelings standing in the room, but Todd was pointing at Hale. Max watched her take a sip of hot chocolate before sitting down at a gigantic wooden spool that used to hold electrical cable. It was set on its end to make a table. Her trading cards and knucklebones were already set up and ready to go.

"Here I figured you'd be out on a date with your girlfriend," Hale said after she saw Max. "You know, dinner and a movie. Isn't that what normal people do on a Friday night?"

The air started to shimmer around her, and Max watched as Hale's skin bubbled. It looked painful, but she kept smiling. Then she was gone, replaced by Brooke. She winked at Max, who just stood there looking confused. He could vaguely hear everyone's laughter as he struggled for something to say.

"Ignore her," Todd said. "She's trying to get in your head. You know, to psych you out."

"Did I do a good job?" Hale asked after she had turned back to her original form.

"I've seen shape-shifters before," Max said. He was trying to sound confident, but he wasn't sure it was convincing. Max pulled out his knucklebones and his new deck and sat down in his chair.

"Not like me," Hale said.

"Okay," Todd said. "This might not be an officially sanctioned duel, but we're still going to play by the

King's Rules. That means the first person to strike his or her opponent seven times will be the winner, but if neither one of you can—"

"Yeah, we got it," Hale said. "If we can't get seven hits after an hour, whoever has the most points wins."

"Exactly," Ross said.

"Let's roll to see who goes first," Hale said as she shook a pair of knucklebones in her cupped hand. Max grabbed his as well, and after Hale counted down from three, they both cast their roll.

SHOWDOWN

"I hope that's not an omen," Hale said as she looked at the double ones that Max had just rolled. In the game, that was considered automatic failure.

"Don't worry," Max said. "I'm just getting it out of the way."

Hale slipped on her Kinematic goggles before turning on the power.

The MERLIN Tech that surged through the goggles turned a simple trading-card game into a three-dimensional, interactive battle where the duelists became part of the action. In reality, they were still pitting card against card while casting knucklebones to determine their success, but the Kinematic goggles made everything seem real.

Max fired up his goggles, as did everyone standing around the table. It was the only way to watch the real action. The dining room faded and was replaced by the charred remains of a city. The sky was filled with swirling clouds, and rain fell diagonally. When lightning flashed, Max started to second-guess his decision to play with a deck filled with metal clockworks.

"Are you ready?" Hale asked. She was standing under the glow of a gas lamp on the far end of the street.

"Does it matter?"

"Good point." Hale flicked her wrist, sending a Round Table card spinning through the air. In a flash, it disappeared, leaving something that looked like a cross between a lizard and a bird in its place. It was as big as a horse, with a head that looked like a falcon's. Its reptilian body was covered in blue scales, and feathers crested around its neck like a mane.

"Are you going to defend yourself or not?" Hale asked as the monster's forked tail swished back and forth.

Max flipped his card into play, and a small clockwork appeared. It was shaped like a barrel and had tracked wheels. Its head was a turret with a cannon, and as Max saw it standing in front of the monster, he realized it didn't stand a chance.

"Are you serious?" Hale asked. Everyone laughed. Then she cast her knucklebones. The total was added to her monster's attack value, and that released the monster. It ran across the cobblestones before launching into the air with outstretched claws.

Max shook his own knucklebones before releasing them, but the result was pathetic. He was forced to watch as the clockwork fired an errant plasma bolt that hit one of the gas lamps.

Hale's monster landed on top of the machine, ripping off the clockwork's turret with a swipe of its claw. The clockwork sputtered before its gears stopped rotating. It was out of the game.

Max went on the offensive with a clockwork covered in iron plating. Each of its four hands held a plasma revolver as its eye scanned the horizon, looking for an opponent.

"Multiple-attack advantage? Nicely played," Hale said.

She countered with a pixie that looked like a cross between a grasshopper and a little girl. When the clockwork fired its first round, the pixie danced nimbly to the side. Then she stuck out her tongue. The second shot wasn't even close. Max was ready to ditch his knucklebones for a new set, especially after the next shot missed as well.

"Can somebody get Max a hot chocolate with extra marshmallows?" Hale said. "He's going to need something to calm his nerves."

Max tried to ignore her chatter. He scooped up his knucklebones and shook them in his fist. He had one last chance.

"It's about time," Hale said after she saw what he cast.

The clockwork took aim before squeezing the trigger. Hale's pixie tried to fly away, but it wasn't fast enough. When the bolt struck, she exploded in a cloud of shimmering dust that turned back into a Round Table card after it settled on the street. He was on the board with his first point.

"So what's with all the metal, Sumner?" Hale asked.

"They're part of the new expansion set."

"Clockwork Chaos?"

"Yeah."

"It's not even out yet. How'd you get them?"

"If I told you, I'd have to kill you," Max said. "But if you're nice to me, maybe I'll give you my doubles."

"Is that a bribe?" Hale had disappeared only to be replaced by Chief Constable Oxley. His enormous mustache was dripping with water as rain beaded on his hat.

Max smiled. "No strings attached."

"Very well," Oxley said in Hale's voice. "Just make sure you mind yourself—these streets aren't safe for children."

Oxley disappeared, leaving Hale standing in his place. Her green skin glistened in the rain as her antennae swayed. Over her next four turns, she scored three points to take a commanding lead. Max did his best to counter, but he didn't have much luck.

He had no idea how to use the new cards in his deck, but Hale was managing hers expertly. She set traps and took advantage of bonuses that eliminated some of his best cards. It wasn't long before she had five points, while Max was still stuck on two.

Then she sent a Frost dragon after him. The beast roared as it shimmered to life. Its wide mouth was filled with more teeth than Max could count, and everywhere it stepped, the ground turned to ice. It looked hungry.

Max countered with an enormous Nemesis clockwork. As it came to life, he could see the fire burning through a grate in its chest. Clouds of steam poured out from two exhaust pipes that shot up over its shoulders, and the hands on all four of its arms flexed and unflexed.

The dragon roared, but the clockwork didn't budge. It stood with its feet planted firmly as the dragon slammed its tail against the ground. Chunks of frozen bricks shot into the air. Then, with its lip curled back, the dragon launched at the clockwork.

The Nemesis wrapped two hands around the dragon's snout while two others took hold of its neck. Then the clockwork fell back. Its feet shot onto the dragon's chest before it flipped the dragon over. The dragon landed with a thud, and Max struggled to remain standing as the ground shook. The dragon dissipated. Max had won.

He went on the offensive with his Nemesis, and Hale countered with a gnome. Max frowned. It seemed like a ridiculous play. After all, the tip of the gnome's pointed red cap didn't even reach the clockwork's knee.

"Are you serious?" Max asked.

"Do your best," Hale said.

The clockwork charged. With each step it took, brick cracked under its weight. All four arms were outstretched. Its eyes were glowing red. The gnome looked unperturbed. Its eyes were heavy as though it was tired. Then, as the clockwork closed in, the gnome reached into a pouch hanging from its belt. In a single motion it tossed seeds onto the ground.

The rain continued to fall. The ground rumbled before it broke apart. The Nemesis was about to grab the tiny gnome when giant vines sprang from the ground. Like the tentacles of a hungry octopus, the vines wrapped around the clockwork. They twisted around its neck, legs, waist, and arms before hoisting the Nemesis into the air.

Its arms and legs flailed, then bolts of electricity coursed over the vines before shooting into the clockwork. The machine convulsed as smoke rose out from its eyes. The vines threw the lifeless metal husk to the ground. A moment later the clockwork fizzled before it turned back into a Round Table card.

Max slammed his fist on the table.

"You realize we should be tied, right?" Hale said.

"Yeah, right."

"You get too emotional, and then you lose focus."

"It's your move," Max said. Losing was one thing, but getting a lecture was unbearable.

Hale tossed a card into the air. It vanished with a pop before an armored zeppelin appeared in the sky. Max wished he had his regular deck. He would have sent a swarm of Fireball Pixies to rupture the zeppelin's envelope.

Instead, he had to settle on a massive machine called a Magnetron. According to the description on the card, it was capable of creating a magnetic field that would devour anything made of metal once it was in range.

"Nice try," Hale said. "Too bad missiles are made of metal, too."

As Hale cast her knucklebones, Max closed his eyes. The magnetic field would make sure that the zeppelin's missiles didn't miss. They roared through the sky before hitting the Magnetron. The ground shook as the machine exploded, sending a shower of scorched metal into the air.

"Time's up," Ross said before Max had a chance to go on the offensive. "And our winner is . . . Hale!"

Everyone cheered.

Max peeled off his Kinematic goggles and threw them onto the table. It took a moment for his eyes to adjust, but he was back in the dining room of the abandoned house.

"Shake it off," Harley said as the crowd dispersed. Most of the group ended up in the kitchen, where Ross and Todd had set out snacks. For the Toad brothers, the duel was nothing more than a chance to sell more *Toad Reports*, so they didn't skimp on the treats as part of their bribe to entice new business.

"If I play like that, I'm not going to make the team," Max said.

"If you focus, you will," Hale said, joining them.

"Yeah, right."

"Listen, Sumner. Did you know that I got kicked out of a tournament last year for flipping a table over?"

"What happened?"

"I was upset because an unranked player scored against me on consecutive turns. If that wasn't bad enough, he started taunting me," Hale said. "I told him to shut his mouth, but he kept on chirping, so I stood up, threw the table out of the way, and then I punched him."

"During a school tournament?"

Hale nodded. "I got suspended for the rest of the season. It was my own fault. I mean, I had a shot at becoming the youngest champion in the history of the Templar academies, but thanks to my temper, I blew it."

"So that's how Xander won the title," Max said.

"Who knows, maybe he would have beat me anyway," Hale said, shrugging. "But yeah, I think about it every day. If you don't keep yourself in check, you're going to have the same regrets. You can't let your emotions get the best of you . . . not at this level."

"Here." Max offered her his Round Table cards.

"I don't need your charity."

"It's not charity," Max said. "I told you, I have doubles. Besides, after what just happened, I'm never playing with those cards again. Either you take them or I'm going to burn them. It's your choice."

"What are you talking about?" Todd said.

146

"Yeah," Ross said. "Do you know how much money we could get for those?"

Before the Toad brothers could snatch them away, Hale took the cards. Then she placed them in her satchel. "As long as these are doubles, I guess I could take them off your hands."

"By the way," Max said, "thanks for the duel...and the advice."

"No problem," Hale said. "Next time, bring your best deck. I heard you almost beat a Grandmaster."

"That was just luck."

"There's no such thing."

CONVERSATIONS WITH THE UNDEAD

Natalia spent Saturday in the Iron Bridge library, researching the writings of Sir Walter Windham.

She had written the name down after seeing it inside the visual memory linked to Von Strife's journal. Windham was the author of some books on Von Strife's desk.

Natalia had been hoping to find a direct link between Windham and Von Strife, but she wasn't having much luck. Most of Windham's writing was on the subject of time travel, which was a controversial subject at best. Then again, a man who was desperate to save his daughter might be willing to try anything to save her.

Then Natalia came across an old article in the *New Victoria Chronicle.*

"You had me come down here to read the obituary of some guy who died over a hundred years ago?" said Raven, who was sitting at a table with Natalia.

"Please lower your voices," the librarian said from behind the checkout desk.

Raven rolled her eyes.

"Don't you recognize who this is?" Natalia asked in a whisper.

"Should I?"

"He wrote the books that were in the memory you showed us, and guess where he's buried?"

"Underneath the school?"

"You're close," Natalia said. "He's buried at the cemetery behind the Cathedral of St. Peter."

"What good does that do us? He's kind of dead, right?"

"I was thinking," Natalia said, "what if Von Strife visited his grave?"

"So you want me to talk to a gravestone, is that it?" Raven asked. "Are you serious?"

Natalia got Raven to agree to her plan, and within an hour, the girls exited the *Zephyr* at the Walpole Road platform. A light drizzle fell as the weak gas lamps fought to give meager light.

"Is New Victoria always this dreary?" Natalia asked, opening her umbrella.

"Pretty much," Raven said. Her heels clicked on the sidewalk as they headed toward the iron gate that stood protectively around the cemetery lawns.

There was a gust of wind, followed by a low moaning sound. Both girls stopped.

"That was just my imagination, right?" Natalia asked.

"Let's hope so," Raven said.

Though the cemetery was closed to visitors after five o'clock in the evening, the length of chain that held the gate shut had been cut away. Natalia crouched down to find at least two distinct footprints.

"You still want to do this?" Raven asked.

Natalia swallowed and nodded.

"After you," Raven said, holding the gate open.

As they moved down a line of crumbling vaults, Raven said, "I can't believe I let you talk me into this." Rain was beading on the hood of her jacket, and her lips were blue from the cold.

She stopped at one of the crypts. The iron door leading inside was choked with weeds. Raven brushed them aside to reveal a plaque:

WALTER WINDHAM
The Marquis of Time
d. 1880
"TEMPUS RERUM IMPERATOR"

"Is that your man?" Raven asked.

"It looks like it," Natalia said.

Raven closed her eyes and placed her hand on the plaque. Then she frowned.

"What's wrong?" Natalia asked.

"Von Strife hasn't been here," Raven said. Her head was tilted to the side as though she was confused. "But Strange was here a few weeks ago, and he went inside."

"Obadiah Strange?"

"I know, it doesn't make any sense," Raven said. Then she fished out a flashlight from her backpack.

"What are you doing?" Natalia asked.

"We're going inside."

"Why?"

"Don't you want to know why Strange was here?"

There were more moaning sounds, and Natalia spun around to see the silhouettes of walking corpses approaching. Their heads hung at odd angles as they dragged their legs through the mud.

The first zombie was a woman who reminded Natalia of her mother. She had long, stringy red hair that was matted to her gaunt face. There were dark circles under her eyes, and her jaw hung too low, as though someone had tried to pull it off its hinges.

Natalia stood, transfixed, as Raven pushed open the door to Windham's crypt. She rushed inside, pulling Natalia in, and shut the door.

"What were you doing?" Raven asked. Her breathing was shallow, and her eyes were wild.

"I...I don't know," Natalia said as though she were waking from a dream.

Their only light came from the flashlight in Raven's hand, but the crypt was so choked by darkness that they couldn't see much of anything. Cobwebs hung from the low ceiling, and a fat spider scampered out of the light and back into the comfort of the shadows.

"Were those actually zombies?" Natalia asked.

"I'm not sure, but it looked like it."

Raven had her back braced against the door as though she was expecting the zombies to try to follow them, but they didn't.

"That's strange," Raven said.

"What?"

"It's not like I'm an expert or anything, but aren't zombies supposed to be able to smell blood?"

"I guess so," Natalia said.

"Then why aren't they trying to break down the door to eat our brains?"

"Wait, what are you doing?" Natalia asked as Raven

opened the door a crack. She peeked out, then pulled it open wide.

"They're gone," Raven said before slipping back out to the cemetery grounds.

The girls could still see the zombies in the distance, but they lost sight of the walking dead when a swirl of fog crossed the path.

"What should we do?" Natalia asked.

"Run!"

The girls ran through crooked trees and rough thickets, trying to get away, but no matter where they went, they were surrounded by the eerie sound of dead people moaning. It was as though the entire cemetery had come to life.

"Natalia!" Raven shouted.

When Natalia spun around, Raven was gone.

"Raven! Where are you?"

There was no response, and Natalia had lost track of which direction they'd been heading. She spun in circles calling Raven's name, but there was no answer. Then Natalia tripped on something. At first she thought it was an arm, but when she looked closer, she could see it was a shovel.

She took a step back but felt nothing underneath her foot. She screamed as she fell into an open grave, where she hit her head on a stone. The world went black.

When Natalia finally opened her eyes, she didn't know where she was. It was dark and raining. Her fingers dug into the wet earth as she moaned. Natalia tried to sit up, but she slipped before sloshing in a puddle. Her clothes were caked in mud, and her head was pounding.

"It came from over here," Natalia heard someone say through the haze of semiconsciousness. There was a moment when she wasn't sure if she was in a dream.

"You're sure?" a second voice asked.

Natalia realized that the nightmare was real. She'd fallen into an open grave and hit her head. Natalia raised her hand to her forehead, and when she pulled it away there was a spot of blood thinned by rain.

"Yeah, I heard someone scream," the first voice said as Natalia struggled to stand. Her feet sank in the sloshing mud, and she could taste her own blood as it fell on her lips.

"I don't see anyone."

The voices were close. Natalia was worried she might be spotted. She figured that whatever had happened to Raven was probably the speakers' doing, yet the voices were familiar. Natalia couldn't place them, though.

"I'm telling you, someone is in here. Do you think it's the Agents of Justice?" one of the voices said.

"I doubt it. Those nitwits have no idea what we're up

to. Besides, they're supposed to be down at the pier in Bludgeon Town tonight. We need to hurry if we're going to catch them."

Natalia's eyes lit up. That was Smoke — she was sure of it. Her heart started pounding. If they were after the Agents of Justice, that meant Ernie was in trouble. Natalia fought to climb out of the grave, but the walls were too slick, and she slipped back down into the mud.

"How long have you been able to do this?" she heard Smoke say.

"What?" the other voice answered.

"Animate dead people."

The other boy laughed. "Why? Are you scared or something?"

"I don't get scared," Smoke said. "Besides, don't forget that you're just a diversion to keep the THOR agents busy."

"What does that make you?"

"Your babysitter," Smoke said. "He sent me to make sure you don't screw up."

The voices trailed off, and so did the moaning from the zombies. Though her head was starting to clear, Natalia still felt groggy. At least, she thought, there weren't any bodies in the grave with her.

"Natalia?" Raven's voice wasn't much louder than a whisper.

"Raven?"

"Where are you?" Raven's voice was closer that time.

"I fell into a grave," Natalia said. It wasn't long before she saw Raven's face looking down at her.

"Nice hiding spot." Raven extended her hand, which Natalia grabbed, and she climbed out of the grave. Then she wrapped her arms around Raven's neck and held her tight. "Thank you," she repeated several times.

Raven gently pushed her away as a bolt of lightning shot through the sky. "What happened to you?" she asked. "If I didn't know better, I would have thought you were one of the zombies. Are you okay?"

"I'm fine," Natalia said. "I was worried that something happened to you."

"Yeah, well, I tripped on a tree root."

Natalia looked down to see that Raven's pants were ripped at the knees. "I didn't mean to leave you."

"I know," Raven said before looking over her shoulder at a zombie walking toward the horizon. "Everything is going to be okay."

"Did you see Smoke?" Natalia asked.

"Here?"

"I heard two people talking, and I'm positive he was one of them," Natalia said. "They mentioned Von Strife... and that the zombies are just diversions."

"From what?"

"I'm not sure, but they're heading down to the pier to look for Ernie."

TURNABOUT

Natalia called Max and Harley, who were at Monti's workshop. They tried to reach Ernie, but he wasn't answering his communicator. The boys promised to meet the girls down at the pier in Bludgeon Town.

With lungs burning and legs aching, Natalia and Raven splashed through puddles and skirted around beggars, hoping to avoid trouble as they raced through the underbelly of the city. It wasn't long before they could hear waves crashing against the rocky shoreline.

"We're getting close," Natalia said between pants. They had stopped to catch their breaths beneath the awning of a barbershop. Across the street, a long pier stretched toward the horizon. It was lighted with gas lamps hanging on wire poles, but they couldn't see much of anything else through the haze.

A dog started yapping, and its cries set off a chain reaction until the streets echoed with the sounds of upset canines. Then a horse tried to break free from its tether. It yanked its head and kicked with its hooves, but it didn't have any luck.

"The way those animals are spooked, I bet the zombies are close," Natalia said as she started to cross the street.

As Natalia made her way down the pier, she imagined undead sailors with worms slithering in their eye sockets, but she pushed those thoughts away and kept going. "Ernie?" she said, whispering loudly. "Are you out here?"

"I have a bad feeling about this," Raven said. "If those things show up, we're going to be trapped."

Fishing boats were moored to the pier, all of them empty as they swayed with the current. The wood beams creaked, and on one of the ships, the door to the tiny cabin kept opening and closing in the wind.

A wooden frigate stood twenty feet above the water. Its red sails billowed against the rolling banks of fog as seagulls glided around the masts, but by the time the girls reached the end of the dock, they hadn't seen a single soul.

That's when they heard footfalls on the planks. A moment later, two silhouettes appeared. They were walking through the fog toward them. Next came the agonizing moans that carried over the water. Natalia grabbed Raven's arm.

"Wait," Raven said, her eyes narrowing as she craned her neck. "Those aren't zombies."

"No kidding," Harley said as he walked out of the fog.

Natalia let go of Raven before running over to give Harley a hug.

"What was that for?" he asked.

"I don't know," she said before embracing Max. "I guess I'm glad neither of you are...well, zombies. Did you call Logan?"

"Not yet," Max said. "I think we need to do this one on our own."

"He's trying to show Ernie that we're there for him," Harley said. "All I know is that whatever we do, we need to hurry. The zombies are only a couple of blocks away, and there are more than we could count."

A pelican landed on the dock nearby, startling Natalia. Then it morphed into Sprig, who started licking her front paw.

"Have you seen Ernie?" Max asked.

"We haven't seen anybody," Natalia said.

"Here," Harley said, handing Natalia a small pistol.

"What is it?"

"A freeze ray. It's supposed to stop zombies."

"What about me?" Raven asked.

"It's just a prototype, so we only have one," Harley said before handing her a crowbar. "The rest of us get these."

"Gee, thanks," Raven said, letting it hang at her side.

"You aren't going to use those, are you?" Natalia asked.

Harley looked at her sideways. "How else are you supposed to kill a zombie?"

"I don't think they're zombies," Natalia said. "Someone is controlling them, kind of like puppets."

"Either way, they're still dead, so they won't feel a thing," Harley said.

"I still don't think we should hurt them," Natalia said, unwilling to let it go. "They used to be people's parents or grandparents....I even saw kids. It's just...I don't know. It's wrong, that's all."

"What about Smoke?" Max asked.

"What about me?" Smoke said as he flashed into view, blocking their path back to the shore.

Harley raised his crowbar as Sprig morphed into a white tiger and stood protectively in front of Max.

"I'd be careful if I were you," Smoke said. He disappeared before popping up in front of Harley. Then he wrapped his hand around the crowbar before vanishing again. He reappeared back where he started and dropped the crowbar into the water.

Sprig roared.

"Before this is over, Von Strife is going to turn on you," Natalia said. "He's going to rip your soul out and stuff it into a machine, just like he did with Robert."

"Von Strife doesn't want to kill anybody," Smoke said. "He's saving us. Don't you get it?"

"He is a liar," Sprig said.

Smoke sneered at the faerie. "What would you know? You're nothing more than a wild animal that can do a few parlor tricks."

"Tell that to Robert," Raven said as Sprig revealed her fangs.

Smoke closed his eyes and took two deep breaths. Then he looked straight at Raven. "Look, I'm here to help."

"Sure you are."

"The day is going to come when that faerie essence takes over your body," Smoke said. "You won't remember your name... where you live.... You won't even recognize your own parents. Is that what you want?"

Raven only glared.

There was a chorus of groaning as a mass of bodies stumbled down the pier.

"The only person who can help us is Von Strife," Smoke said.

"No, thanks," Raven said. "I'd rather get my brains eaten."

"Don't say I didn't offer." With that, Smoke was gone.

"Get behind me," Max said as the first zombie broke out of the fog. He reached down and twisted the iron ring on his finger. It shimmered before turning into the gauntlet.

"There're too many," Natalia said. She thought about jumping over the side of the dock, but when she looked down, all she saw was angry water swirling against the rocks.

"Don't give up on me," Max said. Blue flames ignited around his gauntlet. The zombies stopped, confused by the strange fire, but their confusion didn't last.

The first zombies slouched as they ambled with arms raised. Rotting skin clung to their bodies, and some were missing ears, lips, and even eyelids. With each step they took, the world seemed to grow darker, more hopeless.

Natalia swallowed hard before raising the ray gun.

"Shoot them!" Harley shouted.

The zombie closest to her was enormous. The hair from his balding head had fallen away, revealing pieces of his scalp. He was missing one eye, and a black liquid dripped down his face and onto his white shirt. His arms flailed as he dragged his back foot toward her.

Natalia could smell the rot of death. She screamed, and then she fired.

Liquid ice sprang from the barrel of the pistol before hitting the dead man. Ice crystals spread across his chest, encasing his entire body. He howled as he tried to break free, but he couldn't. Then he fell off the dock and into the raging water.

Natalia took aim and hit a second zombie. Then she shot at an old woman in a flowered dress who was missing most of her teeth, along with her left arm.

Max unleashed a stream of blue fire from his gauntlet, creating a wall in front of the zombies. The mass of the undead groaned louder, fearful of the flames that crackled in front of them. Sprig pawed at the air in warning, showing the undead her massive claws.

There was shouting coming from the end of the pier. The fog was too thick for any of them to see much of anything, but something was upsetting the zombies. As one, they turned before dragging themselves back to shore.

"Where are they going?" Natalia asked. The ray gun was shaking in her hands.

"I don't know, but this is our chance," Max said. He grabbed Natalia by the sleeve before stepping over the dying flames. Then he ran to shore.

The streets were filled with pandemonium as six costumed changelings drew the zombies away from the pier. A dozen of the undead lay frozen on the ground, victims of Nadya, the changeling who could turn moisture into ice. Yi was there as well. His body was shrouded in flames as he pushed the zombies toward a cliff that overlooked the water.

There was a blur of motion, and suddenly Ernie was

standing in front of them. "What are you guys doing here?" He sounded upset.

"We came to help you fight zombies," Natalia said.

The blare of sirens cut through the night. Ernie looked over his shoulder to see the first of the flashing lights. "You better go before the constables show up."

"What about you?" Natalia asked.

"I'll be fine."

"Come with us."

Ernie bit his lower lip. "I can't," he said. "I'm not going to leave anyone behind."

"But—"

"We'll be fine."

"Natalia thinks a changeling is controlling the zombies," Max said. "If you take him out, that should stop them."

Ernie paused. Then he nodded. "Thanks."

"Smoke's here, too."

"We're ready for him," Ernie said before taking off in a blur.

"Let's go," Max said as his gauntlet turned back into a ring.

"Yes," Sprig agreed. "We should leave this place."

"We're not going to abandon them, are we?" Natalia asked. "We can help."

"You heard him," Max said. "They don't need us."

"Max!" Natalia shouted.

Max spun around as one of the zombies reached for

him. The man's hair and beard were wild, and patches of his skin were torn away, revealing yellowed bone. Max ducked out of the way, infuriating the dead man.

Something grabbed Max's ankle. He tried to kick free and heard the crunch of bone as his heel connected with something, but he couldn't see who or what it was. More hands grabbed at him. Max looked up to see the remains of an elderly woman whose arm was swinging like a pendulum while her other arm reached toward Natalia.

Sprig swatted at a zombie as it lurched for Max, knocking it to the ground. Natalia screamed. Before the undead woman could grab her, Harley tackled the corpse. Then the remains of a young girl in a white dress smeared with mud approached. Her lips were pulled back in a snarl as she dragged one leg, relying on the other for her momentum.

"Get away from me!" Natalia shouted as she flailed with her arms. The girl's corpse tried to bite her but missed.

A rotting hand grabbed Max around the throat. The dead flesh felt like ice. Another hand grabbed his wrist. Max didn't want to give way to panic, but the walking dead were more horrific than monsters and faerie creatures combined. The nature of their movement was disturbing, and the stench of their flesh was vile.

Sprig pounced, biting into one of the zombies before throwing it to the side. She roared. The sound had the effect of a bucket of cold water as Max woke from his

165

daydream. Before scrambling to his feet, he pulled away from the zombie that held his arm.

Max watched as one of the undead slipped an arm around Harley's neck. Another wrapped around Harley's waist. Then there were more, and Harley fought to stay standing.

All of a sudden, the zombies fell lifeless to the ground.

"What was that?" Harley asked as he kicked free from the fallen corpses.

"I think he did it," Natalia said. "Ernie stopped the zombies!"

Max was breathing heavily. Then he smiled, but only for a moment. Corpses littered the streets and sidewalks, and the stench of death reeked in his nostrils. He felt sorry for whoever had to clean up the disgusting mess.

"We better get going before Oxley brings me in for another round of questioning," Max said as Sprig nuzzled against him.

IF AT FIRST YOU
DON'T SUCCEED

Obadiah Strange had promised a unique experience, and that's just what his class had become. Instead of being tethered to their desks or reading archaic books, his students met in the SIM Chamber, a hyper-real holographic training room.

To the naked eye, the SIM Chamber was little more than a stark dome with iron grating for a floor. There were no paintings, wallpaper, knickknacks, or decor of any sort. However, once it was activated, the SIM Chamber could transform into anything from a lush rain forest to the dark side of the moon. There were no limits to the scenarios that the instructors at Iron Bridge could run.

"I'm curious," Strange said from the observation platform inside the chamber. "Did anyone happen to read the front page of the *Chronicle* yesterday morning?"

Max caught Ernie looking at Yi and then Denton before turning back to Strange. Nobody said a word.

"I was fascinated to learn that our Agents of Justice have expanded their endeavors. Zombie extermination can be a nasty business."

Natalia raised her hand.

"Yes, Miss Romanov?"

"I'm not sure they're actually zombies," she said.

"Is that so?" Strange asked with a cocked eyebrow. "And what makes you say that?"

"Well, zombies are driven by hunger for human brains, but...well, there were no fatalities."

"So you did read the article?" Strange asked.

Natalia nodded.

"Any theories?"

"What if someone was controlling them?" Natalia asked. "You know, like puppets."

"Interesting," Strange said, scratching his beard. "There are, in fact, documented cases of changelings with the ability to control corpses, though never at this magnitude."

"Like I said, it's just a theory."

Strange's eyes lingered on Natalia before he turned his attention to the rest of the class. "Now then," he said. "Today we'll start our team exercises. I'll need Max,

Natalia, Yi, and Agent Thunderbolt to stay where you are. The rest of you can join me on the observation platform."

"What about Sprig?" Max asked as the Bounder Faerie nuzzled against him.

"She'll be part of the scenario as well," Strange said. "The goal will be simple. All you need to do is open the box and bring the contents to me."

"That's it?" Yi asked.

Strange smiled, revealing his wooden teeth. "That's it."

As the rest of the class walked up a spiral staircase that led to the observation platform, the atmosphere shimmered. The SIM Chamber was gone and was replaced by a room that looked like an ancient temple.

Creeping vines covered the brick walls, and the floor was little more than compacted dirt and sand. There was a stream of light that came down from an opening in the ceiling, bathing a pedestal and the box it held in a golden glow.

"Hold on," Max said, catching Yi's shoulder before he could take a step.

Yi pulled away. "Hands off, Sumner. I'm not one of your Grey Griffin groupies," he said as flames sparked in his eyes. Sprig morphed into a white tiger and started growling. Her ears were pinned back and her head was lowered.

"You realize the floor is covered with traps, right?" Max asked.

"So?" Yi said, setting his jaw.

"Look, I know you don't like me, and that's fine," Max said. "But this isn't a competition. Strange picked the four of us for a reason, so we're going to have to work as a team. When it's over, you can go back to hating me, but I don't want my grade to suffer, and I'm pretty sure you don't, either."

Yi hesitated when Max extended his hand, but he shook it and said, "Fine, but you're not in charge."

Max resisted the urge to roll his eyes. Instead, he turned to Ernie. "It's your call."

Ernie frowned. It was as though he was trying to gauge whether Max was serious, but Max just stood there with Natalia and Yi waiting for Ernie's instructions.

"Well," Ernie said as he adjusted his goggles, "Natalia should probably check for traps in the faerie spectrum."

Max nodded his approval, which appeared to put Ernie at ease. He looked around the room while Natalia pulled out her Phantasmoscope. "Yi, we could probably use a little more light," Ernie said.

"No problem." Yi's arms burst into flames, pushing back the darkness.

"I'm not finding much of anything," Natalia said. "There's some trace around the box, but that's it."

"I could probably run fast enough to get there and back without triggering any traps, but something doesn't seem right," Ernie said, shuffling his feet.

After hearing a scraping sound, Ernie knelt down to rub the sand away. When he was done, he found a circular stone that was roughly the size of a car tire.

"I wonder if there're more," Natalia said.

Ernie remained on his hands and knees as he swept the sand away from a second stone. Then he found a third before he stopped. "It could be a path," he said as he started to clear off a fourth stone.

Ernie slipped, putting his full weight on the stone. It started to sink, and then the ground started to rumble.

"That's not good," Ernie said.

The sand started to swirl before it fell away like water draining from a bathtub. "Get to the stones!" Ernie shouted.

Yi fell back. He was fighting against the sand, but it was sucking him under. Ernie knelt on a stone, which wasn't a stone at all. As it rose out of the ground, like all the others, he saw that the stones were actually the tops of pillars that stood over twenty feet tall.

As Ernie reached for Yi, he had to pull his hand back. Yi's entire body had erupted into fire. The more frightened he got, the higher the flames grew, and the sand around Yi started turning into glass.

Sprig morphed into a winged monkey with bright blue fur. Nearby, Max had latched onto one of the stone pillars. He was hanging over the pit of falling sand by his fingertips while Natalia scrambled to the top of a pillar a few feet away.

"Sprig!" Max called out as his fingers slipped. She pinned her wings back before diving. Then, as Max fell, she grabbed his wrists with her monkey hands, but Max was too heavy. Now, instead of Max falling to his death, they both were.

The spriggan morphed into a griffin with fur the color of honey. She beat her wings, fighting against gravity as she tried to fly to safety. It wasn't working, but Sprig strained, her wings pounding as she started to climb. Then she flew to a pillar, where she dropped Max before morphing back into a winged monkey.

Max breathed heavily as he wiped the sweat from his brow. "Thanks," he said, patting Sprig on the head. She jumped in place, clapping her hands, and did a backflip.

Nearby, Yi had managed to scramble across the slick glass to join Ernie on his pillar. Natalia stood alone on another.

"Now what?" she asked.

Ernie turned to Max, his face a mask of confusion.

"It's your call," Max said, trying to reassure him.

There was a grinding sound before the entire room started to shake. Then the pillars started to drop. It was slow at first, but it didn't take long before they picked up speed.

The ground trembled, and Yi fell. He screamed, and Ernie tried to reach for him, but it was too late. Yi was gone. "Somebody do something!" Ernie shouted.

"Go get the box," Max said to his Bounder Faerie.

172

Sprig nodded and took flight. The ceiling started to crumble. Some of the debris was large enough to crush the pillars, which crumbled under the weight.

Sprig zigged and zagged as she flew. Then, just as her fingertips touched the box, there was an explosion of light. The remaining pillars disintegrated into dust, sending Max, Natalia, and Ernie falling into the depths of the pit.

As the temple disappeared and the SIM Chamber came back into focus, Max was on his hands and knees. His breathing was shallow and his eyes wide as Sprig shuddered next to him.

"If I were grading you on effort, I might give you all passing grades," Strange said. "However, effort isn't enough. If this were a real expedition, we'd be attending your funerals tomorrow."

He looked at his pocket watch before shaking his head. "I'd like to run the simulation again, but I'm afraid we don't have time. I'll expect a marked improvement tomorrow."

The next two groups didn't do much better than the first. Catalina's Bounder imp ended up getting trapped in a hunter's snare. He started screeching as he reached for Catalina, who was sobbing. Between the two of them, they attracted some kind of monster that looked like a panther with a serpent's tail.

While the class wound down, Strange massaged his forehead. "We're not as far along as I'd hoped, but there were some promising moments," he said. Then he sighed. "Since we only have a few minutes, I believe Miss Romanov has something that she'd like to discuss. Is that correct?"

Natalia looked over to Brooke and then to Raven before taking a deep breath. "Have you ever heard of Walter Windham?"

"I knew him well," Strange said. "Why do you ask?"

"It's just that, well... I found some old articles that he had written on time travel, and I wanted to know what you thought about it."

Strange frowned. He turned to Raven, who looked away. "You realize he wasn't referring to time travel per se," Strange finally said. "Rather, it involves traveling to an alternate reality."

"Using a Paragon Engine, right?" Natalia asked.

"Yes, that's right."

"Could a Paragon Engine open up a gateway to the Shadowlands?"

"It's certainly an interesting thought," Strange said. "You're referring to Otto Von Strife, of course."

Natalia nodded.

"I can tell you with confidence that Von Strife does not have the components required to build a Paragon Engine, if that's where this is leading," Strange said. "But we fear he may be close. In fact, the business of Paragon Engines is why this class was formed to begin with."

174

"Do we get to jump through one?" Todd asked.

"I'm afraid not," Strange said. "However, we've been given a mission of utmost importance. For our field test, we will be taking an expedition to find the Schrödinger Box."

Strange paused, looking around the room as he waited for a reaction that didn't come. "Am I to understand that none of you have heard of the Schrödinger Box?"

His question was met with silence.

"Very well." Strange sighed. "The box is a critical component of any device that allows you to travel between worlds. Without it, you would be pulled into a million fragments the moment you stepped through the portal."

"That's wicked," Ross said.

"Yeah," Todd said. "Wicked awesome."

Strange frowned, as though gauging the sincerity of the comment. "From this point forward everything we do in this class will be in preparation to procure that box. If Von Strife finds it before we do, all hope for mankind may be lost."

The bell rang, but the students sat in their seats.

"Well?" Strange said. "What are you just sitting there for?"

"We want you to tell us more about the box," Ross said. "Especially the part where it keeps you from being torn apart."

There was a general murmur of agreement from the other students.

"It will have to wait until tomorrow," Strange said. "Now get going before your parents blame me for keeping you here too long."

SORRY, WE'RE CLOSED

A week had passed, and all discussion of Paragon Engines and Otto Von Strife had given way to the excitement of the upcoming Round Table tournament.

Max and the other Griffins had grown up thinking Round Table was just another game. They had no idea that in Templar culture, it was a phenomenon.

Top players were treated like rock stars, which explained—at least in part—why Xander Swift was so popular. Before he transferred to Iron Bridge, he had won the Merlin Cup. That was the trophy given to the best amateur player in the world. At only fourteen years and three months, he had been the youngest person ever to win.

Along with Xander, Max was one of sixteen students left in the school tournament, but there were only eight spots on the varsity team. Harley, who had been eliminated, wanted to get Max a gift for good luck.

"I don't really need a new pair of knucklebones," Max said.

"People don't give you gifts because you need something," Harley said. "Otherwise all you'd get for Christmas is underwear and socks."

"It's your money."

"Exactly, so stop complaining."

As the boys walked down Avalon's Main Street, Sprig skittered across the awnings overhead as a rambunctious raccoon.

Max looked up at the clock tower. "We better hurry," he said. "The Spider's Web is supposed to close in five minutes. Besides, it's freezing out here."

"You live in Minnesota—it's supposed to be cold," Harley said.

In order to reach the Spider's Web, they had to walk past the Shoppe of Antiquities. It was an odd little store that offered everything from antique lamps to knight's armor, but it closed when the proprietor, Olaf Iverson, went missing. Now the windows were boarded up, and there was police tape across the door.

Max could feel his chest tighten as the powerful feeling of loss became unbearable. Iver, as that's what everyone had called him, was more than a simple shop owner. Like

Monti, he had also been a part of the secret Templar society. More important, Iver had become a surrogate grandfather to Max and his friends, and there wasn't a day when Max didn't think about him.

Iver had been the one who'd introduced the Grey Griffins to Round Table. All the while, he was teaching them how to protect themselves against goblins, werewolves, and trolls without any of them realizing it.

"I was wondering," Harley said. "Maybe we should go back in there. You know, to see if we can find what that clockwork was looking for."

Before the winter break, Max and Harley had ventured into the Shoppe of Antiquities, hoping to find clues that would tell them Iver was still alive. After all, there were strange circumstances surrounding his death. Most notably, that Max's father supposedly killed Iver, and the body was never found.

Once inside the store, the boys had found a clockwork rummaging through Iver's belongings. They chased it off, but the commotion attracted the sheriff, and they had to leave before they became suspects. Neither one had been back since.

"Not tonight," Max said.

Harley looked at him. Then he patted Max on the back. "Yeah, maybe another time."

When the boys reached the comic shop, Ken was already locking the front door. Monti had hired him to help out until things slowed down in the workshop, but it was starting to look permanent, which Max found depressing.

The store wasn't the same without Monti. Ken was the kind of employee who liked to show up late, and he wasn't afraid to leave early.

He usually sat behind the counter reading comic books or surfing the Internet, and when someone had a question, all Ken would do was grunt. Business had suffered, but Monti couldn't find it in his heart to fire Ken. After all, Ken had been out of work for three months before Monti hired him. Max was starting to see why Ken couldn't get a job.

Harley grabbed the handle just as the bolt clicked. He jiggled the door a few times, but Ken simply pointed at his wristwatch. "Sorry, we're closed."

"Come on," Harley said. "All I need is a pair of knucklebones."

Ken brushed a long strand of black hair out of his face and scratched his straggly beard. "Come back tomorrow. We open at ten."

"I can't. We have school."

"That's not my problem." With that, Ken flipped off the lights before disappearing into the back of the shop.

"What a jerk," Harley said as he leaned against the door with his arms crossed.

Max was about to suggest that they head over to the arcade to wait for their ride when he saw someone with a cane limping down the sidewalk. "Is that Monti?"

"Where?"

"What are you troublemakers up to?" Monti asked when he saw the boys standing under the awning of his comic shop.

"Aren't you supposed to be resting?" Harley asked.

"I was craving Leonardo's bow tie pasta with the garlic cream sauce," Monti said, holding up the white paper bag in his hand. When he saw that the lights were off inside the store, he frowned. "Have you seen Ken?"

"Yeah, he slammed the door in my face before he went home," Harley said.

Monti raised his eyebrows.

"It wasn't that bad," Max said, "but he did close a few minutes early."

"Were you going to pick up your subscriptions?"

"No, we got those on Wednesday," Harley said. "The Round Table qualifying tournament starts back up tomorrow, and I wanted to grab a new pair of knucklebones for Max. I was even thinking about getting some for Ernie, but I'm not sure. He's still acting like a jerk."

"You're a good man, Harley," Monti said before turning to Max. "So who are you going to be dueling against?"

"Catalina Mendez."

Monti narrowed his eyes as he tried to put a face with the name.

"She's the one with the Digger imp."

"Ah, yes," Monti said. "The last time she was in the store, her Bounder had . . . well, let's call it an accident."

"What kind of accident?" Harley asked.

"It wouldn't have been so bad if it hadn't come out of both ends," Monti said. "I replaced the carpet, but on a hot day, I can still smell it."

"I wonder how Catalina got stuck with that thing," Harley said.

"She's never talked about it," Max said.

"Speaking of Bounders, where's yours?" Monti asked.

A cat screeched as they heard a trash can being tipped over. Its lid clanked on the ground, followed by the sound of glass breaking. Then something howled.

"I'd say she's torturing the strays that live in the alley."

"Let's get inside," Monti said. He placed his cane between his knees so he had a free hand to fish for his keys. As Monti pulled out a thick ring, he started to cough.

"I hate traditional keys. They're so last century," he said as he fumbled to find the right one. "Come on in."

"Are you sure?" Max asked as Monti flipped on the lights.

"Of course," Monti said. "I'd love the company."

The Spider's Web wasn't a big store, but it still held over 250,000 comic books, not to mention vintage toys and action figures and an impressive collection of Round Table trading cards that he kept in the glass case next to the cash register.

"Is it just me, or does it smell like a dog in here?"

Monti asked. He set his food on the counter before he had another coughing fit.

"No, it definitely smells like a dog," Max said. "I think Ken's German shepherd has a gas problem. Why do you let him bring that thing in here?"

"I don't know," Monti said as he knelt down to check what was left in the minifridge behind the counter. He took out three bottles of root beer and set them on the display case. "Well, then," he said. "Did you have some knucklebones in mind?"

"Those," Harley said, walking over to the glass case. He was pointing to a pair that looked like they had been taken from the knuckles of a dragon, which was exactly how the dice got their name.

"I had a pair just like that when I played for Stirling Academy," Monti said. He unlocked the display to pull the knucklebones out and slipped them into a black velvet bag. "Not a bad choice."

Harley continued to scan the display case until he spotted a red pair with silver numbers. "I guess I'll take those for Ernie. They match his Agent Thunderbolt costume."

"An interesting choice," Monti said. He pulled them out and tossed them up and down in his hand. "Nice balance, metallic finish. Bartameaus Butler used a pair just like this to beat me in the quarterfinals my senior year."

"I could pick another set."

"No, no," Monti said. "He went on to win the Merlin

Cup that year. Let's hope they bring Ernie some luck as well."

Harley pulled out a wallet connected to his belt loop by a length of chain. "Here you go," he said as he handed Monti his money.

"Much appreciated," Monti said. He started coughing.

"You still sound terrible," Harley said.

"It's nothing."

The front door opened, and Ross and Todd bounded into the store. Their cheeks and ears were bright red. Their teeth were chattering.

"How do people live in Minnesota?" Todd asked. "It's so cold that I can't even feel my tongue."

"What are you two doing here?" Harley asked.

"Looking for Max," Ross said before handing Max a large manila envelope.

"I already have a *Toad Report* on Catalina," Max said without bothering to open it.

"This is an update," Todd said.

"You could have sent it to my DE Tablet."

"We needed to make sure you got it," Ross said. "Catalina has a new battle deck, and from what we could gather, it's nasty. I guess she's pretty upset after what you said."

"What are you talking about?"

"You know, how you called her Bounder disgusting," Ross said. "She's out for blood."

"I didn't say that," Max said. Then he pointed to Harley. "He did."

Harley just shrugged.

"Ouch," Monti said. "You shouldn't talk about people's Bounders like that. Especially not to their faces."

"I didn't think she'd hear me," Harley said.

"How bad is it?" Max asked.

"Bad, but you still have fourteen hours before the duel," Ross said.

"More like thirteen and a half," Todd said.

"Either way," Ross said. "That's plenty of time to put together a deck that can counter hers."

"I'll take a look at it when I get home."

"What's with Monti?" Todd said after he glanced over at the counter.

"He's been sick," Harley said.

"I know, but look at him," Todd said. "I mean, I don't think people are supposed to have skin that color. It looks like chalk."

Max turned in time to see Monti sway before he fell backward into a table behind the cash register. By the time Max reached Monti, Monti was lying on the floor, unconscious.

UNFORGIVEN

Max was about to dial emergency services, but he decided to call Logan first. Within minutes an unmarked car that looked more like a hearse than an ambulance showed up. Monti was conscious, but when he tried to stand, he stumbled and fell.

The Templar paramedic took an instrument that looked like a metal wand and swiped it across Monti's forehead. The device it was attached to lit up, and then the paramedic entered a few more bits of information before putting it into his pack. A second paramedic strapped an oxygen mask over Monti's nose and mouth before injecting something into his neck.

"Just a little something to help him sleep," the paramedic said when he saw the nervous look in Harley's eyes. "Now please, step back."

Two more men brought a stretcher into the shop. They strapped Monti in it, then covered him with a blanket. With his pale skin and the dark circles under his eyes, Monti looked near death.

"Where are you taking him?" Harley asked.

"The hospital down by the mayor's office in New Victoria."

"He'll be all right," Max said as he placed his hand on Harley's shoulder.

"I hope so."

When he finally got home, Max tried to stay up so he could study the updated *Toad Report* on Catalina, but he didn't last long. He was exhausted. Besides, it was hard to sleep knowing that Monti was lying in the hospital and nobody knew what was wrong with him.

From what Max could see, the changes to Catalina's deck weren't nearly as drastic as the Toad brothers had made them out to be. Max decided to stick with his usual battle deck for the most part, though he made a few changes that he hoped Catalina wouldn't expect.

The first two rounds of the Iron Bridge qualifying tournament had been an elaborate affair. They were held in the auditorium in front of nearly a thousand people. The mayor of New Victoria had been there, as had a number of Templar dignitaries from around the globe.

Things were going to be different in the third round.

When Max arrived the next morning, armed guards escorted the sixteen remaining duelists to the dining hall. The room had been cleared—even the clockworks were gone.

Soldiers armed with nullifier nets and tranquilizer guns were stationed at every door and window, just in case Smoke decided to make an appearance. With only two changelings remaining in the tournament, it was doubtful that he would, but the staff decided it was better to be safe than sorry.

"Good morning," Ms. Merical, Max's homeroom teacher, said from behind the registration table. She was smiling, as always. "Hurry now. I'll need to scan and weigh your knucklebones, and then Ms. Butama will test your Kinematic goggles. Once we're finished, Dr. Thistlebrow will say a few words, and then we'll begin."

Max watched as Catalina handed her knucklebones to Ms. Merical. The dice were a strange combination of brown and green, which reminded Max of something that might have come out the backside of the Digger imp that was holding her hand.

"They passed," Ms. Merical said, "but I'm afraid your Bounder will have to wait outside."

"I can't just leave him."

"I'm sorry, dear," Ms. Merical said. "It's official policy, no exceptions. He'll be fine, though. Just send him out to the pond. It's nice and dreary out, and there are plenty of places for him to burrow."

The imp scampered up Catalina as though he were climbing a tree before settling in her arms. "It'll be okay," Catalina said. "I'll come looking for you as soon as I'm done."

Scuttlebutt looked like he was on the verge of tears as Catalina stroked the top of his lumpy head. Then she bent down to place the imp on the floor. Scuttlebutt started to whimper as Catalina took him by the hand to lead him out of the dining hall.

As the imp was leaving, Ernie burst into the room in a streak of light. When he finally stopped, his face was frantic. "Am I late?"

"You aren't early," Hale said from the back of the registration line.

Max watched Ernie walk over to her. He pulled out his battle deck, and they went through the cards together.

"Not bad," Hale said. "That's a good one, too. You know when to play it, right?"

As Max watched them, he had an empty feeling in his stomach. His missed the times when Ernie came to him for advice. When Hale was done giving him pointers, Ernie stuffed them back into the front pocket of his jeans. Then he made eye contact with Max.

"Good luck," Ernie said.

"Yeah, you, too," Max said. He remembered the extra set of knucklebones in his pocket. "I almost forgot, Harley bought these for you."

Ernie frowned. "He did?"

Max reached into his pocket to pull out the small velvet bag with the gold drawstring. Ernie took the bag and dumped the contents into his hand.

"He thought they'd match your costume," Max said.

Ernie stared at the gift before bouncing them in his hand. "They're amazing."

Max noticed that Ernie was wearing a black armband with the letters *RH* written in white. Max smiled, though the expression was laced with sadness. He was certain the band was in homage to their fallen friend, Robert Hernandez. "Where did you get that?" he asked.

Ernie looked down at the armband. "My mom made it."

"Anyway." Max didn't know what else to say.

"Yeah, I better get back in line." Ernie hesitated before walking back to stand next to Hale.

Max turned around to watch Xander hand Ms. Butama his goggles.

"These are beautiful," she said.

"Thanks," Xander said. "My dad had them custom-made in Milan. I think they've turned out pretty okay."

"I would say so."

When it was his turn in line, Max opened the drawstrings of his pouch and dumped his new knucklebones into Ms. Merical's palm.

"You look exhausted," she said.

"I was up kind of late last night."

"Yes, I heard about Monti. That's terrible."

"The doctors want to run some more tests, but I guess he's up and walking around," Max said.

"I'm glad to hear it." Ms. Merical retrieved the knucklebones from the measuring scale and handed them back to Max. "They run that poor man ragged. What he needs is a nice vacation somewhere warm."

Max placed the knucklebones back into his pouch. Ms. Merical reached out and took him by the wrist. "Your grandfather would have been so proud of the young man that you've become," she said. Then she let go before patting him on the top of his hand. "You go on now, and good luck."

Ms. Butama, the Bounder Care teacher, was seated next to Ms. Merical. Though she was born in Nairobi, she'd spent most of her youth in London, where she picked up her accent. "So this is it," she said as Max handed her his Kinematic goggles. "What will you do if you win?"

Max shrugged. "My mom thinks we should invite everyone over for pizza or something, but I don't know."

"Team building is a very good thing." She smiled. "Now let me take a look at these." Ms. Butama pulled his goggles over her eyes before flipping the switch to turn them on. Then she lifted a series of cards in front of the lenses. "Everything appears to be in order."

Next, Dr. Archimedes Thistlebrow logged the cards that Max had selected for his battle deck. "Now you're sure about this one, are you?" the Arithmetick teacher said as he held up a Blight Spider card.

The creature wasn't much bigger than a spriggan. It stood on two legs and had six arms, each ending in a clawed hand. The Blight Spider also had eight large eyes and a snub nose, and its body was covered in grey bristles.

"Not really," Max said.

"Pardon the pun, but Blights are a bit of a wild card," Dr. Thistlebrow said. "They can surprise you in more ways than one, if you catch my meaning, so be careful."

"I will," Max said. The Toad brothers hadn't told him any of that when they suggested he add the card to his battle deck. Unfortunately, once a card was logged, it couldn't be replaced, so Max was stuck.

When Dr. Thistlebrow finished, Max was directed to join Catalina at a table near the back wall. She refused to look at him as she sat down, which wasn't a good sign. Catalina had always been friendly, but Max understood why she hadn't been speaking to him. Even if it was a misunderstanding.

"Hey, Sumner."

Max turned around to see that Hale had left her place in line. "How's it going?" he asked.

"I'm good. So are you going to keep that temper of yours in check today?"

Max let a half smile cross his lips. "I'll try."

"Watch out," Hale said, nodding toward Catalina. "I hear she's out to get you."

"Thanks to Harley's big mouth."

"Just remember, there's no such thing as luck. Stay focused and you'll make the team." With that, Hale walked to her table.

"Hi," Max said as he approached Catalina at their table.

Catalina already had her cards and knucklebones out. She rolled her eyes.

"Look, I kind of heard that you were upset with me, and—"

"If you're trying to distract me, it's not going to work," Catalina said as Max sat down. Her eyes were narrowed and her lips were pursed.

"I didn't say anything about Scuttlebutt. That was Harley."

"It doesn't matter," Catalina said. "You were laughing with everyone else. Besides, he's your friend."

"I didn't laugh. I mean, maybe I could have told him to knock it off or something, but I would never make fun of your Bounder. Trust me, Natalia does it to me all the time. She hates Sprig, and I know how it feels when people say stuff like that."

Catalina's eyes softened for a moment, but then the scowl returned. "Nice try."

Max wanted to defend himself, but he thought better of it. Catalina was upset, and nothing he could say would change her mind. Instead, Max slipped his Kinematic goggles over his eyes and waited for the duel to begin.

"If I could have your attention," Dr. Thistlebrow said as he walked to the center of the dining hall. "I won't bother with the rules. If you don't know them by now, then you shouldn't be in the room. However, I do want to congratulate you for making it this far."

There was an obligatory round of applause, but Dr. Thistlebrow was quick to raise his hand to wave them off. "Now I know we all recall the events of last December with heavy hearts. The staff very nearly canceled this tournament, but Robert's parents asked that we move forward with our heads held high in his honor."

The applause grew louder.

"The winners of today's duels will be awarded one of the coveted spots on the varsity team. From there we will select two additional alternates based on an array of criteria. The attitude you display in defeat counts as much as your skill. Now then, please begin."

ROUND THREE

Max turned his goggles on. As they came into focus, he saw Catalina standing in a field with clear skies overhead. Max could smell lilacs in the wind, the sunshine was warm on his face, and he could taste the salt from the ocean air as waves crashed in the distance. It was a welcome break after the long Minnesota winter, but he knew the relaxed feeling wasn't going to last.

They had already cast knucklebones to determine who would go first. Catalina won, and she planned to take full advantage of her opening move. Max barely had time to blink before she released a kite that looked like a dragon. It rose into the sky and bounced in the wind as she held the strings in her hand.

Catalina cast her knucklebones. Once they settled, the artificial dragon opened its mouth to reveal a length of metal tubing. It roared, and a ball of fire erupted from the tubing to fly at Max.

He didn't have much time to react. Quick as he could, Max scanned his cards. He tossed one into the air, and, with a pop, it turned into a doorway. Max could feel the heat of the fireball as it raged toward him. He shook his knucklebones, hoping to block the dragon.

Max smiled after a great roll. The door opened in time to let the fireball pass through. It slammed shut before disappearing in a puff of smoke.

"Sorry," Max said.

"I bet you are."

For his opening attack, Max summoned a Templar THOR unit. Ten men dressed in camouflaged body armor appeared in the middle of the field. They were almost invisible as they crept toward Catalina with weapons drawn.

She rolled her eyes, as though to say his play was either obvious or weak. Her contempt angered Max, but he didn't say anything. Instead, he watched as she made, at least from his vantage point, a bizarre play. Catalina had countered with an Inferno imp.

It was a tiny creature covered in a red hide, with leathery wings and a hawkish nose. The imp looked sad, if that were possible. Max cast his knucklebones. It wasn't a very good roll, but it was enough to eliminate the imp.

As the THOR agents closed in, Catalina bit her lower lip. Then she released her knucklebones. Double sixes! She may have lost her imp for the duration of the duel, but the perfect roll meant that she'd eliminated Max's THOR unit as well.

Max watched as the imp's skin erupted in flames. The THOR commander called for a retreat, but it was too late. The Inferno imp exploded. The force from the blast spread through the field, enveloping the THOR agents. In a flash of light, they all disappeared.

Part of Max's strategy was to get an early lead, but it didn't look like that was going to happen. Apparently, Catalina had the same thought. She didn't waste time before she sent a massive man with the head of a boar charging after Max.

According to legend, the giant's name was Jimmy Squarefoot, and he smelled as terrible as he looked. Saliva dripped from curved tusks that sprouted from his jaw, his oddly shaped feet were wrapped in calico bands, and his tiny eyes were filled with rage.

Max countered with Water Leapers. As he threw his card into play, there was a pop. The air became thick with winged frogs that had tails with stingers instead of hind feet. They swarmed over Jimmy, who tried to swat at them with his long arms. There were too many, though. Leapers lashed out with their tails while others sank hooked fangs into his flesh. Jimmy fell and then disappeared.

Max sent the Water Leapers after Catalina. Her eyes grew wide as the hideous flying frogs closed in. She reached to play a card, but it slipped out of her hand. She fell to her knees, her hands reaching blindly for the card.

The first frog was about to strike when she threw her card into play. It was a spriggan. After a flash of light, the tiny creature simply sat on its haunches, licking its front paw. "Do something!" Catalina shouted.

The spriggan looked at her, as though agitated. Then it turned to see a Water Leaper bearing down at them. Before the Leaper had a chance to sting it, the spriggan morphed into an undead horse called a Kelpie.

Its nostrils flared; then it opened its mouth to swallow the Water Leaper whole. The other winged frogs tried to flee, but the hungry Kelpie was too quick. It ate at least a dozen before the others disappeared.

The game went back and forth. Max would take the lead, but Catalina would storm right back and tie the game. For one move, she used a plasma tank to obliterate one of the watchtowers Max had built. He destroyed her tank with a catapult, but Catalina tied the game with a flying warship called *Winged Victory*.

Max had been hoping to save the card, but he decided to put a squadron of griffins into play. Some of the griffins tore at the warship's sails, while others swooped down to pluck members of the crew from their stations.

Catalina watched helplessly as *Winged Victory* fell from the sky. The warship rammed into the earth, shaking the ground and sending dirt into the air.

Once everything settled, *Winged Victory* was little more than a massive pile of scrap. The wreckage shimmered before disappearing back into Catalina's card.

"This is your ten-minute warning," Dr. Thistlebrow's voice boomed.

Though he was starting to feel desperate, Max could hear Hale's voice telling him to control his emotions. That was easier said than done. The game was tied, and even if he scored on this turn, with the way things were going, he wasn't sure that it was going to be enough.

Max tossed a card into the air. It turned into a dozen iron spheres the size of basketballs. Griffins pinned their wings against their bodies before diving for the plasma bombs. They caught the bombs in their talons and then snapped their wings to fly toward Catalina.

The griffins released them as Catalina put a two-headed giant that wielded an oak tree as a club into play. Its left head shouted at the griffins as the right head spit on the ground, leaving enough saliva to fill a swimming pool.

The giant raised its club and swung. It knocked the first bomb over a line of trees and into the ocean, where

199

it exploded with a splash, but there were too many griffins with too many plasma bombs. The giant tried to bat them away, but he couldn't. Plasma bombs erupted, forming craters in the ground. Moments later the giant was eliminated, and Max had scored another point.

With time winding down, Max wasn't sure if he was going to get another opportunity to go on the offensive. He needed to keep Catalina from scoring, or the game was going to end in a tie. If that happened, the duel would go into sudden death.

Max watched as Catalina studied her cards. There was no room for mistakes, and she knew it. She started to pull one but put it back into her deck. Then she reached for another but thought better of it. Finally, she tossed a card into play. The air shimmered before a wingless dragon stood on the scorched earth where the Inferno imp had combusted.

"Have you ever seen a Sonoran Whiptail?" she asked.

Max shook his head.

"They get two attacks per turn," Catalina said. "I just thought you should know."

Max didn't need to be a math wizard to understand why Catalina was acting smug. If she broke through and scored with both attacks, she was going to win.

The best defensive card he had left was the Blight Spider, but after Dr. Thistlebrow's warning, Max wasn't in a hurry to put it into play. But his Stone Golem was too slow, and the Fireball Pixie swarm wouldn't hold up. Max looked at the clock. There was a little over three minutes left. His hands were sweating.

"I'm counting on you," he said. He tossed the Blight Spider into play. The air shimmered and the Blight Spider appeared, but the bizarre creature just yawned as the wind blew through its spiny coat.

Catalina looked confident as her dragon charged, its claws ripping at the dirt. Max watched, horrified, as the Blight Spider's body started to stretch before tearing in two. Light flashed. Now, instead of one Blight Spider, there were two. Both repeated the process, as did the next batch, until there were sixteen bristling Blights spread across the field.

Before the dragon could reach Max, one of the Blight Spiders opened its mouth, releasing a sticky white substance that looked like spiderweb silk. It latched around the Whiptail's front leg just as a second Blight Spider spit a web of its own. Soon all sixteen Blights had vomited streams of webbing until the dragon was caught in a network of sticky goop.

The Whiptail fell, and, as the dragon tossed its head from side to side, the ground shook. The webbing stretched, but it didn't break until Max and Catalina collected their knucklebones for the second attack.

Finally free, the dragon stamped its feet and slashed its tail, but the Blight Spiders didn't budge. Catalina looked over at the clock. There was less than a minute. The dragon threw its head back and roared before leaping at Max with jaws spread wide.

Max was certain that the Whiptail was going to swallow him whole. He could see down the dragon's throat as it rose over him. Its breath was hot, and its teeth were deadly. Then, at the last possible moment, one of the Blight Spiders shot webbing that latched around the dragon's snout. The webbing looped under its jaw, cinching its mouth shut. The other Blights joined in the attack. Moments later the dragon was lying on the ground in a cocoon.

Catalina threw her remaining cards on the table. She ripped off her Kinematic goggles, knocked her chair down, and then stormed out the door.

"Congratulations, Mr. Sumner," Dr. Thistlebrow said. "You've made the team."

As Max took off his goggles, he could hear everyone in the room cheering.

"Welcome to the big leagues, Sumner," Hale said as she threw her arm around his shoulder. Considering the tension between the Grey Griffins and the changelings, it was quite a gesture.

"Thanks," Max said. He was scanning the room, trying to determine who else had made the team. It wasn't difficult to spot them. Ms. Merical had given each a sash to wear for the rest of the day.

Predictably, Xander was wearing one. So was Hale,

along with four other eighth graders. That's when he saw Ernic with an enormous smile plastered across his face. More important, he was wearing one of the sashes.

"You made it?" Max asked.

Ernic nodded.

Despite the distance that had grown between them, Max wanted to high-five him, or shake his hand, or something, but Ms. Merical stepped between them.

"I can't wait to call your grandmother," she said as she slipped the sash over Max's head.

Pushing Their Luck

Max was back on the front page of the *New Victoria Chronicle* the next morning, but this time he was joined by the other members of the Iron Bridge varsity Round Table team.

Everyone was talking about the results, and the Toad brothers were ready to capitalize. They boarded the *Zephyr* with oversized duffel bags stuffed with T-shirts, pennants, buttons, and just about anything else that would hold the Iron Bridge Academy team logo. They were sold out of merchandise before they reached the second subway car, but they continued to take orders throughout the day.

Teachers had a difficult time maintaining control in

their classrooms. They were all thankful that seventh period had been canceled in favor of a school assembly.

Once the last class filed into the auditorium, Dr. Thistlebrow led the team to the stage as the band played the school fight song. The students in the audience cheered as each member of the varsity team was introduced.

The changelings were sequestered in the balcony with Dean Nipkin, yet they were no less enthusiastic. When Ernie's name was called, they started calling out, "Thunderbolt!" The other students joined in the chant as Ernie took a bow. He was about to take another when he felt Dr. Thistlebrow's hand on his shoulder.

"Very good, Mr. Tweeny," he said. "Now let's move along."

Ernie was reluctant to give up the spotlight, but he did—though not before blowing a kiss to the audience. Max, on the other hand, didn't want to be introduced at all. He hesitated when Dr. Thistlebrow called his name, and he might not have gone forward at all if Hale hadn't pushed him.

"Now," Dr. Thistlebrow said, "though it's a bit unusual, I've decided that we shall have two team captains this year, Xander Swift and Stephanie Hale!"

The excitement over the Round Table tournament lasted through the week. Ross and Todd spent long hours every night creating more merchandise to sell at school. Each day they went with overflowing duffel bags, and each day they were sold out by the lunch hour.

When Saturday finally rolled around, the Toad brothers decided to head over to Mad Meriwether's Gadgetry Shoppe. Between the merchandising and the *Toad Reports*, they had made a tidy profit, and they were ready to go on a shopping spree. That's when they spotted Barnabas Glover and Titus O'Shea coming out of a pub called the Burning Boar. Both were known slavers.

"Let's follow them," Todd said as he pulled his collar up around his face and the brim of his hat down over his eyes.

"I don't know," Ross said. "Maybe we should let Ernie handle it. Remember, we don't have superpowers like the other Agents of Justice."

"Just until we know where they're hiding out," Todd said. "Then we'll call it in."

Ross agreed, and the brothers followed the slavers through the streets of New Victoria and into Bludgeon Town. They did their best to be inconspicuous, but it wasn't easy. There weren't many kids running around down there, so they stood out.

"Good afternoon, gentlemen," a heavyset woman wearing a dress that looked to be at least four sizes too small said to the boys. Through the meager light from the gas lamp, the Toad brothers could see that her face was plastered with enough makeup that they wondered if she wasn't an escaped clown from the circus.

Of course, they didn't bother to say what they thought. It would have been rude, if not dangerous. She looked more like a professional wrestler than whatever she was supposed to be.

"Can I interest you in a bit of entertainment?" she asked.

Todd looked up to see the marquee that hung above the door. It read: THE SPOTTED KILT PROUDLY PRESENTS POLLY KNIGHT'S VAUDEVILLE SHOW.

"Thanks, but, um...well, we have somewhere that we have to be, don't we?" Todd said as he nudged his brother in the ribs.

"Yeah, we gotta go," Ross said.

The boys ran across the fog-drenched street before disappearing into the crowd.

"Did you see where Glover went?" Todd asked. He was craning his neck as a man with a patch over his eye bumped into him.

"Sorry," the man said with a tip of his cap.

"He's over there," Ross said, pointing to a man who was standing beneath a gas lamp.

Glover turned to look at Ross, and then he frowned.

"He saw me," Ross said before ducking into the entry to an abandoned store. The glass had been knocked out of the door, replaced by wood slats with knotholes. Ross looked inside through the window to see a rat creeping across the floor.

"You're sure?" Todd asked.

"Of course I'm sure."

Todd ventured a look at the street, but he couldn't see much through the fog. Then he pulled back before taking a second look. "They're gone."

The boys snuck back out to the sidewalk and down to the corner.

"There's O'Shea," Todd whispered as he pointed at a man who was walking into a pub. Titus O'Shea was easy enough to spot, even in a crowd. He was a stout man with thick arms and a thicker neck. He always wore suspenders and a derby, but it was his waxed mustache that gave him away.

"And there's Glover," Ross said, watching a man walking down an empty street toward an abandoned brick building. "It looks like we found their hideout."

An hour later, the Agents of Justice had gathered outside the abandoned building. Ernie split them into two teams. He was with Ross, Todd, Yi, and Denton behind a trash bin near the back door. Hale, Geppetto, Nadya, and Tejan were in an alley across the street, watching the front.

"How many others were there?" Ernie asked in a hushed voice.

"We saw two more go in, but we aren't sure who they are," Todd said. "They weren't in any of the reports."

"What about O'Shea?"

Ross shook his head. "As far as we know, he's still in that pub."

"We need to hit them while we know they're in there," Denton said.

"I know, I just don't want any surprises," Ernie said before speaking into a walkie-talkie. "This is Alpha leader, over."

"*Copy, Alpha leader,*" Hale's voice replied.

"Is there any movement out there?"

"*Nothing.*"

"What do you think?"

"*The longer we wait, the tougher it's going to get. Bludgeon Town comes alive once the sun goes down...not that you ever get to see the sun around here.*"

"Let's do it."

Ernie brought his fingers to his lips to remind the Toad brothers to keep quiet. He slipped from behind the trash bin and darted toward the back door of the apartment building. With his back against the wall, he reached over and checked to see if it was locked. The brass handle clicked open, and Ernie gave the signal for the others to follow.

Todd tried to follow Yi and Denton, but he tripped over his pant leg and fell on his face.

"Those two are going to get us killed," Denton said as Ross ran over to help his brother.

"They'll be okay," Ernie said.

The Toad brothers were huffing when they finally reached the wall. Todd's pants were ripped at the knee, where he was bleeding.

"Sorry," Todd said.

Ernie shook his head and pushed the door open. The hinges squeaked. His heart started to pound.

Denton dipped his head inside before pulling back. "Nothing."

After a nod from Ernie, Denton ducked into the building. Yi was right behind him. "You two go next," Ernie said. He grabbed Todd by the arm and pushed him inside.

"Maybe I should stay out here," Ross said. "You know, as a lookout."

Ernie shoved Ross into the building and followed him. When he pulled the door shut, everything went pitch-black.

"I can't see anything," Todd whispered.

Yi took the hint. His hands ignited like torches, pushing back the darkness as the others followed him down a long hallway lined with doors.

AMBUSHED

"You have the handcuffs, right?" Ernie asked as they stumbled through the half-lit darkness.

Todd nodded.

The hallway led to a foyer where errant strands of light streamed through broken windows. The floor was covered with plaster, along with the shattered remains of a crystal chandelier. There were overturned furniture and piles of charred paper, but no slavers.

Hale was standing with her team in the middle of the mess. "They're not here," she said.

"What about upstairs?" Ernie asked. He didn't bother whispering.

"Unless they can fly, I don't see how they'd get up there. Look." Hale pointed to a curved staircase that rose over the front desk. At one time it must have been an impressive sight, but it looked like a bomb had taken out half the steps.

"The elevator doesn't work, either," Tejan said. He was standing by the open doors looking down the shaft.

"So where are they?" Ernie asked.

"Are you looking for me, then?" asked a man standing on the balcony. He had a distinctly British accent, along with a robotic left arm that reminded Ernie of Doc Trimble's. The man was also holding a rifle with a grenade launcher attached under the barrel.

The changelings looked to Ernie, waiting for orders. Ernie, however, didn't say anything. His breath grew shallow as his chest constricted. He licked his dry lips once, then twice.

"What's wrong?" the man asked. "Cat got your tongue?"

"Maybe you didn't notice," Ernie finally said, hoping he didn't sound nervous, "but you're kind of outnumbered."

"Ah, you must be the famous Agent Thunderbolt," the man said, lowering his weapon before he leaned casually on the rail. "The name is Barnabas Glover, though I believe you know my brother, Tom. After all, he's in prison thanks to you."

212

"How does he like his cell?" Ernie asked. It was an attempt to match Glover's relaxed tone, but nervous sweat trickled down his cheek, betraying him.

"Oh, I don't think he plans on staying too terribly long," Glover said. "Now which one of you is the shape-shifter?" His eyes roved over the changelings like a hog buyer at the county fair.

"It doesn't matter, because you're going to join your brother tonight," Ernie said.

Glover laughed. "Is that so?"

Ernie gritted his teeth.

"Do you know how much money I could get for the lot of you?" Glover asked. "I could make enough money that my great-grandchildren would never have to work."

"Come and get us, then," Yi said. Flames erupted in his hands.

"Actually, I'm willing to make you a deal," Glover said before removing his hat. Then he wiped the sweat from his brow before replacing it. "All you have to do is hand over the shape-shifter, and I'll let the rest of you walk away. It's as simple as that."

"We don't make deals with slavers," Ernie said.

"This is your last chance," Glover said. "I'd hate for things to get ugly."

Ernie crossed his arms over his chest.

"Don't say I didn't offer," Glover said. He reached into a pocket inside his duster jacket and pulled out a small device. After he entered a code, a red light started to flash. Then sheets of metal rolled down to cover the windows and doors, blotting out the light.

The changelings were trapped.

Yi hurled a fireball at Glover. It struck the railing and exploded, sending the slaver ducking for cover. Yi's next shot burst across the ceiling, drowning it in fire.

"That'll cost you," Glover said as he rolled to his knees. He took aim with his rifle. When he pulled the trigger, a canister exploded from his grenade launcher. The lid opened up, releasing a net.

In a blur of motion, Ernie darted across the room to grab a lamp. He threw it like a spear so the net wrapped around the lamp instead of Yi.

"Thanks," Yi said.

"More slavers!" someone shouted.

Ernie spun around to see dark figures running through the shadows. One snuck up behind Nadya, who was preoccupied with shooting ice at any movement in front of her.

"Look out!" Ernie shouted. He stripped his backpack from his shoulders and pulled out a length of rope. Within a second, he leaped over a couch, ran around a pillar, and reached Nadya, just as the slaver was about to inject some kind of tranquilizing serum into her neck. Ernie wrapped the rope around the man's shoulders again and again until the slaver couldn't move his arms.

Ernie was moving so fast that the man didn't realize what was happening until he was tied up. "Don't move," Ernie said after kicking him to the ground.

Nadya turned on the slaver. "You look a little hot," she said. "Let me help you cool off." She inhaled before a stream of liquid ice spat from her mouth to encase the man up to his neck. "One down," she said.

Across the room, another slaver was pointing a dart gun at Geppetto, but the changeling just smiled. "What's so funny?" the slaver asked.

"I don't think you want to shoot me with that," Geppetto said.

"You don't?"

"Nah, I think you're going to shoot yourself instead."

The slaver's eyes shot wide when his hand started to shake. As the barrel of the gun moved from Geppetto to his own neck, the slaver started to whimper. "Get out of my head! What are you doing to me?"

Geppetto narrowed his eyes. "Bang!" he shouted.

The slaver pulled the trigger, and the dart shot into his skin. He crumpled to the floor.

At the same time, Glover fired one of his nets at Hale, but she morphed into a hummingbird before darting out of the way.

"It looks like we found our shape-shifter!" Glover said.

"Heads up!" Yi shouted through the pandemonium. "They brought clocks!"

Ernie could see the burning eyes of a clockwork moving through the darkness. Fire burned inside its chest as steam poured out of two pipes lodged into its back.

Denton was closest. He took three steps before launching himself at the clockwork. The momentum sent them rolling until they crashed into the front desk.

Taking advantage of the distraction, Glover aimed at the hummingbird. He fired a series of errant darts that disappeared into the shadows, skittering across the floor or sinking into the wall. Glover reached into a pouch on his belt and pulled out a canister that he loaded into the grenade launcher.

The clockwork threw Denton into a burning couch. The machine rose to its feet, ready to finish Denton off, but Hale had turned from a hummingbird into a grizzly bear. She was standing on her hind legs, roaring as her massive paws stretched wide. The clockwork hesitated as a dart caught Hale in the shoulder. Then a second hit her stomach. She staggered before morphing back to her natural form.

"That's it, boys," Glover called out as Hale collapsed. "Let's wrap it up." With that, he fired a net that fell over the changeling. Energy surged over the surface, sending her into convulsions.

"No!" Yi shouted. His body was wrapped in flames, and the air around him bent under the heat.

The clockwork picked Hale up and tossed her over its shoulder. Nadya tried to hit the machine with a blast of ice, but it didn't work. The heat from Yi's fire was eating up the moisture. Without it, her changeling ability was useless.

216

"We have to get out of here!" Todd screamed as the inferno spread. He was hiding behind a broken sofa with his brother. "This place is going to blow!"

"Everybody fall back!" Ernie said.

"Where?" Nadya asked. Her eyes were wild. "There's no way out!"

The sound of cracking wood echoed through the foyer. Ernie looked up as a beam snapped in two before it fell. The ground shook as burning debris whipped through the air. One of the slavers brought the leg of a chair down on Denton's back. Nadya was hit in the neck by a dart. Then Tejan fell.

Ernie didn't see Glover's net as it spun toward him. It wrapped around his body, causing him to lose his footing. Ernie fought to break free, but somehow his power was gone. The net had stolen his speed. He stopped struggling long enough to watch the clockwork that was carrying Hale disappear down a trapdoor and out of reach.

JOYRIDE

It had been nearly a week since Monti was admitted to the hospital. His sickness had become a mystery that was proving impossible to solve. Blood samples and X-rays of his chest had been sent to specialists around the globe, but nobody could pinpoint a cause.

Some wondered if it was fatigue, others thought the coughing might be caused by acid reflux. There were suggestions of pneumonia and whooping cough, and one doctor wondered if Monti had contracted a fungal infection called valley fever. None of them were right.

The pressure to finish the portal scanner was more than he could handle, and more than once, Monti tried to escape. One time, a nurse caught him dressed in a janitor's jumpsuit, pushing a bucket and a mop down the hall. If the sensor in his medical bracelet hadn't tripped the alarm, he would have made it out. After that, the nurse threatened to handcuff him to his bed if he tried to leave again.

That left Harley alone in the workshop with Monti's clockwork mechanics. Monti called him as often as the nurses would allow, which they soon limited to twice per day. He spent the rest of the time reviewing the scanner's specifications as well as any results from tests that Harley had run.

Monti's growing frustration only served to exacerbate his symptoms, so Doc Trimble prescribed medication that put Monti to sleep. Even then, his dreams were fitful. He thrashed and moaned, tearing the sheets from his bed. Nothing helped.

Harley wasn't getting much sleep, either. Between homework and his new responsibilities at the workshop, there wasn't much time for rest. Though the portal scanner ate up most of his day, there were other responsibilities as well. Clockwork mechanics broke down, conveyor belts snapped, and pipes burst. In addition, gadgets coming off the assembly lines required testing.

Despite all that, Harley decided to throw a party for Max and Ernie late Saturday afternoon. Making the varsity Round Table team was an impressive accomplishment—especially for Ernie, who hadn't been expected to survive the first round of the tournament.

Harley thought it was important for the Grey Griffins to celebrate together, and Monti gave his blessing to host the party at his workshop. Besides, Monti had decided to pay Harley for all the work that he'd been doing. For the first time in his life, Harley had spending money.

He assigned some of the clockworks to clean out an area big enough for a table loaded with cookies, punch, and a sheet cake that looked like the back of a Round Table card. There were balloons tied to folding chairs and a DJ booth manned by a clockwork with a digital music player and speakers built into its chest.

"You did this all by yourself?" Natalia asked.

"Jasper and some of the other clockworks helped," Harley said, deflecting the attention.

"Well, I think that it's brilliant," Natalia said.

Harley blushed.

"Where's Ernie?" Max asked.

"I left him a message, but I never heard back," Harley said.

"He'll be here," Natalia said.

"I wouldn't bet on it," Max said.

"The pizzas are nearly finished, sir," Jasper said.

"You made pizza?" Natalia asked.

"They don't have pizza in New Victoria, so I brought some over from Leonardo's," Harley said. "They've been sitting in the freezer. Jasper is just warming them up."

"How about some punch?" Jasper asked.

"I'd love some," Natalia said.

"Me too," Max said.

"Sir?" Jasper asked, turning to Harley.

"Sure, thanks."

"Very well, then," Jasper said. "I'll be right back."

"Maybe we should call Ernie," Natalia suggested as the clockwork walked over to the snack table that Harley had set out.

"What's the point?" Max asked. "He's not going to pick up when he sees that it's us."

"I suppose you're right," Natalia said. "But it's infuriating. I mean, I don't know if I should feel sorry for him or be angry."

Harley shrugged. "Either way, it doesn't matter. He'll come around or he won't, and nothing that we do or say is going to change that."

"Here we are," Jasper said. He was holding a tray with plastic cups filled with punch. "I'm sorry that we don't have better tableware, but this is the first gathering that the master of the house has held at our humble workshop."

"It's perfect," Natalia said before taking a sip.

"How's that pizza coming?" Harley asked.

"It should be just about done," Jasper said.

The clockwork was about to return to the kitchen when the music stopped. Then static started to blare through the speakers before a voice spoke.

"...I repeat, this is not a drill. All available emergency

221

vehicles should report to number Eight Harbor Drive. A group of masked vigilantes, presumed to be the Agents of Justice, have entered the abandoned apartment building. Smoke is pouring out from the second- and third-story windows...."

"That has to be Ernie," Natalia said.

"How far away is that apartment building?" Max asked.

"Eleven point four miles," Jasper said.

"Is there a subway stop nearby?"

"The nearest is next to Drummond Park, four blocks away."

"We'll never make it," Max said.

"Yes, we will," Harley said. "Monti has a team of clockwork mechanics working on Logan's aerocar. Most of the structural work is done. So is the engine. All it needs is some paint."

"It only holds two people," Max said.

"That's not a problem," Harley said. Then he smiled. "I have my own ride."

Even without the fog, it would have been difficult for Max and Natalia to see the streets from the sky. It was only six o'clock, but the streets of Bludgeon Town were already wrapped in darkness. Besides, the aerocar was moving so fast that the world below was a blur.

The headlights weren't helping much, even with the

high beams. All Max could see were swirling vapors and an occasional seagull that would dive out of the way as they tore through the sky. There were gas lamps meant to light the streets, but most were either snuffed out or shattered.

Flying with Logan had been unnerving. Flying without him was terrifying. Max gripped the steering wheel until his knuckles were white. His jaws were clenched and his breathing was shallow. "Do you have the map working yet?" he asked just as a church steeple emerged through the fog.

Max jerked the steering wheel to the left, and the aerocar followed. At the insane speed they were traveling, the slightest adjustment was amplified. The aerocar dipped, sending Max into the driver's side window as Natalia's head snapped hard to the left.

"What are you doing?" she asked. Her chest was heaving and her eyes were wild with worry.

"Sorry," Max said as the aerocar leveled out, "but it's hard to see in this mess."

Natalia tried to compose herself, pushing out thoughts of splattering into the side of a building. She hit a series of buttons on the panel until a screen showing a grid of the city came to life. "That must be us," she said, pointing to a flashing light.

"Where's the fire?"

Natalia typed the address into a keyboard below the display. When she hit Enter, a red dot appeared. "We're close."

Pulling his eyes away, even for a moment, was risky. There were clotheslines draped between the buildings like strands of a spiderweb, not to mention a forest of chimneys releasing steam from factories and smoke from fireplaces. Still, Max looked at the map.

They were off course, but not by much, so Max nudged the steering wheel until the green light was heading directly toward the red dot.

"Can you see Harley?" Max asked as he shifted his attention to the horizon.

"I can't see much of anything," she said as she strained to look at the streets below.

"What about the comlink?"

"I'll try," Natalia said. "Harley, can you hear me?"

There was a crackling sound.

"Harley, are you out there?" she asked.

More static.

"There must be some kind of interference," Natalia said.

"*Natalia,*" Harley finally said, though the connection was poor. "*Where are you?*"

"Where are you?" Natalia asked.

"*It's hard to say,*" Harley said. "*What about you?*"

"We'll be there any minute."

"*Don't do anything crazy until I get there. I brought some heavy firepower.*"

224

FALLING

Maneuvering through the narrow streets in the Mark Four armor would have been difficult under ideal conditions, but the fog was making it nearly impossible. Lights shined from lamps attached above both shoulders, and even though there were two more planted in the Mark Four's chest, none of them were helping much.

The armor drew attention as it plodded along like an overgrown toddler learning to walk. It was so heavy that the streets and sidewalks couldn't support it. Harley left potholes with each step. He knocked over light posts and crushed shrubs, but there wasn't time to feel guilty. For the moment, all Harley cared about was saving Ernie from the slavers.

It wasn't a smooth ride. Harley's teeth chattered under the roar of the engines as the cab of the armor shook. Still, he worked the levers and pulleys to keep the Mark Four upright and on track as he headed to the abandoned apartment building where Ernie and the other change-lings were trapped.

Harley decided to take a shortcut through a park. A flock of pigeons took to the sky once he broke through a line of trees. An old man on a park bench watched with his mouth agape as the strange machine emerged from behind a bank of fog.

Visibility was obscured. When Harley finally noticed the enormous water fountain, it was too late. He wasn't sure if he could change his trajectory without tipping over. Harley slowed the pedals, but he knew it wouldn't be enough. His only choice was to stop.

Harley applied the brake mechanism, but he was going too fast. The armor's knees locked, and then the machine started to topple. He moved the left foot forward, hoping that would stabilize it before he fell into the fountain. The machine swayed and then fell forward. Harley put his hands out to brace for the impact, and the armor followed.

Its massive arms held steady on the rim of the foun-tain, causing stone to crack. The armor shook, and the engine chugged as steam spit out of the exhaust. Harley gritted his teeth before pushing off. It was too strong.

226

Now, instead of falling forward, the Mark Four threatened to topple backward.

It took unsteady steps backward as Harley fought for control. He waved his arms, hoping that would help compensate for the lost balance. The old man on the bench was right behind him. If the armor fell, it was going to crush him, but the old man couldn't move.

Harley planted his right foot, and the armor stopped teetering. Harley closed his eyes and exhaled. Sweat poured from his brow. The engines below burned hot, but the perspiration was as much from nerves as it was from the suffocating heat.

Harley pressed forward.

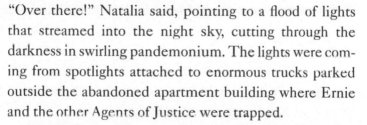

"Over there!" Natalia said, pointing to a flood of lights that streamed into the night sky, cutting through the darkness in swirling pandemonium. The lights were coming from spotlights attached to enormous trucks parked outside the abandoned apartment building where Ernie and the other Agents of Justice were trapped.

Max steered the aerocar toward the chaos. Below he could see red and blue lights flashing from the fleet of emergency vehicles pouring into the street. Sirens screamed and constables shouted at the growing crowd, warning onlookers to stay clear.

An explosion shook the building. Max watched as

227

constables, firefighters, paramedics, and spectators were thrown to the ground. He pulled up in time to avoid a ladder that jutted up from the fire truck, only to fly into wet sheets hanging from a clothesline. They plastered the windshield like papier-mâché.

"Where are the windshield wipers on this thing?" Max asked. As he felt around the steering wheel, the aerocar dipped right, then left, and then right again.

"I don't know, but you need to do something!" Natalia shouted.

"I'm trying."

Natalia decided to take matters into her own hands before they crashed into the side of a building. She unbuckled her seat belt and rolled down her window to lean out. The cold wind tore at her face as her braids flailed.

"What are you doing?" Max asked. "Get back in here before you fall out!"

Natalia stretched, reaching her arm around at an odd angle, but the sheet was just out of reach. She leaned out farther as a gust of wind blasted the aerocar, knocking it off course. Natalia screamed as Max lunged.

He grabbed the back of her coat, keeping her from falling out the window while he tried to steer the aerocar. His momentum took him too far. They tilted to the right until the wings of the aerocar were perpendicular to the ground.

Natalia continued to scream as Max let go of the steer-

228

ing wheel. He grabbed her with both hands this time and pulled with all his might. Natalia shot back into the cab of the aerocar, but not before grabbing the sheet.

The aerocar started to spin out of control. Max took hold of the steering wheel as Natalia let go of the sheet. It lifted into the air and floated off. She fumbled to strap back into her seat belt, but her hands were shaking too much.

Max fought to regain control as a red light flashed on the dashboard. The map on the display screen disappeared, only to be replaced by a video image of Logan. He looked upset. *"Do I even need to say it?"*

The aerocar was spiraling out of control. "Hold on!" Max shouted through chattering teeth.

"What's going on?"

"We're going to crash!" Natalia shouted as she watched the ground closing in on them below.

"You're what?"

"Pull up!" Natalia said. Her hands were gripped tightly to the sides of her bucket seat.

"I'm trying," Max said.

"Try harder."

Max yanked back on the steering wheel. He gritted his teeth, and the veins on his neck popped out. The belly of the aerocar sparked as it scraped against the cobblestones. The grating sound was worse than fingernails raked over a chalkboard.

Max pushed on the throttle, and the aerocar shot back

into the sky, rising over the tops of the buildings and out of the fog. As he leaned back into the headrest, Max closed his eyes and exhaled.

"Are you okay?" Logan asked through the speakers.

"I think so," Max said as he turned to Natalia. "How about you?"

All she could manage to do was nod.

"Good," Logan said. *"Now I want you to turn around and head back to Monti's workshop before you go and get yourselves killed."*

"We can't," Max said.

"Let's forget about how many laws you're breaking," Logan said. *"Do you have any idea what kind of men these slavers are?"*

"Probably not," Max said, "but I can't let them take Ernie."

"The chief constable and his men are already there."

"We saw them."

"So turn around. They have it covered."

"I'm not leaving him...not this time," Max said.

"Listen to me," Logan said. *"I'm giving you a direct—"*

Max reached over and turned off the screen.

"What are you doing?" Natalia asked, her eyes wide.

"We're not leaving him," Max said. He was determined as he steered the aerocar toward the apartment building. They cut through a bank of fog, and one of the beams from a floodlight hit Max in the eye, temporarily blinding him.

230

"There's a clockwork in the window," Natalia said. "It has some kind of weapon. Max, look out!"

There was a burst, like cannon fire. Something hit the side of the aerocar and exploded. The aerocar shook, spinning out of control. Max managed to regain control long enough to avoid hitting the side of the building, but he couldn't change course before they smashed into a chimney.

Brick and dust sprayed into the air as the aerocar careened against the wall of an old warehouse. The impact tore the left wing from the body. "Do something!" Natalia shouted.

Max pulled on the controls, but the aerocar wouldn't respond. The hull twisted once they struck the pavement. Sparks flew as the aerocar slid across the cobblestone street. It teetered before hitting a curb, flipping it over onto its hood and crumpling it.

It smashed into the side of a warehouse, where its nose punctured the wall, sending bricks down on the aerocar. Max groaned as he shook his head. He was disoriented, and it didn't help that he was hanging upside down.

Smoke seeped from the engine. A spark flashed and flames erupted. He looked over and saw that Natalia was unconscious. He tried to reach her, but his arm was pinned. Blood was seeping from a gash on her forehead. The windshield was shattered. She hadn't been wearing a seat belt.

"Natalia," Max said. His voice was weak. She didn't respond.

The flames grew higher. The heat was unbearable. Max fumbled to find the seat belt release, but his fingers wouldn't cooperate. He was fighting to maintain consciousness, but he was losing the fight.

"There they are!"

Max turned his head. He could see silhouettes running toward him through the smoke and flames. Max started to cough. It was so hot in the cabin that components on the dashboard were melting.

"Get them out of there before it blows!" someone cried out before the door was ripped open. Frantic hands searched for Max's seat belt release but couldn't find it. There was a flash of steel. A knife cut through the fabric of the seat belt. Max fell on his head before someone dragged him out of the cabin and into the street.

"I've got you."

Max was being cradled like an infant. Whoever it was, they were running. Max tried to open his eyes, but he couldn't. Right before he drifted off, he heard an explosion.

TOO LATE

As the Mark Four trudged down the street, Harley could see the lights from emergency vehicles flashing behind a barricade that Chief Constable Oxley's men had built. The curious crowd of spectators was growing. They didn't understand the danger they were in.

"I'm here," Harley said through his comlink, but his only response was static. He tapped the speaker in his ear. "Max...Natalia, are you there?"

Harley continued to march. The ground shook with each step he took, catching the attention of constables. With weapons drawn, they turned their attention to the monstrosity of metal that approached.

"What is that thing?" one said.

"I think it's one of them clockwork killers," another answered.

"Stop!" a constable shouted. His plasma pistol was quavering in his hand, but to his credit, he stood his ground.

Harley didn't stop. In fact, he didn't even bother to slow down.

As the shadow of the Mark Four passed over the constable, he closed his eyes and fired. The blast ricocheted off the armor, leaving a burn mark but nothing more. Harley kept his momentum, and the constable rolled out of the way.

Harley ignored the constables as he broke through the barricade. Shots were fired from somewhere in the dark, and like before, they bounced off the armor and landed in the street. Harley stopped. His searchlights scanned the darkness for his attacker, but he couldn't see anyone.

More shots were fired. One hit the protective glass that covered the armor's cockpit, leaving a crack. A clockwork was standing in a window up above with a rifle in its mechanical hands.

Harley stopped the armor, twisting a crank that controlled the cannon on his right shoulder. The cannon moved to the right, but it went too far. He adjusted, bringing it back to his left. Then he leveled the barrel until it was pointed up at the clockwork.

The clockwork blasted three more rounds from its sniper rifle, but Harley's armor was too thick. He returned fire with a missile shot from the cannon. Harley watched as it screamed through the night before blasting into the wall. Brick was turned to powder as the missile put a hole in the side of the building, knocking the clockwork out of the window.

Someone shouted. The clockwork didn't make a sound until it struck the pavement, where the metal casing blew open. It released a shower of cogs and gears that bounced before skittering down the street and into the darkness.

Harley turned his attention to the front door and shot a second missile from the cannon. There was an explosion, but when the smoke settled, Harley could see that the only damage was a dent. Two more missiles struck the wall next to the door, puncturing a hole in the building that was big enough for a double-decker bus.

"I'm going in," Harley said. He waited for a reply from Max, but it didn't come. "I repeat, I'm going in." Still nothing. Figuring that he was in some kind of communication dead zone, Harley decided to press forward. Smoke poured from the gash in the wall as Harley guided the armor into the burning building. The machine scraped against brick, creating a shower of sparks as he squeezed through.

The heat from the inferno was intense. Heavy smoke obscured his view, but Harley could still see Barnabas Glover standing on the balcony. He spotted at least two other slavers on the ground, along with another clockwork.

The machine raised an arm that ended in a Gatling

gun instead of a hand. The barrel spun as it released a ferocious barrage of bullets that pounded against the Mark Four. Harley fought to keep it from tumbling over as it staggered, but then it hit a wall.

Once the armor regained its footing, Harley charged with hands raised. He brought the mechanical arms down on top of the clockwork, and the machine crumpled.

Across the room he could see Yi burning out of control as the fire around him rose higher. Other changelings were unconscious on the ground. Harley scanned the rest of the room and spotted Ernie trapped under a net. He looked terrified.

"Ernie!"

Ernie was holding some kind of handheld device as he pushed a series of buttons. A moment later, there was a flash. Ernie was gone. The net fell to the ground, empty.

Harley didn't have time to wonder how Ernie had vanished. Glover fired a grenade that struck the Mark Four in the shoulder. The impact from the explosion tipped the armor off balance. Harley could feel it teeter as he fought for control. A second grenade hit the ground near the Mark Four's foot, forming a crater.

As the armor fell, Harley reached out to grab a pillar. The wood started to splinter as it threatened to break in half. Harley quickly planted his back foot and felt the machine correct itself. There was another explosion, and the ground shook. Hot ash swirled in the room as the inferno blazed around him. The metal inside the cockpit was hot to the touch, but Harley ignored the pain.

He reached up to crank the winch that controlled the cannon on the armor's shoulder. Harley aimed at the balcony and fired his last missile. There was an explosion, and the balcony buckled. Plaster fell. The entire balcony followed.

"They have Hale!" Nadya shouted.

Harley turned to see the last slaver disappear down an escape hatch in the floor. There was no way he could follow them inside the armor. Instead, he turned to get the changelings out of the building before it could collapse on them.

"What are you doing?" Nadya said.

"We need to get everyone out of here."

"They're going to kill her!" Tears were streaming from Nadya's eyes.

"This place is surrounded by constables," Harley said. "They won't be able to get very far." He reached down with the Mark Four's arm to pick up Tejan, who was unconscious. "Come on," Harley said. "We don't have much time."

Harley didn't bother to duck through the opening. The broad shoulders of the armor tore into the brick, forming a gaping hole. Smoke poured out, wafting into the sky. Harley walked over to lay Tejan next to an ambulance. The Toad brothers were coughing as they ran to the police barrier.

"Where're the others?" Harley asked.

Todd tried to answer, but he started to cough.

"They're still inside," Ross said. Then he started coughing, too.

Harley turned the armor around and headed back into the building, where he found Yi leaning over Denton, shielding him from the flames. Across the floor, Geppetto was dragging an unconscious slaver to safety. His face was covered in ash and streaked by sweat.

There was a cracking sound, followed by another. "The roof is caving in!" Harley shouted.

"I can't wake him up," Yi said.

Chunks of plaster fell from the ceiling, bouncing off the armor. Harley knew there was a chance that they wouldn't make it out. Still, he couldn't leave Denton to die. He bashed a couch with his arm, sending it flying across the room before stomping over to where Denton lay.

"I'll get him," Harley said. "You get out of here."

Yi hesitated, but he nodded before running out of the building. Nadya was already outside. So were Geppetto and the slaver.

Wood cracked overhead, and more plaster rained down. Debris bounced off the armor's back as Harley picked Denton up. A beam engulfed in fire fell, punching through the floor. Harley teetered as he tried to sidestep the hole. Denton started to slip, but Harley tightened the machine's grasp on him. Denton groaned.

Another beam fell, shaking the ground. Harley hesitated, scanning the inferno for any sign of Ernie. Denton started to cough as he was pulled back to consciousness.

"Ernie!" Harley called out.

The only answer was the crack of flames as the fire grew. Then there was a loud snapping sound. Harley looked up just as the ceiling fell. In three long strides he was back outside, a whoosh of flame, ash, and smoke behind him.

When everything settled, Harley was holding Denton in the arms of the Mark Four as a dozen constables leveled guns at them.

"Don't move!" Chief Constable Oxley shouted.

Harley opened up the hatch and put his hands in the air.

"It's just a kid," someone said.

"Look! They're pointing their guns at a kid!" another called out.

"Lower your weapons," Oxley said to his men.

"If you want to see my driver's license," Harley said, "I don't have one."

PART THREE

REUNITED

WHEN FLOWERS
AREN'T ENOUGH

Natalia woke up to the smell of fresh flowers. Her first thought was that she must have fallen asleep in a garden, but when she opened her eyes, Natalia could see that she was in a hospital room. The walls were white, as was her bedding, but the stark monotony was broken by an explosion of colorful flowers bursting from more than a dozen vases.

With her arm in a sling, Natalia lay on her pillow and looked at the ceiling. She remembered falling from the sky and a terrible explosion, but after that she was drawing a blank. Then it came to her....

"Max?"

He had been with her in the aerocar, but something went wrong. There was fire and blood. Panic struck her. Natalia tried to sit up, but she didn't have the strength. She kicked at her sheets, but all she managed to do was cause a tangle. Natalia yanked with her good arm, but there were tubes in the top of her hand connected to an IV drip next to her bed. She touched her head and felt bandages.

"Let me out of here," she said. Her head was swimming, and she was starting to feel nauseated, but Natalia reached over to rip the tubes out of her hand. She was too weak. Natalia could feel tears of frustration starting to form as she rocked her head from side to side.

"It's okay," a voice spoke as someone approached from her periphery.

"Get away from me!" Natalia said as she lashed out at gentle hands that were trying to soothe her.

"It's me, Brooke."

Natalia stopped flailing and turned to see Brooke Lundgren looking down at her. Honeysuckle was there as well, hovering over Brooke's shoulder. Even though faeries weren't supposed to be in the infirmary, she had snuck in inside Brooke's handbag.

"Here, let me help you," Brooke said. She placed one hand behind Natalia's neck and another on her elbow to help Natalia prop herself up. She then walked over to a closet and fished out another pillow, which she slid behind Natalia's back.

"Where are we?"

"The infirmary at Iron Bridge," Brooke said. "You've been here for over a week."

"But..." Pain shot through her temples. Natalia winced, closing her eyes as her shoulders bunched.

"Just relax," Brooke said.

When Natalia opened her eyes, she saw Honeysuckle land on the nightstand by her bed and watched as she uncorked a crystal vial that was nearly as tall as she was. The pixie managed to lift it and pour a bit of the red liquid into a thimble.

Honeysuckle picked it up, flew over to Natalia, and hovered at her lips. Natalia looked at Brooke, who simply nodded.

"It's okay," Brooke said. "Doc Trimble left it for you."

"What is it?"

"A special nectar," Brooke said. "I forget the name of the flower, but he prescribed some for me when I wasn't feeling well. It tastes a bit like strawberries and cream. Go on, try it."

Natalia parted her lips, and Honeysuckle poured the nectar into her mouth. It felt warm as it went down Natalia's throat and into her stomach. Within seconds the feelings of nausea were gone, along with the headache.

"See?"

Honeysuckle smiled as Natalia licked her lips to savor every drop of the liquid.

"That was…"

"Like magic?"

"Yeah." Natalia paused. "Where's Max?"

"I'm not sure," Brooke said.

Panic returned to Natalia's eyes.

"Oh, he's fine," Brooke said. "Nobody knows how he did it, but he walked away without a scratch. He almost got a ticket for flying that aerocar without a license, but Logan got him out of it."

"What about Harley?"

"He's a hero," Brooke said. "They had a big article about him in the paper. That Mark Four he was driving is all people are talking about."

Natalia closed her eyes and exhaled. "Have you seen my parents?"

"The nurse said that your mom left about an hour ago, but I think your dad stayed here with your sister last night. He should be here in a while, though. He's going to be excited to find you awake."

"What about Ernie?"

"Harley said it was a miracle that he's even alive," Brooke said. "He was caught in a slaver's net, and then he disappeared. Literally."

"He's fast, but he's not that fast."

"It wasn't his changeling speed," Brooke said. "The nets those slavers used nullify changeling powers."

"Then how'd he disappear?"

"Nobody knows," Brooke said, "and Ernie won't say."

"That's weird," Natalia said, her eyes drifting to the ceiling as she pondered how Ernie could have pulled it off. "Oh, well," she finally said. "I can't believe I was out for a week."

"It was more like ten days," Brooke said. "You wouldn't believe how many visitors you've had."

"Really?"

"Most of your teachers, Raven, Max, Harley... Ernie's been here more than any of them, though."

"Ernie?"

"He does his homework over there," Brooke said, pointing to a small table in the corner of the room. "The nurse has to kick him out when visiting hours are over, and somehow he still manages to sneak back inside."

"That doesn't make any sense," Natalia said. "He's been acting like he hates us."

"I think he feels like all of this is his fault," Brooke said. "Either that, or he needs a friend. The other changelings are blaming him for what happened."

"That's ridiculous."

"I told him that, but he won't listen to me."

Natalia felt her stomach rumble. "I'm starving."

"You should be," Brooke said. "I'll call the nurse to see if she can bring you some food."

Brooke was about to ring for the nurse when someone knocked on the door.

"Come in," Natalia said.

The door slowly opened, and Ernie walked in.

"I'll go check on your breakfast," Brooke said. Honeysuckle slipped into Brooke's bag before she left.

Ernie was holding a small vase filled with carnations as he stood by the bed with his head hung low.

"Are those for me?" Natalia asked.

Ernie nodded and set them on the dresser next to a massive bouquet from Max.

"They're beautiful."

"You don't have to say that."

"I mean it," Natalia said. "They really are."

"I also got you this," Ernie said and took his backpack off. He unzipped the front compartment and pulled out a small package wrapped in white paper.

Natalia took it in her hands and gently unwrapped it. Inside was a porcelain unicorn standing on its hind legs. Its head was thrown to the side, and its mane and tail looked as if they were blowing in the wind.

"Where did you find it?" she asked.

"I had to order it," Ernie said. "I didn't think you had this one in your collection yet."

"It's perfect. In fact, I have the perfect place for it in my bedroom. So thank you."

"You're welcome," Ernie said.

"Brooke told me that you've been spending a lot of time here."

"I just needed a quiet place to do my homework."

Natalia smiled. "You know, Ernie, this isn't your fault."

"Yes, it is. I should have listened to you."

"What do you mean?"

"You told me that I couldn't handle it, and you were right," Ernie said. "I led everyone into that trap, and now Hale is gone...and I almost got you killed."

"Wait, what happened?"

"We heard that some of the slavers were hiding in an abandoned building, but it was a setup," Ernie said. "They were waiting for us with nets and restraining collars. The only reason I got out was because..." Ernie almost let it slip that Obadiah Strange had given him the IPA, which helped him phase in and out like a ghost.

"Because why?" Natalia asked.

"Well, I got lucky, that's all, but now Hale is gone, and it's all my fault."

"You didn't know."

"Maybe I should have." Ernie looked down. "Everyone thinks that I've been telling Von Strife where we're going so he can send the slavers after us. All I wanted to do was make Von Strife pay for what he did to Robert."

"It's going to be okay."

Ernie bowed his head. "Not this time."

"You should talk to Max," she said.

"I've been such a jerk," Ernie said. "I doubt he wants to talk to me."

Natalia reached out to touch Ernie's hand. "Yes, he does," she said gently. Ernie looked up. She could see that his eyes were red. "Friends forgive each other, Ernie. Max understands how much pain you're in, and he wants to help. We all do."

Ernie wiped his eyes with his sleeve and stood up. "I have to get going," he said.

"Promise me that you'll talk to Max."

Ernie nodded. "I'll try."

A VIAL OF PILLS

There was still no medical explanation for Monti's illness, but the coughing had subsided, the color had returned to his skin, and his eyes had stopped drooping. Doc Trimble wanted to keep him under lock and key until he knew what was going on, but Monti had become unbearable with his incessant requests to be released from the hospital.

Against his better judgment, Doc Trimble signed Monti's release papers. There was no real excuse to keep him, but Doc Trimble was sure Monti would be back. Monti, of course, went straight to work. To make up for lost time, he had his automated workforce laboring around the clock, but that only made things worse. The clockworks started to break down, and in Monti's condition, he couldn't fix them.

Harley was coming by after school and on the weekends, but it wasn't enough. When he arrived at the workshop Saturday morning, he found Monti pale, feverish, and weak. Against Monti's wishes, Harley had Jasper call Doc Trimble. The doctor was there within the hour.

"I want you to take these. They should help with the anxiety until things settle down a bit," Trimble said, handing Monti a vial of pills.

"I don't think so," Monti said, handing the pills back to the doctor.

"If you keel over from a heart attack, you won't be much use to any of us," Trimble said. "So are you going to take them, or am I going to have to come here and stuff them down your gullet myself?"

"Fine."

"Isn't there someone who could help around here?"

"Not really," Monti said.

"What about the boy?" Doc Trimble asked as he pointed his mechanical arm at Harley. He was standing at the docking bay watching a delivery truck back in.

"He's brilliant, but he's only twelve."

"What does that matter? Does he have what it takes or doesn't he?"

Monti sighed. "Yes."

"Then you've found your solution," Trimble said.

"What about his classes?"

"You let me take care of that." With that, Trimble tipped his hat and walked out.

When Max showed up at the workshop, Monti was in his office taking a nap, and Harley was preoccupied with what looked like a pile of scrap metal.

"Are those more clockworks?" Max asked as Harley guided a robotic crane with a remote control. A magnetic arm lowered, grabbed hold of battered parts, and lifted it. Harley pushed another button, and the crane rolled along the ceiling tracks.

"It's what's left of the Mark Four armor after Oxley made me take it apart."

"Are you serious?"

Harley sighed and hit another button, making the crane release the load. The metal clanked as it hit the floor.

"Wasn't it in a scrap heap when Monti found it?" Max asked. "If he fixed it once, maybe he could fix it again."

"Not in his condition," Harley said as he put on a pair of gloves.

"You're not kidding," Monti said.

Max turned to see Monti leaning heavily on a cane. He was smiling, but it looked forced. His face was pale, and there were dark circles under his eyes.

"Shouldn't you be in bed?" Harley asked.

"What do you think?" Monti asked, changing the subject. "Is it salvageable?"

Harley shrugged as he inspected the damage to a knee joint. "I'll find a way to fix it."

"I'm sure you will." Monti turned his attention to Max. "How are you feeling?"

"Better than you."

"That isn't saying much."

"I'm still kind of sore, but it could have been a lot worse," Max said. "Logan said I'm lucky that I'm still alive."

"Trust me, I already got an earful," Monti said. "So from now on, I'll be keeping the keys to all my toys locked safely in my office."

"Sorry about that."

"You did it to save Ernie," Monti said. "So how could I be upset?"

"Thanks."

"Speaking of Ernie, how's he holding up?"

"Who knows?" Max said. "He still isn't talking to us."

"And the changelings aren't talking to him," Harley said. "They think he's working for Von Strife."

"That's crazy," Monti said.

Harley shrugged. "Ernie was the one who led them into the trap."

"Making bad decisions is a lot different from sabotage," Monti said.

"The only way Ernie is going to get off the hook is if we finish that scanner and find Hale."

"After you, then," Monti said.

Harley led them through a bank of steam. "By the way," he said as they walked past the shooting range. "Your freeze ray is still jamming."

"I'll add it to the list," Monti said.

ONCE MORE INTO THE PAST

Natalia blinked as the first rays of sunshine poured through the blinds. She stretched as she looked around the hospital room. It still smelled like a spring garden, even though some of the flowers were starting to droop while others had lost their petals.

The days were starting to bleed together, but Natalia was scheduled to go home this week, so her spirits were high. She pulled back her sheets, threw her legs over the side of the bed, and then slid into her fuzzy slippers.

Natalia stretched once more, rising to her tiptoes before walking over to raise the blinds. Then she went to work, trimming the flowers with a pair of scissors she found in the nurses' closet. Natalia hummed a tune as she went from vase to vase, stopping to read each card along the way.

Someone knocked on the door.

"Just a minute," Natalia said. She kicked off her slippers and jumped back under her sheets, doing her best to look exhausted.

"What's going on in here?" Raven asked as she walked into the room.

"Sorry. I thought you were my nurse. I'm not supposed to get out of bed without supervision."

"Then why did you get out of bed?"

"Because I'm fine, see?" Natalia said, bending the arm that had been hurt. "I don't know why I'm still here."

Raven shrugged. "What do doctors and nurses know, right? I mean, it's not like they went to years of school or anything."

"Okay, I get the point," Natalia said.

Raven plopped into the chair next to Natalia's bed. "Have you read any more of Windham's books?"

"I've tried, but they're kind of…"

"Boring?"

"You could say that," Natalia said. "He spends as much time talking about his brilliance as he does about time travel. I did a search using my DE Tablet, but there wasn't much we didn't already know."

"How about Paragon Engines?"

"Oh, there's all kinds of information out there,"

Natalia said. "Of course, most of it is garbage. You can even download blueprints that show you how to make a Paragon Engine using stuff that you can buy at a hardware store."

"I bet the Toad brothers already tried it."

"Probably."

"So what's next?"

"I have some homework that I need to finish," Natalia said. "After that I might try another one of Windham's books. I'm afraid it's going to put me to sleep, though."

"Good luck."

Natalia glanced over at the door before turning back to Raven. "Did you bring it?"

"Yeah." Raven reached into her purse to pull out a bundle wrapped in cloth and tied with a string. Once she unwrapped it, Natalia could see the worn leather cover that had once protected Otto Von Strife's journal.

"Perfect," Natalia said. She threw her blanket to the side before sitting cross-legged on her bed to make room for Raven.

"Do you still think Smoke is right about Von Strife?"

"I never said he was right," Natalia said. "I just think there's more to what's going on than we know. I mean, what if Von Strife is doing all these terrible things, but he really thinks that he's helping people?"

"That just makes him a lunatic," Raven said.

"Maybe he just misses his daughter."

"If you think he's such a great guy, why don't you ask

the parents of all those missing kids what they think? I'm sure they'd have an opinion."

"Look, I'm not trying to justify what he's done," Natalia said. She paused, biting her lower lip as she contemplated what to say next. Raven's friendship meant a lot to Natalia, and she didn't want to push her away. "It's just that... I don't know. If we can uncover Von Strife's motivation, maybe we can stop him before he hurts anyone else."

Raven sighed. "I still say he's a nut job, but since I'm already here..." She tossed the journal cover onto the bed, closed the blinds, and locked the door. Then she sat down at the foot of the bed and placed her hand on what was left of Von Strife's journal.

"Okay, we have to be missing something," Natalia said. "He has to mention where he sent Sophia."

"It's called the Shadowlands," Raven said, though Natalia ignored the sarcasm.

"You might be right," Natalia said, "but we need proof. I mean, what if he sent her to a parallel world where they have the technology that could save her life?"

"Let's just get this over with," Raven said. "If I'm late for first period, Nipkin is going to put me in detention for the rest of the year."

"The nurse isn't supposed to be here for another half hour, so we should be okay."

"What about Brooke?" Raven asked. "Are you sure that she won't be upset if we do this without her?"

"We're fine," Natalia said, placing her hand on top of Raven's.

The hospital room faded as Von Strife's study came into view. A haunting melody played from the phonograph on his desk as Von Strife gazed into what looked like a Paragon Engine that was the size of a large monitor. He was taking notes with a fountain pen, occasionally stopping to adjust some of the knobs on the machine.

"I've heard that song before," Natalia said, "but I'm not sure what it is."

"I think it's Tchaikovsky's Piano Concerto number one," Raven said.

"Wait, how did you know that?"

"I grew up on that kind of music. My mom's a composer."

"That's amazing," Natalia said.

"I guess," Raven said with little enthusiasm. "Now shhh…"

The door opened and a clockwork researcher stepped into the office and saw Von Strife. "Sir," the clockwork said, "you have studied nearly a thousand worlds. The odds of finding Sophia are —"

"Thank you, but I have no interest in the odds," Von Strife said. His eyes never left the machine in front of him.

"Why is that?"

"One day you'll understand that nothing can come between a father and his child. Not mathematics. Not even physics."

"My apologies, sir."

"You have nothing to apologize for," Von Strife said. "You were merely trying to help."

"Thank you, sir," the clockwork said. "May I ask a question?"

"Of course."

"What will happen once you find Sophia?"

"I'll go to her."

"Will you take us with you?"

"That's the plan."

"What of the Templar?"

Von Strife sighed and massaged his forehead. "They'll pay for what they have done, but all in due time."

"Is there anything else I can do for you, sir?"

"No, Johnny," Von Strife said. "You may go."

"Wait, did he just call that clockwork Johnny?" Raven asked.

"I thought we were supposed to stop talking," Natalia said.

"As you wish," the clockwork said.

When it turned to leave, Natalia saw the name JOHNNY GEIST engraved on its chest.

"You know who that is, don't you?" Natalia asked.

"The first changeling who went missing," Raven said.

Once the door was closed, Von Strife sat up and cocked his head as though he was listening for something. "Who's there?" he asked.

No one responded.

Von Strife slid his chair back and stood up. He walked over to look behind the door, and then he checked the space behind his desk. "I know you're there," he said. "Show yourself."

Still nothing.

He spun around on his heels before looking up. Natalia could feel his eyes boring into her. "Who are you?" he asked. "What do you want?"

"I think he's talking about us," Natalia said. "But he couldn't be..."

There was a flash of light as the girls were ejected from the scene. Natalia's head slammed against the wall. Raven flew off the bed and slid across the floor and into the dresser. The impact sent Ernie's carnations crashing to the ground. The vase shattered, covering the floor in tiny shards of glass.

"Are you okay?" Natalia asked.

Raven struggled to stand. "I think so. What about you?"

"I'm going to have another headache, but I'm fine."

There was a knock on the door before someone tried to turn the doorknob. "Is everything okay in there?" the nurse asked. "Natalia?"

"Oh. Um...just a minute," Natalia said as she stood up. Then she lowered her voice to a whisper. "What should I tell her?"

"I don't know."

"Natalia," the nurse said, "what's going on?"

"I'll be right there." Natalia went to hand Raven the cover to the journal.

"No way," Raven said. "I'm not touching that thing."

"What am I supposed to do with it?"

"You can burn it for all I care."

"Has that ever happened before?" Natalia asked.

"Never."

"How do you think he saw us?"

"All I know is that this is over our heads." Raven grabbed her purse before opening the door and storming past the surprised nurse.

The nurse surveyed the mess on the floor with an open mouth. "What happened?"

"Trust me, you don't want to know."

FROM BAD TO WORSE

Natalia hid the cover of Von Strife's journal under her bed, but after a restless night filled with dreams of Von Strife experimenting on helpless changelings, she decided to keep it in her backpack on the other side of the room.

It didn't stop the nightmares. That Von Strife had somehow seen them through Raven's vision was terrifying. As long as she had visitors, Natalia was fine. The moment she was alone, panic set in. However, the bigger problem was explaining everything to her parents.

As would be expected, they were ready to take Natalia out of Iron Bridge Academy, and all of Templar society for that matter. In their estimation, the dangers were too great and the costs were too high.

"We don't want to lose you," her father said one morning at the hospital a few days after Natalia woke up. He was looking down at Natalia through square-framed glasses that couldn't hide the worry in his eyes. Reaching over, he brushed a strand of hair from her forehead.

"I know," Natalia said, grabbing him by the hand, "but running away from all of this isn't going to change anything. The world is a scary place, and you and Mom can't save me from that. If you take me out of Iron Bridge, it's only going to make things worse. I mean, they're teaching us how to fight against things the real world can't even comprehend. Besides, I was chosen to do this. Don't you want me to be prepared?"

Her father reached up to wipe a stray tear and sighed. "Of course we do," he said. "We're just not sure that this is the best way. Look at you. You have a black eye, you suffered a concussion, and the doctor had to use twenty stitches to close up that cut."

"But, Daddy, I survived," Natalia said, sitting up. "Look, as strange as this may sound, I think we were called into this for a reason, and I don't want to stop. I can't stop. I want to protect you and Mom and our whole family, and I won't be able to do that if I leave."

Mr. Romanov scratched at what little of the auburn hair remained on his scalp. Then he stood up, shook his head, and smiled. "I can't believe I'm saying this, but okay."

"I can stay?" Natalia couldn't hide her shock.

"I'll talk to your mother about this, but I have a feeling she isn't going to be happy. Either way, there're going to be some conditions," he said, trying to sound stern but failing miserably. He couldn't help but sound proud. "No more joyrides in flying cars. In fact, I don't want you in flying cars at all."

"Agreed."

"And other than your classes, I don't want you coming into this city."

"Wait, you mean New Victoria?"

"Yes."

Natalia was about to protest, but she decided against it. After all, considering everything that had happened, Natalia knew that she was lucky. She didn't think there would be a chance that she'd be able to stay, and her father wasn't asking for much.

He'd been sleeping on an uncomfortable cot in her room every night since the accident, while Natalia's mother stayed with her sister, Katarina, at their house. It was a sacrifice. After all, Mr. Romanov was a tall man, and his legs were far too long for the cot. Yet he never complained, not once.

Instead, he stayed up half the night trying to catch up on paperwork that he'd neglected in order to spend more time with Natalia. Occasionally he'd leave to pick up something at his office, but only if Brooke or someone else was there to keep Natalia company.

When Doc Trimble finally signed her release papers, Natalia wasn't sure what to do with the cover of Von Strife's journal. Her first thought was to tie it to a rock and throw it to the bottom of Lake Avalon. She figured it couldn't harm anyone from there.

Still, despite the fact that it gave her nightmares, the journal had proved useful so far. As much as the thought of traveling back inside its memories terrified her, Natalia knew that the journal cover might come in handy down the line. She decided to hide it in the records room inside the school library. Natalia was fairly certain she was the only person who went in there, besides Mrs. Prosser, the head librarian.

Ernie had told his parents that he needed to stay after school to work on a project. Instead, he ended up outside Obadiah Strange's office. He took a deep breath before knocking on the door.

"Come in."

Ernie found Strange standing as he stared at several maps strewn across his desk. An antique phonograph played classical music as a fire crackled in the hearth nearby. There was ash on the floor, likely from the stack of papers that were burning atop the logs.

"I thought you were someone else," Strange said, looking up.

"Oh, sorry."

"Nonsense. Please, have a seat." Strange pointed to the leather chairs in front of his desk, took a deep draft of tea, and joined Ernie.

"What are all the maps for?"

"Your field test," Strange said. "We'll use the jump station to transport here." He pointed to a clearing in the middle of an enormous forest on one of the maps. He slid his finger to a dark area that looked like it might be a hill. "And this is where we should find the Schrödinger Box."

"What does that thing do again?"

"Theoretically, it will ensure that you're not torn apart when you travel from one universe to another."

"How do you know it's still there?"

"I don't," Strange said.

Ernie stood up and walked over to a shelf where he had spotted some tin soldiers next to a small box. They were lined up as though they were in a battle. Some stood with rifles aimed, while others rode on horseback. Then he saw tin clockworks scattered among the soldiers. There was even a suit of Mark Four armor just like the one Harley had worn.

"Where did you get these?" he asked as he picked the armor up.

"They were a gift from a man by the name of Wilhelm the First," Strange said.

"Was he a king or something?"

"Yes, for a time."

"What's this?" Ernie asked. He set the tin armor down and touched the box.

"Please be careful, it's quite delicate."

Ernie unfastened the latch and pushed the lid back to reveal a porcelain ballerina that started to pirouette as music played. "Natalia has one of these."

"Many young girls do," Strange said.

"Then why do you have one?"

"Let's just say it has sentimental value," Strange said, walking over to shut the lid. He clasped the lock and turned back to Ernie. "Now tell me, what brings you here at this late hour? Are you out of our special brew?"

"I think I have enough," Ernie said, referring to the dragon dung tea that was supposed to stunt the changeling transformation from human to faerie.

"Since you don't have a tail just yet, I'd say it must be working."

"I guess."

"Is something troubling you?"

"I've been thinking," Ernie said after a moment. "You know how you can travel through time?"

"In a manner of speaking, yes," Strange said.

"Do you already know what's going to happen?"

"What do you mean?" Strange walked over to his desk and sat down. He motioned for Ernie to do the same.

"If you already know what's going to happen, you could tell us how to save Hale."

"I'm afraid that my gift doesn't work that way."

"Why not?"

"It's true that because of my changeling gift I travel back to a certain point in time if I die, but there's a twist.... It's never the same world."

"Like Mars?"

Strange sighed. "No, Mr. Tweeny. Though that would simplify things. I'm referring to an alternate universe that may resemble our own, but it's quite different."

"Oh, you mean like in comic books where there's a thousand versions of Superman on a thousand different Earths?"

"Something like that, yes."

"Does that mean there's more than one of me?"

"More than likely."

Ernie sat there trying to grasp the concept, but it wasn't easy. "So what would happen if I met another version of myself? Would the world explode or something?"

"I hope not," Strange said, laughing.

"Do you think there's another version of me here right now?"

"I'd say the odds are against you, but more peculiar things have happened."

Ernie sighed. "I wish I could go to another Earth right now."

"Why would you say that?"

"Because everyone at school thinks that I'm helping Otto Von Strife kidnap the changelings. You know, just like Smoke did."

"Let me ask you a question," Strange said after a moment of contemplation. "When a baseball team doesn't live up to expectations, what happens?"

"I don't know," Ernie said. "I guess they fire the coach."

"Precisely," Strange said. "Right or wrong, the coach becomes the scapegoat for the failures of the team."

"The team didn't fail, though. I did," Ernie said. "I mean, I didn't do it on purpose or anything, but I'm the one who led them into the trap."

"Perhaps, but we all make mistakes," Strange said. "No matter what, we cannot let those mistakes define who we are."

"What am I supposed to do?" Ernie said.

"Only you know that answer, Agent Thunderbolt," Strange said. "But one way or the other, you must win back their confidence."

MAKE THE JUMP

Ernie knew that he had to rescue Hale before Von Strife ripped the soul out of her body and stuffed it into one of his machines. It was the only way the other changelings were going to forgive him. Ernie just wasn't sure how he was going to do it.

A few days after the incident, the *New Victoria Chronicle* ran an article unmasking the Agents of Justice. Once the public learned that the vigilantes were changelings from Iron Bridge Academy, editorial letters about Dean Nipkin's incompetence poured in.

Dean Nipkin decided to take her frustration out on her students. Annie was given daily injections of a serum that negated her powers so she couldn't manipulate the inhibitors. Short of a miracle, the changelings—except for Ernie—were going to be stuck in Sendak Hall until summer break.

There was an exception, however. Obadiah Strange made sure that the changelings were allowed to continue attending his class. Dean Nipkin wasn't happy about it, but Strange had the backing of the Templar academies' governing board, and its word was final.

The Relic Hunters continued to train in the SIM Chamber, despite the friction among the students. After the incident with Hale, Ernie was enemy number one with the other changelings. His relationship with the Grey Griffins wasn't much better. Ernie was still avoiding Max and Harley, despite Natalia's constant urging for them to work things out. They didn't.

Then, just three days after Ernie met with Strange in his office, a clockwork messenger showed up in homeroom. The machine was tall and thin, with a shiny iron casing accented by bits of bronze. It had four eyes, all the same size, stacked in two rows of two, and a hinged jaw and long fingers.

"Excuse me," the clockwork said.

"Yes?" Ms. Merical asked.

"I've been sent to collect the following students: Natalia Romanov, Harley Eisenstein, Ernest Tweeny, and Grayson Sumner," the clockwork said, using Max's formal name.

"Max," Max said, correcting the clockwork.

"Pardon me?"

"My name is Max."

"Never mind," Ms. Merical said. "May I ask why you need to see them?"

The clockwork turned away from Max to face her. "Obadiah Strange requires their presence. They are to be excused from all classes today." It walked over to hand her a slip of paper.

Ms. Merical removed her glasses and rubbed the bridge of her nose. "You tell Obadiah that I expect him to look out for these children. I swear, if one hair on their heads is harmed, I'll come after him."

The clockwork tilted its head as though it was trying to understand the gravity of the threat. At the same time, Max and the other Grey Griffins gathered their belongings and followed the clockwork down the hall, up a flight of steps, and then into a large room, where Strange was standing with the other students from their Archaeological Reconnaissance and Excavation class. Todd and Ross were already there.

"Welcome," Strange said as the Griffins walked in. "Well, now that our class is complete, let's get down to business. We have reason to believe that Von Strife is actively searching for the Schrödinger Box, which means we must act now."

"Wait, does that mean we're going on our field test today?" Todd asked. His eyes were wide.

"I'm afraid so," Strange said.

"But we haven't been able to pass the test in the SIM Chamber," Ross said. "Yesterday I fell into a pit with a Sand Dragon, and Todd got eaten by a colony of Vampire Pixies. Xander hasn't even passed his test yet. I mean, if he can't do it, how are we supposed to survive?"

Though Strange was smiling, it was clear by his stiff posture, if not the intensity of his eyes, that he was just as concerned. "I'm afraid we haven't the time to wait," he said. "I don't have to tell you the gravity of what would happen if Von Strife opens a portal to the Shadowlands. All would be lost."

"What if we can't find it?" Todd said. "Or what if Von Strife already has it?"

"We'll worry about that later," Strange said. "Right now, all you need to focus on is getting into your gear and making the jump."

"Are you talking about a jump station?" Ross asked. "As in a room that can teleport us anywhere in the world?"

"Yes, of course," Strange said.

"When did we get one of those?" Todd asked. "I mean, I thought we weren't allowed to use portals on campus."

"You aren't," Strange said, "but I am."

Even though they had spent weeks preparing for the mission, tensions were high. Catalina's imp vomited, while Kenji's drake flew in circles belching flames. Sprig, however, was asleep in a corner of the room.

"I bet these things are made with that new ballistic

275

fabric," Todd said as he slipped into a camouflage jump-suit that each of the Relic Hunters had been given. "You know, like a bulletproof vest."

Besides the jumpsuit, each Relic Hunter had been given boots, gloves, a helmet, a backpack filled with basic supplies, and a communication device that fastened to their wrists like an oversized watch.

Natalia saw Ernie sitting by himself in the far corner of the room, his eyes focused on the floor as his leg shook up and down thanks to nerves. She walked over and asked, "You haven't talked to Max or Harley yet, have you?"

Ernie shook his head.

"Why not?"

"I don't know," Ernie said. "I guess I'm scared."

"You shouldn't be," Natalia said. "Once you get every-thing out in the open, it's going to be such a relief."

"I guess," Ernie said. "It's just that...I don't know. I guess I've been kind of a jerk, and I don't know if they're going to forgive me."

"You won't know unless you talk to them," Natalia said.

Once the students were dressed in their gear, Strange led them to an elevator that required a key card. "Quickly now," he said as the elevator rumbled to life. The eleva-tor car took them to a large room, where armed soldiers stood watch as a team of engineers manned a series of complex control panels.

276

"Now then," Strange said, clearing his throat, "your test will begin in a few moments, but I wanted to make something clear. Though you may not see me, I will be present at all times. However, my role is simply that of observer. If you get into trouble, you must rely on your wits and one another."

"Wait a minute," Todd said. "What if we fall off a cliff or something? I mean, you're not going to let us die, right?"

"Let's hope that it doesn't come to that," Strange said. He nodded toward one of the engineers.

Harley watched closely as the engineer input a series of commands. Once he pulled a switch, the air was charged with electricity. Jagged bolts of plasma jumped across Tesla coils. There was a flash of light, and then the Relic Hunters were gone.

The jump platform had delivered them into the heart of a rain forest that was blanketed in mist. The sounds of birds and insects echoed all around. Everything was washed in green, from the leaves in the branches to the ocean of ferns that covered the ground. The trees were wrapped in moss and fungi, while flowers clung to creeping vines that drew brightly colored hummingbirds.

"They're actually faeries," Natalia said as she inspected the birds through her Phantasmoscope.

"Of course they are," Strange said as an enormous butterfly landed on his forearm. Strange smiled as he watched the wings of the creature rise and fall.

"That's a—"

"Winged Croaker," Strange said. Faeries could mask their true nature so humans couldn't see them.

"That's a Croaker?" Todd said. "It's disgusting."

"No kidding," Ernie said with a wrinkled nose. "It's almost as ugly as that..." His voice trailed off when he saw Catalina glaring at him. She was standing next to her Digger imp as he splashed in a puddle.

The Croaker looked like a fat toad with stubby wings. Its lumpy body was covered with warts, and two tusks jutted up from its jaw.

"I suppose it's all a matter of perspective," Strange said as the Croaker leaped into the air. Its tiny wings started to beat so fast that they were nearly invisible, but somehow they managed to carry the corpulent faerie into the distant shadows.

"All right," Strange said once the Croaker disappeared. "Mr. Swift, have you checked our coordinates?"

Xander was looking through a pair of binoculars. "We should be less than a quarter mile from the temple."

"Excellent," Strange said. "Lead the way."

Xander entered the thick mist with Strange and the other Relic Hunters trailing behind. Sprig walked next to Max as a white tiger. Her fur was matted from the condensation that dripped from the leaves. She was intrigued by the monkeys that were jumping from tree to tree.

It wasn't long before rushing water drowned out the sounds of the forest. Xander led the Relic Hunters over a fallen tree that spanned a river. In the distance, a waterfall shot down the side of a cliff, feeding the river as it sped beneath the natural bridge.

"Look," Brooke said as fish with rainbow scales jumped into the air and splashed back into the river.

Natalia knelt beside her and watched tiny faeries with tails like mermaids. Their translucent wings were barely perceptible as they shot into the air to hover in front of the girls.

"Come on," Raven said as she walked past the fairies. "We don't want to get left behind in this place."

The Relic Hunters continued to wind their way through the forest until they came to a trail marked by a statue worn from age.

"What is it?" Ernie asked.

"I'm not sure," Todd said. "It kind of looks like an elephant."

"Maybe it's an eagle."

"It's a panther," Xander said, just as something shot out of the branches above.

Kenji's drake leaped from his shoulder. The tiny dragon wrapped his claws around a startled bird before bringing it to the ground.

"Wait, it's a parrot," Natalia said.

The drake turned his head to hiss as she approached.

"I wouldn't do that," Kenji said. "He gets territorial when it comes to food."

Natalia pushed her way past Kenji, and that's when the drake sprang.

A Sticky Situation

With his mouth spread wide, Sparky leaped at Natalia, but Max was quicker. He grabbed the drake by his neck before his tiny teeth could sink into Natalia's nose.

"Be careful!" Kenji shouted as Sparky whimpered. The drake tried to break free. He was flapping his wings and kicking his legs, but Max wouldn't let go.

Kenji rushed over to wrap his arms around the tiny dragon, stroking Sparky's neck as he cried.

Natalia stood rooted to the ground, her face drained of color as she tried to catch her breath.

"Next time, listen to him," Max told Natalia. The drake hissed while Max walked away, but it was nothing more than a false sense of bravado. The Bounder was trying to save face.

The Relic Hunters pressed forward, but the path was choked by vegetation. They tried to use the statues as markers, but most were lost in the thick undergrowth. The sun was fading, and as night set in, tensions in the group mounted.

"I don't think we're going the right way," Yi said. His hands were lit like torches, and even though they provided light, they were also drawing enormous insects.

"Hold up," Xander said.

Yi walked over to where Xander was standing. The flames around his hands revealed a massive spiderweb stretched between two trees like a roadblock.

"I'd hate to see the spider that made this," Ernie said.

"That makes two of us," Todd said.

"Three of us," Ross said.

"Can we go around it?" Kenji asked as his drake landed on his shoulder.

"I'm not sure we'd want to," Xander said.

"Look," Yi said, pointing into the branches overhead.

"I don't see anything," Ross said.

"Maybe not, but I can smell them," Denton said.

"Me too," Ernie said.

"There it is again," Yi said. "Something is up in the trees. I think it's a—"

Yi couldn't finish his sentence, because a white gelatinous substance, like a giant spitball, was covering his mouth. He tried to pull it away, but it stuck to his hands. Max could see the panic in Yi's eyes, but as the changeling's body burst into flames, whatever was choking him burned away, allowing Yi to breathe again.

A second dollop of goop hit Brooke in the face, sending her into the ferns. Honeysuckle tried to pull it off Brooke as another glob struck Kenji's drake, wrapping around his wings so he couldn't fly.

Ross and Todd grabbed flashlights that were hanging from their belts. They shined the beams up into the trees' branches, and then they recoiled.

"They're Blight Spiders," Max said. With their six arms, eight eyes, and bristling hair, they looked just like the monsters on his Round Table card.

"Any suggestions?" Xander asked.

"They hate fire." Max raised his *Codex* gauntlet, and a captivity orb shot from his palm. The Blight Spider that he targeted leaped out of the way, and the orb zipped past and fizzled in the branches of the tree.

Max let three more orbs fly, and though the first two missed, the last struck its target. The Blight Spider screamed as it clawed at the prison. Sparks of energy flew, but it couldn't break free no matter how hard it fought.

"We can't get the webbing off Brooke's face," Natalia said as she struggled with Honeysuckle. "She's suffocating."

"Hold still," Yi said as he raised an index finger to the webbing. A flame leaped from his fingertip, melting the sticky substance.

Brooke's eyes were wild as she gasped for breath.

"Look out," Denton warned.

Max turned in time to see a spray of webbing race toward him. Yi shot it out of the air with a fireball. He shifted and sent another volley at Kenji's drake. The flames melted the web, releasing the tiny dragon so it could join the fight.

Sprig pounced on one of the Blight Spiders before it could reach Raven. Harley took aim at another with his freeze ray. He managed to hit it in the leg, but the rest of his shots missed. The Blights were quick, but they weren't too quick for Ernie.

He ripped off his backpack and dumped the contents onto the forest floor. Then, in a blur of speed, he ran toward one of the Blight Spiders and pulled the backpack over its head. The Blight screamed, trying to break free. Ernie grabbed a vine that was hanging from a branch and used it to wrap the Blight Spider like a spool of thread.

Nearby, Catalina's Bounder imp tore into the soft earth, looking for a place to hide. One of the Blight Spiders jumped down from the branches. It opened its mouth to unleash a torrent of webbing at Catalina, but Max hit it with a captivity orb before it could attack.

At the same time, Denton scaled a tree and launched at one of the Blight Spiders. They both fell off the branch and landed in the ferns below. Somehow the Blight landed on top, but Denton coiled his legs, growled, and kicked hard.

The force sent the monster flying backward. Max unleashed another captivity orb, hitting the monster in the chest. It hovered in the air, howling and screaming as it fought to break free.

"Nicely played," Strange said from a safe distance. He was standing with his arms crossed as though he were observing another scenario in the SIM Chamber.

"Is he just going to stand there and watch us get slaughtered?" Raven asked before she swung a fallen tree branch at one of the Blights.

"Probably," Max said. He watched as a length of webbing spun Todd into a cocoon. Ross was next, and before either of the Toad brothers realized what was happening, they were hanging upside down from one of the branches. They wiggled and writhed, but they couldn't break free.

Another Blight Spider landed on top of Harley and bit him in the shoulder. Even though the Blight's teeth couldn't penetrate the protective fabric of the jumpsuit, the pressure was painful. Harley reached up with his free hand to grab the monster by its neck and flipped it onto the ground.

Kenji's drake swooped down, spraying flames from his mouth. The Blight crouched, covering its head with two of its arms while the other four grasped at the drake.

It didn't see the captivity orb that Max had shot until the ball of energy slammed into its back.

Frightened by the orbs, the rest of the Blights fled to the shadows of the forest. Denton scaled the tree where the Toad brothers dangled like ripe fruit.

"Should we leave them up here?" he asked.

"As much as I'd like to, we better cut them down," Max said. "I doubt we'll score many points for abandoning members of the team—even those two."

With a single swipe of his claws, Denton cut them both down. The Toad brothers landed with an "Oomph!" on the soft forest floor, but it was a long drop.

"Now that every monster in the forest knows we're here, what's the plan?" Raven asked.

"We need to find the temple," Xander said.

"Please tell me somebody has the map," Raven said.

"That was Ross and Todd's responsibility," Natalia said.

Todd, whose legs were still wrapped in webbing, struggled to open his backpack. His gloves stuck to the zipper, and he couldn't break free. He did, however, manage to open the compartment where the map was resting.

"Here, let me help," Ross said as he reached into the backpack. He pulled out the map, but it was stuck to his hand.

"You two are nitwits, do you know that?" Raven said, walking over to pry the map away. There was a loud rip. A portion of it was stuck to Ross's hand while Raven held the rest.

286

"Okay, this is the temple," Raven said, pointing to the center of the map, "and this is where they were supposed to drop us off."

"We're not that far off track," Harley said. "There should be a stream nearby that'll lead us straight there."

"Let's hurry up before something else shows up and tries to turn us into a midnight snack," Todd said.

THE TEMPLE

Finding the stream wasn't difficult. The forest had come to life thanks to luminescent mushrooms that were stuck to virtually every rock and tree. They cast the dense landscape in a strange yet beautiful glow. Firefly Pixies added their glimmer to the mix as they danced through the forest to the musical sounds of night creatures.

"I've never seen anything this beautiful," Natalia said after one of the pixies blew her a kiss.

Being the jealous sort, as most faeries were, Honeysuckle rolled her eyes. She despised others of her kind, particularly if they were beautiful, so when one of the

Firefly Pixies flew too close, she leaped from Brooke's shoulder to chase it away.

"What do you think, Sumner?" Xander asked as the Relic Hunters stood beneath the canopy of trees.

Max looked around the clearing. Yi was glowing like an ember as he stood next to Ernie. Raven had the hood of her jacket pulled tightly over her head, and the Toad brothers kept looking over their shoulders and into the shadows of the forest whenever they heard a noise.

"I think we should send Ernie ahead to scout things out," Max finally said. "According to the map, we should be close, but we don't know if anyone is waiting for us."

Ernie raised his eyebrows, surprised that Max would pick him for the task.

"Like Von Strife?" Denton asked. "Is that why you're sending Tweeny? Because he's going to lead us to another trap?"

"What did you say?" Harley moved toward Denton with clenched fists.

Max stepped between them. "Let it go. Both of you."

"Are you up for it, Agent Thunderbolt?" Xander said, ignoring Denton's protest.

"I guess," Ernie said, shrugging. He looked over at Denton, who was seething.

"Of course he is," Natalia said. She winked at Ernie, who offered a half smile in return.

Without another word, Ernie raced away. Vegetation

swayed as he shot through the forest. He leaped over gnarled tree roots and skirted around oversized toad-stools. Agent Thunderbolt was moving so fast that the night creatures had no idea he had come and gone.

"What took you so long?" Harley asked when Ernie returned less than a minute later. Though he had spanned more than a half mile in less time than it took some people to tie their shoes, he wasn't sweating or breathing abnormally.

"I found the temple," Ernie said to Xander as light from the iridescent mushrooms reflected in his brass goggles. "It's not very far."

"What about Von Strife?" Xander asked.

Ernie lowered his eyes. "I didn't see anyone," he said, his voice barely a whisper.

"Clocks?"

"Nothing."

"Why do I feel like we're walking into a trap?" Xander asked, biting his lower lip.

"See? I'm not the only one," Denton said.

"I don't like it either, but Ernie doesn't have anything to do with it," Max said, his voice terse. "Something isn't right, but I don't think we have much of a choice."

"Here's the thing," Xander said. "If this mission is so important, why is it our field test? I mean, don't you think they should have sent a THOR unit or something?"

"That's what I would have done," Max said. "But Strange doesn't think like most people do. He must have a reason for sending us instead. Let's just hope he's right."

Xander sighed before turning to the rest of the group. "This is it," he said. "I need Denton at the rear. Agent Thunderbolt, you take the lead. Raven and Yi will go in the middle. You guys can see farther than the rest of us. Everybody else, fall in line and keep your eyes open. We could be walking into a trap."

Ernie led the Relic Hunters—including the other change-lings, despite their reluctance to follow him—to a clearing that was dominated by a massive stone structure covered in vines. A waterfall roared in the distance, blanketing the landscape in a thick mist that made it difficult to see.

"It looks just like it did in the SIM Chamber," Todd said.

"That's the point," Raven said. "Let's get this over with so we can go home."

"Hold on," Xander said, grabbing her arm as she started for the path that led to the temple. "Has anyone seen Professor Strange?"

"He said he'd be watching us," Todd said. "Maybe he's using hidden cameras or something."

"He's here; we just can't see him," Max said.

"I hope you're right," Xander said before turning to Catalina. "You're up first."

Catalina nodded, but her Bounder imp shook as he hid behind her. He scampered up her legs and clung to her like a frightened child.

"It's okay, Scuttlebutt," Catalina whispered in his ear. "You're going to do great."

Scuttlebutt's bottom lip quivered. He looked like he was about to cry, but Catalina patted his back before starting through the undergrowth toward the temple. The others followed in single file, watching the shadows for any sign of trouble.

The only way to open the door to the temple was from the inside, which meant that Catalina's Bounder had to dig his way in. She placed him next to the wall and knelt down to stroke his cheek. "Are you ready?"

The imp shook his head.

"Sure you are," Catalina said. "We've done this dozens of times in the SIM Chamber. All you need to do is make a tunnel so you can reach the lever on the wall inside. We'll be back together before you know it."

The Digger imp sighed before wiping a glob of snot from his nose. Then he turned around and went to work. With long fingers, the imp tore into the soft earth. Dirt sprayed into the air, and before long Scuttlebutt had dug a hole deep enough and wide enough that he was already beneath the temple.

"Has anybody seen any Vampire Pixies?" Ross asked.

"Not yet," Todd said. He was wearing a string of garlic around his neck as he carried a wooden stake in one hand and a hammer in the other. Ross had an identical set.

The group heard what sounded like two boulders scraping together before the doorway into the temple slid open. When the dust settled, Scuttlebutt was standing there weeping.

"You did it," Catalina said.

As she smothered the imp with kisses, Natalia adjusted the arms on her Phantasmoscope to check the faerie spectrum for any magical traps or trip wires.

"I don't see anything," Natalia said from the doorway.

Harley slipped his backpack off his shoulders to unzip the front pouch. He pulled out an iron sphere that was the size of a grapefruit and hit a button, and a stem popped out. After Harley wound it up, the gears started to crank, and the sphere came to life. It lifted into the air with at least a dozen beams of blue light shooting into the darkness. He followed that up with five more spheres, and soon the drones were scanning the interior of the temple, looking for traps.

"I made a few adjustments last night," he said as he watched his machines. "The sensors should pick up any loose stones or unusual cracks in the walls."

The drones lit the interior of the temple in a ghostly blue. The only other light was coming from a skylight, which cast a single ray of moonlight over a pedestal.

Thanks to the faerie blood that coursed through him, Ernie didn't need very much light in order to see.

He took a careful step through the doorway, half expecting the door to crash down on his head. It didn't. Once inside, Ernie got down on his hands and knees to wipe the sand away from the floor.

"It's just like the SIM Chamber," he said once he saw the first stone. Then he looked up into the recesses of the ceiling, wondering if there were any Vampire Pixies waiting for them in the shadows.

FINDERS KEEPERS,
LOSERS WEEPERS

A gust of wind swept through the room, swirling until it formed a funnel of sand. Moments later, a creature larger than a troll started to take shape. Its shoulders were wide, its arms long, but it didn't have any eyes or a mouth.

Yi walked into the temple, fire bursting throughout his body. As he raised his hands to unleash a torrent of flames, the sand monster struck. Its arm stretched across the distance like pulled taffy and hit Yi in the chest. The force sent him flying, and his flame was doused as his head struck the ground.

"Go!" Kenji said, instructing his drake to finish the job, but the tiny dragon couldn't produce enough flame to turn the sand to glass. The sand monster wrapped its granular hand around the tiny dragon and threw it against the wall.

Blinded by rage, Kenji ran toward the creature. Raven tried to hold him back, but she couldn't get a very good grip. As Kenji's foot touched the first stone, the ground started to rumble. Just as in the SIM Chamber, the sand started to drain, leaving a forest of columns spanning a deep pit.

Kenji took a running leap at the sand monster as it stood on one of the pillars. He screamed as the monster's arm shot out, pounding him in the chest. Kenji flew backward, gasping as the air left his lungs. There was a sickening crack as his head hit the stone wall. Kenji slumped down, unconscious.

Brooke ran over to help Kenji as Max lifted his gauntlet to unleash a spray of blue fire, which engulfed the sand monster. Its chest turned to glass that quickly spread down its arms and legs, and then up its neck. The monster fought to break free, but cracks spread up its now-glassy arms and legs. It teetered before shattering.

"Let's move!" Xander said. "We have less than a minute to pull this off."

Sprig, who had taken the form of a spider monkey, leaped from Max's shoulder before turning into a griffin. She beat her wings and flew toward Natalia. As Natalia lifted her arms, Sprig grabbed her wrists. They flew over the pit, and Sprig dropped Natalia onto the small island where the pedestal stood.

Natalia mistimed her fall. She landed hard, twisting her ankle as she fell to the ground. Her Phantasmoscope flew from her hand and skittered toward the edge of the island. Natalia winced as she stretched her arm. The handle of her Phantasmoscope slipped over the side. Natalia's fingertips grazed one of the lenses, but she couldn't reach it in time. She watched the Phantasmoscope fall.

"No!" Natalia shouted.

Sprig pinned her wings to her sides before she dove into the shadows of the pit. Natalia had crawled to the edge of the island, where she watched Sprig reach for the Phantasmoscope. There was a clanking sound, and the griffin rose back into the air. Natalia's eyes were wide, and she held her breath as Sprig circled back toward her.

Sprig morphed back into a spider monkey before landing nimbly on the island with the Phantasmoscope grasped firmly in her tail.

"I could kiss you," Natalia said, though she didn't. Instead, she took her Phantasmoscope and turned to the Schrödinger Box, which sat on the pedestal.

"The drone isn't picking anything up," Harley said as one of his inventions hovered over the pedestal.

"Neither am I," Natalia said.

"So what are you waiting for?" a taunting voice rang out. The Relic Hunters recognized the voice, and a wave of panic spread through the team.

Everyone turned to see Smoke standing on one of the

pillars. Sprig started to screech as she did a series of back-flips with her teeth bared.

"Cute pet," Smoke said as he watched Sprig morph back into a griffin. Her claws scraped against the stone of the island as her wings spread wide in a show of aggression.

With Smoke distracted by the faerie, Denton took a running leap before he launched across the chasm to where Smoke was standing. He wrapped his arms around Smoke, and the momentum took both boys over the side. In a flash, they vanished, only to reappear halfway across the room on another pillar.

Denton was on top of Smoke, his knees pinning Smoke's shoulders to the ground. He raised his fist, but Smoke vanished. Denton punched the ground as Smoke reappeared on the island with Sprig and Natalia. Sprig lashed out with her talons, but Smoke was already gone. So was the Schrödinger Box.

"Where did he go?" Xander said.

"I'm right here," Smoke said. He was standing on one of the pillars with his arm wrapped around Raven's neck. She was fighting to break free, but his grip was too tight.

Max raised his gauntlet. It was crackling with energy that reflected in his eyes.

"I hope you have good aim," Smoke said, baiting Max. "I'd hate to see what would happen if you hit her instead of me."

"I don't care!" Raven shouted as Max narrowed his eyes. "Do it!"

"What are you waiting for?" Smoke asked.

"I said, do it!" Raven shouted.

Max lowered his arm.

"That's what I thought," Smoke said.

"Wait," Obadiah Strange said, walking out from the hiding place where he was observing his students.

"Look, everyone, it's the indestructible man," Smoke said mockingly.

Strange raised his hands in surrender. "Perhaps we could strike a bargain before things get messy."

"Why would I, when I can just take what I want?" Smoke said.

"Leave the girl and take me in her place," Strange said.

"No!" Ernie shouted, racing over to stand between Smoke and Strange. "You can take me."

Smoke smiled as he raised an eyebrow. "It's tempting," he said. "It really is, but Von Strife made a special request for this one."

"That's only because I'm a bit out of his league," Strange said.

Smoke frowned. "If I wanted to, I could just take you both."

"I suppose you could try," Strange said, "but I don't think you'd like the results."

"You're bluffing."

"Perhaps."

Smoke stood there, his eyes brimming with indecision as the Relic Hunters watched the terrible negotiation for Raven's life unfold.

"We can take him," Harley said.

"Yeah," agreed Yi.

"If you so much as sneeze, I'm out of here, and I'm taking her with me," Smoke said, his eyes never leaving Strange.

"This is your last opportunity," Strange said. "Choose wisely."

"How do I know this isn't a trick?" Smoke asked.

"You'll have to trust me."

"Yeah, right."

Strange narrowed his eyes as he bared his wooden teeth.

"Fine," Smoke said. He let go of Raven and pushed her in the back.

"Wait," Ernie said, spinning to confront Strange. "You can't just leave us here."

"For all we know, there could be a clockwork army waiting outside," Harley said.

"There isn't, is there, Mr. Thorne?" Strange said.

Smoke shook his head.

"But they'll kill you, just like they killed Robert," Ernie said. His voice was strained with emotion as his body shook.

Obadiah Strange looked down at Ernie, and his eyes

softened. A somber smile spread across his lips as he placed his hand on Ernie's shoulder. "There are some sacrifices worth making," he said.

"But—"

"It will work out in the end," Strange said, following his words with a wink. Then he took Ernie's chin so Ernie had to look him in the eyes. "I promise."

Ernie nodded and turned to Smoke. His eyes were filled with anger, and he spoke with determination. "No matter where you go, I'm going to hunt you down. I don't care if it takes a hundred years. You're not going to get away with this."

"I told you," Smoke said before he disappeared. He reemerged next to Strange with the Schrödinger Box tucked under his arm like a football. "Von Strife isn't the villain."

Before Ernie had a chance to respond, Smoke placed his free hand on Strange's shoulder. Then they vanished, leaving the Relic Hunters alone in the temple.

PIANO CONCERTO NO. 1

When the Relic Hunters missed their check-in, Dr. Thistlebrow, Ms. Merical, Ms. Butama, and her spriggan were sent to look for them. They found the students huddled inside the temple with a raging bonfire just outside the doorway to keep the beasts of the jungle at bay. Needless to say, the teachers were shocked by the news of their colleague's disappearance.

Word of Obadiah Strange's abduction had spread through the Templar community long before the article appeared on the front page of the *Chronicle* the next morning. The fact that Von Strife was brazen enough to take a teacher from Iron Bridge Academy was one thing, but to take one as renowned as Strange was another.

Panic spread as people wondered whom Von Strife would take next. Some went into hiding while others bought weapons. There was talk of clockwork armies marching through the streets of New Victoria under Von Strife's banner, rounding up people to place in camps until their souls could be harvested to power his strange machines.

Ernie was inconsolable in his grief. He refused to go to school, much less answer his phone. Dealing with Robert's death had been difficult, but losing Strange had put him over the edge. When Natalia rode her bike to his house, he refused to answer the door.

Like the others, Harley was upset as well. Instead of sulking, though, he went to work. It had been three days since Strange's disappearance, and Harley had spent every waking hour in Monti's lab, forsaking his classes in order to finish the portal scanner so they could find Strange, as well as Hale.

Harley threw a screwdriver across the room. It hit the wall, bounced off the floor, and ricocheted off Jasper's feet.

"May I be of assistance, sir?" Monti's service clockwork asked.

"I can't get this stupid thing to work," Harley said. "I've checked it a thousand times. The connections are solid, most of the parts are new, and I tested the old ones to make sure they aren't faulty. It should work!"

"Perhaps some tea to calm your nerves?" Jasper said.

"No, thanks," Harley said as he turned the scanner over in his hand. He made a slight adjustment before plugging it back into his test equipment. The moment he did, data started to roll on the monitor, but the results looked the same as before.

Harley's eyes grew heavy, and he yawned. It was getting close to ten thirty, and he needed to get home before his mom got back from her late-night shift at the diner. He shook his head, trying to focus, but it wasn't long before his eyes closed. After it happened a second time, Harley decided to call it a night.

"Will you require an escort to the subway depot?" Jasper asked, his eyes lit up against the dark backdrop of the workshop.

"I'm okay," Harley said as he reached over to turn off the monitor, but something caught his eye. He hit the cursor so the screen would page up, and he paused. There was some kind of anomaly in the data. What should have been static wasn't. Or at least it didn't look like static.

"What is it, sir?" Jasper asked.

"I'll tell you in a minute," Harley said. He opened a drawer and pulled out a set of headphones, sliding them over his ears and plugging them into the test equipment.

There was a tone that Harley couldn't place, but he knew it was significant. It had to be.

Harley walked over to a shelf on the wall next to his workbench. After shuffling through components and boxes of spare parts, he found what he was looking for. Harley blew a layer of dust off the recording device, and set it on the table to hook it up to the machine.

"This better work," he said.

He flipped a button, and the recording device powered up. He began recording. Once he captured a sample, Harley brought the file into a sound-editing program on his DE Tablet. He adjusted the sound waves, clearing out as much static as he could.

As he played the sound back, Harley's eyes lit up. He recognized the melody of the song, but he didn't know which song it was.

"Have you heard this before?" Harley asked as he played it a second time.

"I'm afraid not," Jasper said.

Harley played it a third time, while running a music recognition program. The results were immediate: The words TCHAIKOVSKY'S PIANO CONCERTO NO. 1 were displayed on the screen.

"I got you," Harley said. He was so focused that he didn't hear Monti walk up behind him.

"What are you still doing here?"

"I was getting ready to go, but I think I found him."

305

"Von Strife?" Monti said. "How?"

"It was a fluke," Harley said. He explained what happened with the sound anomaly. Monti asked a few questions, and by the end he was smiling.

"All we need to do is break the encryption so we can translate the song," Monti said. "Once we do that, we'll be able to pinpoint Von Strife."

Harley sighed as he pulled at his hair. "Even if we ran that song through the Difference Engine, it could take months."

"If you were Von Strife, what would you use for a password?" Monti asked.

Harley frowned. "Wait, are you serious? We'd have a better chance at getting struck by lightning."

"Maybe, but we don't have much of a choice."

"I don't know," Harley said after a sigh. "What about his daughter's name?"

"It's a bit obvious, but why not?"

Harley input Sophia's name into his DE Tablet, but it didn't work.

"Not to worry," Monti said. "I think you're on the right track. Von Strife is anything but random. He's going to use something important…something with great meaning."

Harley and Monti tried more than seventy-five combinations over the next hour. Some were complex and some simple. They exchanged numbers and symbols for letters, and they flipped some of the words around. Nothing was working.

"Von Strife is obsessed with changelings, right?" Harley asked as he paced the floor.

"That's a safe assumption," Monti said.

"What if the passkey has something to do with that?"

"Like what?"

"I don't know...maybe a changeling power, or even a type of changeling. What kind of changeling was his daughter?"

"Nobody knows," Monti said. "He kept that a secret."

"Didn't Ernie say that the two of them shared a similar strain of changeling blood?"

"Holfessen-Streigsin."

"If you tell me how to spell it, I'll plug it in," Harley said.

Monti did just that, but it didn't work.

"What about a genetic code?" Harley asked.

Monti's eyes shot wide. "Not bad. Can you do a search for any kind of a common genetic sequence shared by all changelings?"

Harley typed the words into a search feature on his DE Tablet and then entered the answer into the decoder.

"Bingo."

As soon as he hit Enter, the computer started to decrypt the song. Within the hour they knew where to find the Paragon Engine, which meant that they knew where to find Von Strife.

IN HIS DEFENSE

By the time the *Zephyr* arrived at Iron Bridge Academy the next morning, a dozen Templar military airships had assembled in the skies overhead. There were destroyers, battleships, and aircraft carriers, but instead of patrolling the high seas, they were hovering in the air as the rumble from their Merlin TECH engines made the earth tremble.

There was talk of canceling school, but Iron Bridge was the safest place in New Victoria, and probably in the world. The *Zephyr* had been crawling with Templar soldiers assigned to protect the students, and as Max stepped out of the subway depot and onto the front lawn, he saw soldiers stationed at every door.

Clusters of students stood with necks craned so they could watch the spectacle in the sky. Sprig was resting comfortably as a chinchilla in Max's jacket pocket. She stirred when he accidentally knocked into Winston Ainsworth, the boy who had asked Max for his autograph after Max had helped save the six changelings from slavers.

"Sorry," Max said.

"No problem," Winston said. His eyes were focused on the sky like everyone else's.

Max weaved through the throng, trying not to bump into anyone else. It wasn't easy. With all the fog, it was hard to see.

"Does anyone know why there are warships flying over our school?" Max heard Todd ask. He was standing in the middle of a flower garden while an angry garden gnome attempted to push Todd's boot off a patch of tulips.

"Maybe they're looking for Strange," Ross said.

"With the navy?" Todd asked.

Ross shrugged.

"Wait," Todd said as his eyes lit up. "Maybe we've been attacked by an army of clockworks. Did you bring the camera?"

"Yeah," Ross said. "Let's go."

Max shook his head as the Toad brothers ran toward the school, hoping to take snapshots of invading clockworks on the rampage when they probably should have been running for their lives.

"There you are," Harley said, sounding out of breath.

"What's wrong?" Max asked.

"Ernie's in trouble."

"He's here?"

Harley nodded. "The changelings have him cornered near the fountain by Sendak Hall."

Max didn't wait for Harley to finish. He took off, with Harley right behind him. They skirted the crowd and ran up the hill that led to the building where the changelings spent most of their time. Sprig wasn't happy about getting jostled.

"What's going on?" she asked as she poked her head out of the pocket to look around.

"It's Ernie," Max said. "We might need your help."

Sprig yawned, not bothering to cover her mouth with her tiny paw. She skittered out of the pocket and up Max's jacket to sit on his shoulder. "I can't see them, but Sprig can feel the anger," Sprig said.

Max couldn't feel the anger, but he could hear the shouting. He twisted the ring on his finger to activate his gauntlet as Sprig leaped out and turned into a white tiger in midair. Max watched her tail undulate as he followed her up the path. Then he saw them.

Twenty changelings had gathered around Ernie like a pack of wild dogs. Many of them were even snarling as they pressed in. Natalia stood protectively in front of

Ernie. Her eyes were narrowed as she exchanged verbal jabs with the changelings. She didn't have any powers, but she wasn't backing down.

Sprig roared, and the sound reverberated through Max's chest. Changelings stumbled to get out of the way as the predator cat ran toward them. Sprig threw herself in the middle of the chaos. Her ears were pinned back, and her teeth were bared as she pawed at the air in warning.

"Get back!" she warned, her voice rising above the others.

"What's going on?" Max asked as he pushed to reach Ernie. Someone shoved him in the back, and Max stumbled before he could see who it was. When he turned around, he was half expecting to see Smoke. Instead, he saw Tejan Chandra glaring at him.

Max paused. He had always gotten along with Tejan, but something had turned the changelings into an angry mob, and it looked like Ernie was the first target on their list.

"He's a traitor!" someone shouted.

"Yeah, he's just like Smoke!" another voice called out.

There was so much commotion that Max couldn't tell who was talking, not that it mattered. It was clear that the changelings were of one voice. Yi was there, and so was Denton. Then Max saw Nadya and Geppetto. The only changeling Max didn't see was Raven.

"Are you okay?" Max asked.

Ernie nodded, but he didn't say anything.

Someone shoved Max into Natalia as Harley pushed through the crowd. Harley slipped past Max and grabbed Yi by his jacket collar. "What's your problem?"

"You!" Yi said as his eyes sparked with flames.

Sprig roared as Nadya closed in.

"This is crazy," Max said.

"I'm sorry," Ernie said. "I didn't mean to get you guys involved."

"You didn't do anything," Natalia said. Her eyes were frantic, but she was standing her ground.

"Yeah, right," Yi said. "He's working with Von Strife, just like Smoke was."

"Have you lost your mind?" Natalia asked.

"Then how do you explain what happened in Bludgeon Town? He led us into a trap."

"Ross and Todd found those slavers, not Ernie," Natalia said. "So are they working for Von Strife, too?"

"Probably."

"I think you've fried your brain," Natalia said.

Fire ignited in Yi's hands.

"Knock it off, both of you!" Max said.

"Tell us where they are," Tejan said through clenched jaws.

"Yeah, where're Hale and Strange?" Laini, a changeling with bright pink hair and what looked like butterfly wings, cried out.

"We have to do something before this gets out of hand," Max said.

"I think it's too late for that," Harley said.

Sprig threw her head back and roared.

"It's going to take more than a tiger to beat us," Yi said as he stood in the morning haze like a human torch.

"We don't want to fight you," Max said, "but we're not going to let you hurt Ernie. Besides, why would we help Von Strife? Ernie's a changeling, and he's our friend. I'd like to think that we're your friends, too."

"How am I your friend?" Yi asked.

Max rubbed his forehead. "You've never given us a chance."

"That's because we don't trust you," Yi said. "You're not one of us."

"Ernie is, and he's our friend," Max said. "And you didn't second-guess him when he helped you capture the other slavers, so why are you doing it now?"

"We didn't know he was working for Von Strife," Yi said. The comment was met with a murmur of agreement from the other changelings.

"Do you have any proof?"

Yi glared at Max, but he didn't say anything. Max looked at the other changelings, waiting for them to give an account, but no one could.

"This is just what Von Strife would want us to do," Max said. "We're not going to bring him down if we're fighting one another."

313

"You don't know what we've been through," Nadya said. "I can't go anywhere without wondering if someone is going to try to kidnap me.... None of us can. And how do the Templar decide to protect us? With these," she said, pulling her hair back to show Max the inhibitor just above her ear. "They try to snuff out our powers so we can't even protect ourselves."

"That's not Ernie's fault," Max said. "Neither are the kidnappings."

"He's right," Raven said as she walked down the front steps of Sendak Hall to stand next to Max.

"What, you're on their side?" Yi asked as the flames grew in his hands.

"Don't be such a hothead," Raven said, earning a smattering of laughter from the changelings.

"Is that supposed to be funny?" Yi asked.

"You're doing a good enough job making a fool of yourself without me," Raven said.

There was more laughter.

"Standing around here and arguing isn't going to get Hale or Strange back," Max said.

"He's right," Denton said, earning a reluctant murmur of agreement from a few of the others.

"Then if it wasn't Ernie, who set us up?" Yi asked. He had supporters as well.

"We're not sure, but we know where Von Strife is," Harley said. "That's why the ships are here. We're going to war."

314

Yi looked up to the sky. "Then they're not here for us?"

"What? For the changelings?" Max asked.

"Yeah," Yi said.

Max put one arm around Ernie's shoulder and stroked Sprig's neck. "They'd have to go through us first."

EAVESDROPPING

"I don't get it," Ernie said as he walked with the other Grey Griffins to their homeroom. "Why did you do that for me?"

"What do you mean?" Max asked.

"It's just that I've been kind of a jerk lately, but...I don't know. You stood up for me anyway."

"Why wouldn't we?" Max asked as Sprig padded behind them as a white tiger. "Isn't that what Grey Griffins are supposed to do?"

Ernie smiled, though not for long. "So does that mean we're friends again?"

"We never stopped being your friend," Natalia said

as she linked arms with Ernie. "We still love you, even when you act like a jerk."

"Thanks," Ernie said. "For everything."

The second bell had already rung. Dr. Thistlebrow and a few other teachers were on the front lawn wrangling curious students who couldn't stop watching the airships hovering in the sky.

"Hey, is that Logan?" Harley asked, pointing to a man in a black duster jacket.

"I can't tell," Max said.

"It is," Ernie said, confirming Harley's suspicion.

"What's he doing here?" Harley asked.

Max shrugged. "Beats me," he said, "but I bet it has something to do with those warships."

"Let's go find out," Harley said. He headed toward the door Logan disappeared through.

"What about class?" Natalia asked.

"It's just homeroom," Harley said. "All we do is sit there and listen to announcements."

"I don't know."

"You can do what you want, but I'm going," Harley said.

"Me too," Ernie said.

"Sorry," Max said, before following the other two.

"Fine," Natalia said. "Wait for me."

They followed Logan into the building until they came to a set of double doors that led to an off-limits area controlled by the Sciences Council. Even though most of it was still under construction, some of the teachers had offices there. It was also home to a research facility, a small publishing house for academic books, and, from what Max had heard, a library that rivaled the Templar Library off the coast of Iceland.

"They're not going to let us in there," Max said when he saw armed guards stationed at the doors.

"Can't you call Logan?" Harley asked.

"If he wanted us in there, he would have told us about it."

"I might be able to help," Ernie said. He reached into his pocket to pull out a small brass mechanism with dials and a lever.

"What is it?" Harley asked.

"It's called an Interdimensional Phase Adjuster," Ernie said.

"Wait, that's an IPA?" Harley said, a smile creeping across his face. "How did you get one?"

"Are you two going to let us in on your little secret, or are we just going to stand here?" Natalia asked.

"Those things make you invisible," Harley said.

"Actually," Ernie said, "it vibrates your molecules so you can be in two dimensions at the same time. It's kind of like being invisible, but you can walk through walls and stuff like that. You can even scream and nobody will hear you."

"That's what you did to escape the slavers' net, isn't it?" Harley asked.

"Yep."

"Why didn't you tell us about it before?" Natalia said.

"I couldn't," Ernie said.

"Where'd you get it?" Max asked.

Ernie hesitated. His eyes went from Max to the floor, but eventually they landed back on Max. "Look, I shouldn't say anything, but... well, Obadiah gave it to me."

"He just gave it to you?"

"I guess," Ernie said. "He told me it was a late Christmas present."

"That's some present," Harley said. "I'm pretty sure they don't sell them to civilians."

"Anyway," Ernie said as he fumbled with the IPA in his hands, "I was thinking that we could use it to sneak in there and find Logan."

Max smiled. "Will it work on four people?"

"As long as we stay close," Ernie said.

"Is it safe?" Natalia asked.

"I guess," Ernie said. "I mean, it feels kind of weird at first, but you get used to it."

"What do you think?" Max asked, looking at Harley.

"I'm in."

"Me too," Ernie said.

"We all go or none of us do," Max said, turning to Natalia.

"No pressure or anything," she said.

Max smiled.

"Fine."

Ernie twisted a few of the dials before pulling the lever. The scene around them dissolved until the Grey Griffins were all that remained in focus. Everything around them went pale. It looked like an X-ray—once-solid objects were now vague outlines.

"This is awesome," Harley said.

"We can actually walk through walls?" Natalia asked as she studied her translucent hand.

Ernie nodded.

Max walked over to the doors, but he stopped short, waiting for the guards to spot him. When they didn't move, he turned back to the other Griffins. "Here goes nothing," he said. There was a slight tug on his skin as he put his foot through the door, but he still passed right through. A moment later the Griffins were standing together in an unfamiliar hallway.

"Which way did he go?" Harley asked.

"I can hear them," Ernie said, using his advanced changeling senses.

They followed Ernie into a room where at least twenty irate Templar officers in full uniform were sitting around an oval table arguing.

"You're sure they can't see us?" Max asked when he spotted Logan, who sat back in his chair with his arms crossed. He was the only person who wasn't shouting.

"Watch," Ernie said. He hopped up on the table, and

then he started to dance. Max held his breath as he watched Ernie bend down to wave at an officer with a pointy beard and a shiny bald head.

"See what I mean?" Ernie said. "We're perfectly safe."

"At least as long as that thing doesn't short out," Harley said.

Ernie shrugged. "It hasn't yet."

Natalia walked over to pick up a pen, but her hand passed right through it.

"It takes some practice, but you can do it," Ernie said.

She tried a few more times but gave up as a short man with a waxed mustache stood at the head of the table, attempting to talk over the other officers as they shouted. He finally gave up. "This is Colonel Hazard," he said after a sigh. His face was red as he raised his voice. "She's the chief strategist for this joint operation, so perhaps you'll show her some courtesy."

One of video screens on the wall flashed to show a map of Switzerland as Hazard walked to the head of the room. She was tall and slender, with hair like corn silk that was pulled back into a bun.

Instead of trying to talk over them, the colonel simply stood there waiting for everyone to stop talking. When the room was finally silent, she spoke. "Thank you, General Upton," the colonel said with a nod. "And good afternoon, gentlemen. The Paragon Engine is located here, near the borders of France and Italy."

The map tightened to reveal a large complex of buildings nestled in the green countryside.

"It used to be a government research facility, but according to our records it was acquired by someone representing Von Strife nearly twenty years ago," she continued. "His fusion generator produces enough power to run the Paragon Engine as well as an energy shield that could repel our entire fleet."

"What's left of it," a heavyset admiral said as the map rotated and zoomed in. He had been the most boisterous of the crowd when General Upton held the floor.

Hazard ignored the comment. "This joint operation will consist of two stages," she said. "The first will be an effort to deactivate the shield. Once that has been completed, our fleet will move into a position where we'll bombard the facility."

"What if we fail?" the admiral asked. His comment was met with general agreement from the others assembled at the table.

"We can't afford to fail, Admiral Lennox. If Von Strife opens a gateway to the Shadowlands, there is no limit to the number of monsters and other dark creatures that will pour into our world. At worst, we calculate that within forty-eight hours, more than half of the human population would be destroyed. Within the week, our species will be wiped from history."

"You're telling us there's nothing that can be done?" Admiral Lennox said.

Colonel Hazard's face was grave. "We have an evacuation plan for major population centers, but that will only put off the inevitable."

"Evacuate? We have nowhere to go!"

Colonel Hazard stood with her hands behind her back as she waited for the outbursts to subside. "I have every confidence that we'll succeed despite the odds," Hazard said once the quarreling stopped. "In fact, we've just learned that Von Strife is at the facility as we speak. Once he's been neutralized, the clockworks will fall."

There was a rush of angry whispers.

"Are you speaking about an assassination?" Admiral Lennox asked. "Certainly we are better than that!"

"Perhaps," Hazard said, "but we're in desperate times."

"This is outrageous!" Lennox said.

"I'm sorry, Admiral, but I've been given command of this engagement, and my decision is final," Hazard said. She turned to Logan. "Brief your men. We're about to go on full alert. You're scheduled to make the jump in ten minutes."

"Wait, what's she talking about?" Max whispered.

"It sounds like they're sending a team of THOR agents to assassinate Von Strife," Harley said.

"You heard what she said about that place," Max said. "It's a suicide mission."

Natalia put her hand on Max's shoulder. "He'll be fine."

"I've got to talk to him before he goes," Max said.

"What are you going to say?" Harley asked.

"I don't know, but I'll think of it when I get there."

LOST

Logan was already at the jump station by the time the Grey Griffins arrived. He was talking to Colonel Hazard as the other THOR agents stepped onto the circular platform.

"If the Paragon Engine is unattainable, you'll still need to hit your other objectives," Hazard said.

"Understood," Logan said. "We plan on being here for Stage Two, right on schedule."

"I have every confidence that you will," Hazard said. "And Commander—"

"Sir?"

"I'll see personally to the children's safety. That goes for the baron's daughter as well."

"Thank you, sir," Logan said. "That means a great deal."

"Godspeed, Commander."

"Wait, how do you turn that thing off?" Max asked as he reached for the IPA.

"Max, don't!" Harley said, grabbing Max's arm before he could reach the device. "We have to stay hidden. If they see us, they're going to lock us up somewhere."

"But—"

"There's nothing you can do," Harley said. "Besides, Natalia's right. He'll be fine."

Max watched Logan salute before he gave the order to activate the jump platform. Soon the sound of gears and hydraulics echoed in the chamber. A switch was thrown, sending purple plasma arcing across the Tesla coils. There was a flash, and then the THOR agents were gone.

Instead of going back to class, the Griffins went to the one-room schoolhouse where they used to meet for their Relic Hunting class. Max figured nobody would look for them there, but he hadn't expected the wave of emotion that hit when he smelled Strange's pipe tobacco.

"We can go somewhere else," Max said as he looked at Ernie, whose face was stuck in a blank stare.

"That's okay," Ernie said.

"Remember, they can't kill him," Harley said.

"I know," Ernie said. He walked over to sit at Strange's desk.

"We're going to find him, Ernie," Max said. "That goes for Hale, too. I don't care what it takes, but we're going to bring them home."

Ernie looked up and smiled, but he still seemed sad.

"I'm serious," Max said.

"Thanks."

Max looked at the clock. "Logan's been gone almost three hours. Don't you think he should be back by now?"

"It's hard to say," Harley said.

Max jumped in his chair when the first siren sounded.

"What's going on?" Ernie asked.

Max was the first one at the window. Students, faculty, and even service clockworks were evacuating the buildings as Templar soldiers were herding them into the subway depot.

"They failed," Max said. His expression was blank, his voice even. It was a statement of indisputable fact. This was, after all, the evacuation plan that Colonel Hazard had spoken about. There was no other explanation.

"You don't know that," Harley said.

"Yes, we do," Max said.

"Then Logan is..." Natalia's voice faltered.

Max closed his eyes as he pictured Logan, the man who had kept him from harm from the moment that Max drew his first breath. A world without Logan didn't seem possible. Max was numb. There were no tears, no sorrow. Emptiness. That was all that remained.

"Should we go with them?" Ernie asked as he watched the Toad brothers disappear into the shadows of the subway depot.

"I can't leave him down there," Max said.

"What are you talking about?" Natalia asked.

Max turned to Ernie. "I need you to give me the IPA."

"Why?"

"What if he's still alive?" Max asked. "What if they abandoned him?"

"Max..." Natalia said, but when she saw his eyes, she stopped.

"Can I borrow it?"

"No," Ernie said, "because I'm going with you."

Max shook his head. "Look, it's too dangerous."

"I don't care," Ernie said. "You're not going alone."

"You can't make it without the jump station," Harley said. "I saw how they work it, so either I go with you or nobody's going."

"Well, you're not going without me," Natalia said.

"Then it's settled," Harley said.

"Look, you guys," Max said, but Ernie cut him off.

"The Grey Griffins stick together, no matter what," he said.

Ernie activated the IPA, which allowed them to reach the jump station without being stopped. Thanks to the evacuation order, it was deserted.

"What if you mess up, and we end up at the bottom of the ocean or something?" Ernie said, turning off the IPA.

"I guess we'll find out in a minute," Harley said as he walked over to the control panel. He quickly verified the coordinates for where Logan and his THOR agents had jumped to.

"Wait," Natalia said. "We need Raven."

"Why?" Harley asked.

"Because we don't know where we're going," Natalia said. "She'll be able to talk to the walls, and they'll tell her where to go."

"I don't want to risk any more lives," Max said.

"You don't have much of a choice," Natalia said.

"We don't even know if she'll go," Max said.

"She will."

"How are we supposed to find her?"

"Leave that to us," Natalia said, putting her hand on Ernie's shoulder. "If we're not back in ten minutes, go without us."

By the time Natalia and Ernie returned with Raven, there were three minutes to spare. But there was a problem — they'd brought someone else, too.

"What's she doing here?" Max asked when he saw Brooke.

"It's nice to see you, too," Brooke said.

"That's not what I meant. It's just that —"

"Look," Natalia said. "There's a good chance that Logan is injured, and Brooke may be the only person who can help."

"So now she wants to help?" Max said, letting his temper get the best of him.

"What's that supposed to mean?" Brooke said.

"You're the one who's been ignoring me, not the other way around."

Brooke's face flushed.

"Why are you being a jerk?" Natalia asked.

"Me?"

"Do you even know why Brooke was avoiding you?" Max was glowering.

"Because she was embarrassed, that's why."

"That doesn't make any sense," Max said, turning to look at Brooke.

"She's right," Brooke said. "After everything that happened with the Reaper, I don't know...I thought that you'd look down on me or something."

"Why?"

"Because I couldn't handle myself."

"You shouldn't have to," Max said. "It took an entire team of THOR agents to capture that thing. It almost killed me, too."

"I hate to interrupt whatever this is, but I hear footsteps," Harley said. "Everybody on the platform."

There was a bang at the door.

"Let's go," Max said.

"Just about there," Harley said as he fired the last switch to activate the jump station.

The door opened as Max jumped onto the platform, Harley right behind. Colonel Hazard burst through the door with a dozen soldiers behind her, but they were too late.

The Grey Griffins were gone.

HOPELESS

The jump station delivered them beneath the shadows of a massive building surrounded by a thick wall of trees. The air was crisp, and the stars were already shining overhead.

"Why do I feel like I was jammed through a strainer and then put back together?" Ernie said.

"I don't know, but you need to get that IPA working before someone sees us," Harley said, spotting a camera overhead. "I'd feel a lot better if we were ghosts."

Ernie fumbled with the controls of the IPA as a large truck rumbled down the drive toward where they were hiding.

"Let's go," Harley said through gritted teeth.

"I'm trying," Ernie said as the IPA slipped from his hand. Somehow he managed to catch it before it hit the ground. He looked up to see the truck's lights were shining on him. Ernie entered his code, and there was a strange humming sound. A moment later, they disappeared as the truck rolled by.

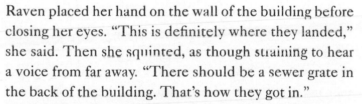

Raven placed her hand on the wall of the building before closing her eyes. "This is definitely where they landed," she said. Then she squinted, as though straining to hear a voice from far away. "There should be a sewer grate in the back of the building. That's how they got in."

Max had Raven lead the way. Despite the IPA, they kept to the shadows as best they could, dodging behind bushes and running when there was no cover. It wasn't long before they found the grate.

"It doesn't smell like a sewer," Harley said.

"Let's hope that's a good sign," Max said, grabbing hold of the iron bars to remove the grate. He lowered himself into the darkness, and the others followed.

The chute dropped them into a narrow passage that was, fortunately, not a sewer. They made good time as they passed into an elevated corridor that led them down another hatch. Clockwork drones were everywhere, scanning the passageways as they looked for intruders.

"I know those things can't see us, but they still freak me out," Ernie said.

"Me too," Max said, patting him on the back. "Let's hurry up and get this over with."

They climbed down a ladder, passed through a maintenance corridor, and entered a hangar filled with helicopters, winged clockworks, and mobile artillery.

Men in grey uniforms inspected the vehicles while Assembler clockworks welded, torched, and upgraded what looked like Dreadnaughts. Covered in thick armor, the massive clockwork war machines were nearly twenty feet tall, with wide chests and small heads. Some had rocket launchers attached to their arms, while others were equipped with Gatling guns fixed to their shoulders. They all looked deadly.

"What if Hale is stuffed inside one of those?" Ernie asked.

"We need to find Logan first," Max said.

"He's right," Natalia said. "But if we can, we'll come back and check, right, Max?"

Max nodded as Raven knelt to place her hand on the ground. "The THOR agents passed through here, and they hadn't been spotted yet," she said.

They pressed on, passing through another hatchway and then around a corner before they entered the heart of the facility. It was nearly as wide as a football field, with intersecting bridges crossing a chasm so deep they couldn't see the bottom. The room hummed with the roar of invisible steam engines and titanic gears as clockwork soldiers patrolled the bridges in squads of ten.

"We need to go that way," Raven said, pointing to a door on the far side of the chamber. It was several flights down, and the stairs didn't have rails.

"Let's move," Max said.

They kept to the center of the bridge as best they could. More than once they had to phase through squads of marching clockworks. Everyone managed to make it down all three flights of stairs without spilling over the edge, but as they crossed the last bridge, they heard what sounded like angry bees following them.

"What are those?" Natalia asked.

Five iron spheres with mechanical arms and lighted eyes had risen from the depths below the bridges. Streams of blue swept across the ground as they closed in.

"They look like my probes on steroids," Harley said, "and they're probably looking for us."

"It doesn't matter, right?" Ernie said. "We're ghosts."

"What do you think?" Harley asked, turning to Max.

"Let's not push it."

"Agreed."

They raced for the hatchway as the probes closed in. The door was shut, but with their IPA, it didn't matter.

Max leaped as the first drone was about to overtake them. He phased through the hatch and into the darkness, hoping the others would follow.

Once his eyes adjusted, Max could see that he was in a narrow passage that looked like it had been bombed, bulldozed, and then bombed again.

The others spilled in, and if it hadn't been for the IPA, they wouldn't have been able to make it through the thicket of smoldering pipe works or the snapping plasma conduits.

"They were overwhelmed," Raven said after taking her hand from the wall.

"What about Logan?" Max asked. Through the darkness, he could see the fallen forms of THOR agents amid the rubble.

"He made it out, but he was one of the few."

"We better keep moving." Max was relieved that Logan was still alive, but he had to push thoughts of the fallen THOR agents out of his mind. It was overwhelming, but they had to keep moving.

Raven led them to an abyss that was impossible to cross. "It's an elevator shaft," she explained. "The clockworks blew it up."

"The THOR agents were trapped," Max said.

Raven nodded.

"Look at this," Harley said. He was kneeling beside the remains of a clockwork with rocket launchers on its shoulders. It had a hole punched through its chest, and its innards had melted into slag. Behind the machine was a hidden air shaft.

"Two men went through here," Raven said. She looked at Max. "Are you sure you want to do this?"

"Why?"

"It's just that..." Raven's voice faltered. "I have a bad feeling, that's all."

"Is there something you're not telling us?"

"No."

"Then let's go." Max was the first to disappear into the small passage. The air shaft twisted like a roller coaster at an amusement park. He held his arms against his sides and pointed his feet forward. At one point, Max was going so fast around a turn that he ended up riding along the top of the tubing.

He could hear the others screaming behind him. Then, just when Max wondered if the ride was going to end, his feet pounded against a grate that shot through the air, ricocheting off the wall and then hitting the floor.

"Whoa!" Max shouted as he hurtled through the air. He braced for impact against the wall, but his shoulder phased right through. Max ended up in some kind of storage facility with metal shelves filled with neatly stacked bins.

Moments later Harley landed on top of him, and the others weren't far behind.

"Where are we?" Natalia asked.

"In the wrong place," Max said before walking back through the wall and into the hallway, where he saw the sunglasses lying on the floor.

"Are those Logan's?" Harley asked.

Max walked over to pick them up. The lenses were shattered and the frame bent. Max stopped breathing.

"Nice of you to drop in."

A ONE-WAY TICKET

Startled by the familiar voice, Max whipped around. In the dim light, he spotted Logan tucked behind an engine of some sort. He was sitting against a pipe that was emitting a thick cloud of steam.

"Whoever you are, I know you're there," Logan said.

"Ernie, turn it off," Max said.

Ernie shut down the IPA, and the world became solid once again.

Max rushed to Logan, whose side was bleeding. He forced a smile, then winced. "Now how did I know that was going to be you?"

"What happened?" Max asked.

Logan snorted and then coughed. "Clocks."

Max looked at the wound in Logan's side. His jacket was drenched with blood, and his skin was pale. "We have to get you out of here."

"I don't think that's going to happen," Logan said.

"Don't say that."

Logan smiled as he reached up to pat Max on the cheek. "We're all going to meet our maker one day," he said, coughing again. "How did you miscreants get your hands on an IPA, anyway?"

Max looked back at Ernie. "Strange gave it to him."

"Strange?" Logan asked, frowning.

"Yeah, he said it was a Christmas present," Ernie said.

"That's some—" Logan coughed. "That's quite a gift."

"He said it wasn't illegal."

Logan smiled, but it faded too quickly. He closed his eyes.

"Come on," Max said to the others. "Help me get him up."

"Don't worry about me," Logan said.

"If we were using an IPA, how did you know we were here?" Natalia asked.

"I have a handy little device that can see through them," Logan said. "Apparently Von Strife does, too. That's the only way his machines could have spotted us."

"Wait," Max said. "If he can see through the IPA, then why didn't he stop us?"

Logan sighed before resting his head against the wall. "There's the million-dollar question."

"Maybe he didn't think we were a threat," Natalia said.

"I don't think that's the case," Logan said. He licked his dry lips.

"Does anyone have water?" Max asked.

Ernie uncapped his water bottle and handed it to Max, who helped Logan take a sip.

"I can help him," Brooke said.

"Maybe not," Logan said with a grimace. "They got me good."

"You have to let her try."

Logan struggled to push his rucksack toward Max.

"What's that?" Max asked.

"The explosives."

"And you want us to set them?"

"I don't think we have much of a choice."

"What about Von Strife?" Natalia asked.

"I haven't seen him." Logan turned to Ernie. "We didn't see Hale or Strange, either, but that doesn't mean they aren't here."

Ernie nodded.

"Are you going to let Brooke take a look at that?" Max said.

Logan sighed. "I'll make you a deal."

"It depends."

"If you follow my orders without question, I'll let her give it a go."

Max hesitated, his eyes narrowed. "No tricks."

"Fine."

Max extended his hand.

Logan took Max's hand to accept the deal. Logan instructed Max and Harley on how to set the bombs that would blow up the Paragon Engine. When he was convinced they could do it without blowing themselves up instead, he sent them off and asked Natalia and Ernie to go stand watch. Raven hung back with Brooke as she tried to heal Logan.

"That's amazing," Natalia said. She was standing with Max, Harley, and Ernie on a causeway that overlooked the Paragon Engine. The machine's core shimmered with waves of energy as scientists and clockworks scuttled about like ants at a picnic.

"I'm going down," Max said, backing onto the ladder that led to the floor below.

Harley was next, then Natalia, with Ernie taking up the rear. Once they were all on the ground, the Griffins made their way through the network of activity until they came to the base of the Paragon Engine.

"Is that the Brimstone Key?" Natalia asked, pointing to a large cylinder made of meteoric iron. It acted as the bridge between the engine and the main power conduit from the fusion generator.

"I think so," Harley said after a brief glance. He set his pack down and went to work, pulling out the adhesive putty before setting three bombs on the ground.

"What about Von Strife?" Ernie asked.

"I haven't seen him," Max said as Harley handed him a bomb.

"Maybe he went through already."

"If he did, he kind of forgot his army," Harley said before standing up with a bomb in his hand.

"Either that or Natalia was right," Max said. "Maybe he's just looking for his daughter."

Harley stuck the bomb onto the Paragon Engine. Then he punched a code before turning the dial, while Max did the same with his bomb.

"What if he took Hale and Strange with him?" Ernie asked. "If we destroy the Paragon Engine, we'll never see them again."

"We don't even know if he's gone through," Harley said as he prepared the last bomb. "Besides, this way Von Strife won't be able to send any more changelings away."

Ernie grabbed Harley's wrist. Harley tried to pull away, but he couldn't. "I'm not going to let you kill them," Ernie said. "Not this time."

"Listen to me," Max said. "You're not the only one who cares about them. We all do, but if we don't shut it down now, Von Strife will never stop."

"I'll stop him," Ernie said.

"How?"

"I don't know, I just will."

Max placed his hand on Ernie's shoulder. "It may not seem like it, but saying good-bye to Robert was hard on all of us," Max said. "I have nightmares about what happened, but we did the right thing....And we're doing the right thing now."

"What about Hale?" Ernie asked, looking defeated.

"Let's hope Von Strife is the only one who went through," Max said. "Either way, we're going to save a lot of lives."

Ernie shut his eyes, lowering his head as he let go of Harley's wrist. Then the IPA flashed, and the phase-adjusted world faded away. They were now visible to all the clockwork soldiers around them.

"What's going on?" Ernie asked. He was shaking the IPA as though that would make it work again.

It didn't.

Max activated the gauntlet, unleashing a stream of energy at the nearest clockwork, scorching its iron hide. The mechanical soldier fell back, but another took its place. A clockwork with four arms ran at Harley, who managed to duck out of the way, but the machine turned around to take another swipe.

It closed in on Harley, and Max leaped. He caught the clockwork in the chest with his gauntlet, and a blue light erupted as the clock's protective casing crumbled. It staggered and fell to the floor. Then its eyes faded.

The sound of gears turning echoed throughout the

344

chamber. The surface of the Paragon Engine shimmered before revealing a field of stars that shined brightly in the night sky. Max could feel the hair on his head and arms rise as he watched Ernie unhinge one of the clockwork's arms with a screwdriver he had found.

Ernie was a blur of motion. The clockwork had no idea what was happening until it was too late. It lost one arm and then the next. Ernie dismantled one of its knee joints, sending the clockwork tumbling to the ground.

Natalia screamed as one of the clockworks closed in on her. Max tried to help, but he felt something tug at him. He looked up at the Paragon Engine to see a strong wind rip Ernie's helmet from his head. It tumbled through the portal and disappeared with a flash. One of the clockworks was sucked through, a moment later, Ernie followed.

"No!" Max fought against the pull of the Paragon Engine, but he was losing ground. Natalia cried out before she was sucked in. Harley reached out to grab her ankle, but in the process he lost his grip.

When Harley disappeared, Max lost his will to fight. He closed his eyes, and then he was gone.

THROUGH THE
LOOKING GLASS

The only survivors were Logan, Brooke, and Raven. The
other THOR agents had fallen in combat, but when the
rescue team found them, Brooke didn't want to leave —
not until someone went through the portal to retrieve her
friends. She sobbed as she tried to break free from the
THOR agent who led her away, even though she knew
there was nothing they could do.

Brooke had overheard that most of Von Strife's
employees had fled the facility. Those who hadn't were
arrested, but none could so much as remember his or
her name. It was as though their memories had been
erased.

Most of the clockworks, including the machines that had attacked the Griffins, had been shut down by the time the rescue team arrived. The few that still worked were service models that performed mundane tasks like emptying trash cans and sweeping floors. The only explanation Brooke could think of was that Von Strife accomplished his objective.

The problem was that nobody knew what that objective was, including Raven. She had attempted to get the walls, machines, and every inanimate object she could find to tell her, but they were silent. Either they didn't know, or like the employees, their memories had been wiped clean.

At least no monsters or dark faeries had poured through the Paragon Engine, which meant that a gateway to the Shadowlands hadn't been opened. Still, Brooke had seen video footage taken from the facility showing the Grey Griffins—her friends—being pulled through the Paragon Engine before it was shut down.

It was over a week later, and she was still having trouble sleeping. Every night, she lay in bed looking at the ceiling as the realization that her friends were lost forever burned in her mind. Then late one night a light caught her eye. It had come from the lamp on her writing desk. The lamp flickered like the erratic beats of a moth's wings. Figuring it was just a short in the cord, she pulled her blankets off and walked over to unplug the lamp from the wall.

She bent down to unplug it, but then her jaw dropped. "That's funny," she said. The lamp hadn't been plugged in.

As Brooke stood up, all the lights in her room started to flicker. Brooke moved to the mirror, where she could see the hair on her head standing on end. It was as if her whole room was charged with electricity.

Then she noticed frost creeping across the edges of the mirror as the surface turned ghostly blue. Brooke gasped when her reflection faded and was replaced by an image of Max, with the other Grey Griffins standing behind him.

"Brooke, is that you?"

"Yes," she said. "Where are you?"

"How long have we been gone?"

"A week."

"That's impossible."

"What do you mean?"

"I'll have to explain later," Max said. "Look, I think we found a way back, but we need help."

"Anything."

"Tell your dad to initiate the Omega Option. He'll know what that means."

She nodded.

"You have to hurry. When Strange finds out we've escaped, we won't have much time."

"Wait, did you mean to say Von Strife?"

"It's the same person."

"What?" Brooke said. She shook her head as her mind raced, trying to grasp what Max had said. Had he just told her that Obadiah Strange, one of the teachers at Iron Bridge Academy, was actually Otto Von Strife in disguise? It was impossible.

She frowned and then tilted her head. She had so many questions that she didn't know where to begin. Unfortunately, she didn't have a chance to ask any of them.

"We have to go now," Max said. "Send word to our families. We're coming home."

"Max, wait!" Brooke said, desperate to hold on to the image. She needed to know that it was real, that she wasn't dreaming, but Max was gone.

WILL THE
GREY GRIFFINS
MAKE IT BACK HOME?

CAN THEY FINALLY
DEFEAT THE
CLOCKWORK KING?

THE EXCITING ADVENTURES
CONTINUE IN BOOK 3 OF

The Paragon Prison

AVAILABLE MAY 2012!

TURN THE PAGE FOR A SNEAK PEEK.

Born Again

Max Sumner awoke to a blaze of swirling light. Everything around him spun like the inside of a fiery cosmic drain. He tried to get his bearings, wondering if this was only another dream or if this was real. All he knew was that moments before, Max and the Grey Griffins had been staring at the Paragon Engine, wondering how to blow up the interdimensional gateway, before Otto Von Strife's clockworks stopped them. It hadn't worked out as planned. Now they were seemingly tumbling across a kaleidoscope of dimensions. Lights flashed. Worlds swept by. And always the humming of the wormhole that funneled them to some unknown destination. It smelled of bleach.

Then the walls of the wormhole collapsed. Max saw—or thought he saw—a massive ringlike structure ahead. Another Paragon Engine? But as it neared, something else seemed to catch hold of him and pull him away. The lights blurred as he moved sideways through several doors of light.

With a flash, he was tossed out of the wormhole and onto wet grass. He heard shouting, and before he could roll out of the way, the other three Griffins tumbled on top of him. There was another flash, and the wormhole disappeared.

They were in a midnight forest so suffocated with shadows that the only sounds they could hear, besides their own breathing, was the soft patter of rain overhead.

"Did we screw that up or what?" Harley Eisenstein groaned. "One second, we're about to blow up the Paragon Engine, and the next, someone throws a switch and we're sucked into the very machine we were supposed to destroy. I bet Von Strife planned it all along."

"I don't care what he planned," said Max anxiously. "We left Logan back there, with Brooke and Raven. If we don't get back fast, the clockworks will finish them off."

"Well, at least we're alive. I don't suppose anyone thought to be thankful for that," Natalia Romanov said, fixing her braids and cleaning her sweater of leaves. Her summer glow had long since faded, along with her freckles, thanks to a cold winter fighting monsters. She looked through the lens of her Phantasmoscope, an ornate cousin of the magnifying glass, but instead of magnifying words, it made the invisible world visible. Not even the fingerprint of a pixie could escape her notice. "Wherever here is. Say, this place looks awfully familiar."

Ernie—the half faerie, teen super speedster known as Agent Thunderbolt—took off his helmet, slid his goggles up on his forehead, and scanned the dense woods. "You're right. It's like we're back in Avalon. These are the Old Woods. But why would the Paragon Engine send us back home? I thought we were going to another world."

"The trees are taller here," said Max, squinting up in the darkness. "Anyway, wasn't Von Strife going to use the Paragon Engine to invade the Shadowlands? Maybe that's where we ended up." Max hoped he was wrong. The Shadowlands was a wild, magical world controlled by the dark king Oberon, who had an unfortunate and ugly grudge against Max. Meeting him this way, in his own world and on his own terms, would probably result in the Griffins' being hand-fed to a nest of dragons.

Harley's pocket flashed twice. He pulled out his communicator. "Wherever we are, they've got phone service. Full bars!" The Griffins sighed in relief.

Natalia took the phone from Harley and flipped through the screens as he protested. "If you have reception, that means you have GPS. Let's figure out where we are!" The Griffins gathered around the communicator and watched it zoom in on a familiar map. A moment later, Max backed away.

"If this is correct," Max said, "my grandma's house is right over there." He pointed through the trees. "What I don't get is, what happened to all the snow? Look at the trees. Some of them have leaves already. What's going on?"

Natalia looked at the phone again. "Midnight of March twenty-first."

"We were stuck in the Paragon Engine for a month?" asked Ernie, turning pale. His thoughts returned to Raven, the changeling girl who he'd come to think was the prettiest and scariest girl in the world. "What if Raven's dead? Do you think...? Oh, no. And she was just starting to like me."

"She's a tough girl," said Harley, patting his skinny friend on the back. "I'm sure she's fine. And when we see her again, you can tell her what it was like to go through a Paragon Engine." Ernie brightened at the thought. It would certainly be nice to have something to brag about.

"We need to take a look around," Max said, who wasn't as optimistic as Harley on the topic of their friends' survival. For now, he had to focus. He turned to Ernie. "How's your super speed, Agent Thunderbolt? Working?"

Ernie replaced his goggles and helmet, then zipped across the forest floor in a blur. He went faster and faster until, with a flash, he disappeared completely. A moment later, he was back with a bug-smeared grin. "Holycowthisissoawesomelyawesome. NotonlyamIworking, butI'm-fasterthanever!"

"How fast?" asked Natalia. "And try to slow down, okay?"

Ernie took a breath and began again. "The whole world freezes. It's sick fast." Ernie wiped away the bugs from his goggles and grinned. His teeth were a traffic pileup of insect fatalities. "I think I need a windshield."

Natalia blanched at the sight. "Or a mouth guard."

"So what did you see?" asked Max.

"Let's just say that your grandma's house is there, all right. So is Avalon. Although it looks kind of weird. But it's night, so who knows?"

Max grabbed his backpack.

"Where do you think you are going, Grayson Maximillian Sumner?" Natalia exclaimed. "We need to be careful. Ernie's super speed may not be the only changes around here."

"Well, we're not sleeping out here," said Max, wiping a slick of mud from his knees. "Let's head to the red barn. At least it will be dry."

The others agreed, and they quickly slipped out of the woods, trudged along the cold and barren rows of corn in the neighbor's field, and rounded the murky old pond. They soon opened the barn's back door and stepped into the darkness. Harley switched on his flashlight.

"Sure looks the same," he whispered.

"Smells the same, too," complained Ernie. He covered his nose as he stepped over a pile of fresh horse manure.

They were in the main section, which was broad and dirt-floored. To their left were the tack rooms and the horse stalls. To their right was a door leading into the milk room, which was filled with all the usual junk: lawn mowers, bicycles, tin cans, jam jars, and chain saws. Confident they were alone, Max circled back to the main room and led the way up into the loft.

"Oh, hey, Mouser!" Max whispered, after nearly stepping on the familiar black cat. It sniffed Max's outstretched fingers, then coiled back into a hiss. With a yelp, it disappeared behind a crate and howled. The rest of the barn cats fled the loft like rats leaving a sinking ship.

"That was weird," said Natalia.

"Mouser's always been weird."

The Griffins piled onto the mountain of hay bales, making sure their flashlights couldn't be seen through the loose sideboards. "Well, so far so good," Harley said.

"And we're dry," Natalia added, wiping her wet hands on her jeans. She took off her shoes and wiggled her toes. "Or we will be. My socks feel like oatmeal. Anyone bring an extra pair?"

Ernie dug through his pack, then whimpered.

"What's wrong?"

"I only have one candy bar left. Agh! What was I thinking? It's times like these I hate being a changeling. I mean, I love eating. But why does it have to be every second?" He wasn't exaggerating. Ernie's faerie metabolism burned through calories. And if he didn't get enough calories, he passed out.

"Not that I mind carrying you," Harley said, "but you don't always smell so good."

"Hardy har har." Ernie snorted. "And it's my changeling medicine that smells bad, not me. Speaking of which, I didn't bring any dragon dung tea with me, Natalia...."

Natalia looked over at Max with concern. Hunger was one thing, but this was serious. If Ernie didn't have his special tea, his changeling blood would start to take over. Good-bye Ernie, hello monster—or whatever it was he might become. Nobody would know for sure until it actually happened. "We'll get you some more. Don't you worry, Ernest."

"Fine. But I'm still starving. First chance I get, I'm raiding his grandma's refrigerator."

"Oh no, you're not," Max said.

Natalia stretched her damp toes. "You know what bothers me about this whole thing? Paragon Engines only work in pairs. The one we went through in our world had to be connected to one in another world. But instead, we were dumped off in the woods like a sack of unwanted kittens. It doesn't make any sense."

"The Paragon Engine is just a big clockwork computer, and computers have glitches," said Harley, an engineering genius. There wasn't anything he couldn't learn or couldn't build. He sure didn't look the boy-scientist part, though. A head taller than most boys his age, he fit the action-hero description much better than Ernie did.

"A glitch?" asked Natalia. "A glitch just wiped out a month of our lives? Is that what you call a glitch?"

"A month is better than dead," said Max bleakly. "Which is what Logan, Brooke, and Raven might be." He sighed. "I feel horrible. Like somehow it's my fault they were left behind." He stood up and paced the floor. "Don't you guys ever think about it? I mean, what we are and what we do? Nothing's simple anymore. And no one is safe. Don't you just ever wish we could go back before everything got so crazy? Before we met the Templar? Before I found the *Codex*?" He paused, his voice growing quiet. "Before Dad left…"

The Griffins regarded Max silently. He was a great leader. The bravest of the brave, and the truest of the true. They'd been through thick and thin together. Each of the Griffins had had these same thoughts. They knew. They understood in a way that only the very best of friends could.

"Max," said Natalia, placing a hand on his shoulder, "we were trying to save the world. And if you haven't noticed, the world's still here. That means that somehow, whatever it was we did, it worked. There's every chance in the world they are alive. Just wait and see. In the morning, everything will look different. I promise."

Max nodded. He was exhausted. Too tired to think. They all were. Maybe Natalia was right. Maybe things would be better after all. They turned off their flashlights, and the Grey Griffins went to sleep one by one.

DISCOVERIES

Max awoke to the sound of a car engine rumbling to life. He rolled off the bale of hay, nearly kicking Ernie in the head, and sprang to look out. It was Grandma Caliburn. He caught just a glimpse as she pulled out of the white gravel driveway.

"Did you see her?" asked Natalia as she joined Max.

"Sure looked like her," he replied with a smile. He never realized how relieved this fact would make him feel. And what if things had turned out just fine for everyone? Maybe Logan was out there somewhere, tuning up his Ferrari's engine. Maybe Brooke was curled up in a chair with her favorite book. Maybe everything had worked out after all. Then Max spotted Ernie popping a hard-boiled egg into his mouth.

"Hey, where'd you get that?"

"From your grandma's kitchen—where do you think? She should really lock her door. It's not safe."

"Ernie! I told you not to do that. What if someone saw you?"

Ernie brought out a tray of carrot sticks and gnawed away. "I don't think so. I'm pretty fast. You should try your Skyfire, Max. I bet you are all powered up, too."

Max looked down at his magical ring—the *Codex Spiritus.* A little more awake now, he could definitely sense something had changed. Was it the enchanted Skyfire that coursed through his veins? Or perhaps his shape-shifting ring, which could turn into a gauntlet of power or a magical book? Max would have to figure it out. "So inside the house—it's all the same?" he asked.

"Looked the same to me. Man, I love the way your grandma always keeps the carrots so crispy in the water tray." He munched a dozen sticks in rapid succession. "I was only in the kitchen. Want me to go back? There's a pecan pie on the counter I had my eye on." Before Max could answer, Ernie disappeared...and reappeared again. His careless smile had vanished, and his hands were behind his back.

"What's the matter?" asked Harley. "What have you got there?"

Ernie squirmed. "I, ah...here!" He thrust a photograph

into Harley's hand. In it, Harley saw himself, standing next to his mother. Beside them stood a man Harley had never seen before. "Check the writing on the back," Ernie prompted meekly.

The Eisensteins. Summer at Lake Waconia. Harley, Candi, and Henry.

"Holy smokes, Harley!" Max gasped. "That's your missing dad! You look just like him."

Harley said nothing. His finger traced the figures. He'd never known his father. Never even seen a picture.

"Henry," Natalia read aloud. "That's a really nice name." She studied Harley closely and saw a frown forming.

"What sort of sick joke is this?" Harley growled.

"Guys," Ernie said, "that's not all." He pulled out a newspaper clipping. It was a picture of all four Griffins standing together on the grounds of Iron Bridge Academy. They were dressed in their monster-hunting gear and looked very grim. More grim, however, was the headline: MISSING TEENS PRONOUNCED DEAD.

"Dead?" exclaimed Max.

"Well, I certainly don't remember this picture being taken," said Natalia. "Even if it was, how do you explain the earrings in that picture? My ears aren't even pierced!"

"Keep reading," Ernie said.

Harley Davidson Eisenstein, Natalia Felicia Anastasia Romanov, Grayson Maximillian Sumner III, and Ernest Bartholomew Tweeny—the intrepid Agent Thunderbolt—have been declared dead by the Avalon crimes unit. The four teens went missing on December 24 last year while on assignment with the Templar. An anonymous tip led investigators to Sumner's bodyguard, a man known only by the name Logan. The man was questioned, but he denied involvement, then injured several officers—including Sheriff Wilfred Oxley—in his escape. At this time, the bodyguard is still at large and considered extremely dangerous.

Ernie sat down and sighed. "I feel so weird. Is this what it's supposed to feel like when you're dead? Why would Logan kill me? Do you think he was mad because we left them behind?"

"Wait," said Max. "I don't get it. December twenty-fourth? Is this the future, or the past?"

Natalia scanned the clipping again. "Neither. You're totally missing the point."

"What do you mean?"

"The photo. It was taken in front of Iron Bridge Academy, right? But this is the Avalon newspaper. Last I knew, no one in Avalon knew Iron Bridge existed, except us. They aren't supposed to know about the Templar, about monster-hunting, and they certainly shouldn't know Ernie is called Agent Thunderbolt."

Max's and Natalia's eyes locked. They spoke at the same time: "This isn't our world!"

"You mean the Paragon Engine worked?" asked Ernie.

Natalia looked up from the newspaper clipping. "It gets weirder. This paper calls itself the *New Avalon Times*. And look, there're advertisements on the other side for dwarf-made furniture and pixie-dust elixirs. I don't know what weird, parallel world we just discovered, but magic isn't a secret here. It's as normal as a box of Cheerios." Natalia quietly scribbled some notes into her *Book of Clues*—her pink detective notebook that had been with her on every mission.

"Once Grandma discovers the missing food," said Max, "she'll call the cops. We need to find someplace else to hide until we figure this out."

"Do you have a place in mind?" asked Harley.

"If the Griffins here are dead, no one will be looking for us in our old tree fort, right?"

"Maybe we should take a look around town first," said Ernie. "Just to see how much has changed. I can do it. No one will see me."

"We can't take any chances on getting caught, Ernie," said Natalia. "We should stay together, at least until we know more."

They agreed, and after Ernie gathered up enough food for all of them, they crept out of the loft and through the back door, and tromped down an old, familiar path back to the Old Woods, where they'd hide out until dark. This was the very path that the other Griffins might once have taken. They were dead now. As Max regarded the well-worn footprints, he shivered. If the other Griffins could be killed, then so could they.

When the sun went down, the Griffins snuck out of their hiding place in the Old Woods and took the dusty road leading toward the outskirts of town.

"I still don't understand why we're taking the long way around the woods," said Ernie. "There's a shortcut to the tree house from your grandma's."

Natalia sighed. "Like I've told you already, Ernest, there's no telling what's lurking in those woods at night. With your speed, maybe you'd be all right. But the rest of us are safer walking *around* the woods. Trust me."

They soon crossed a pungent field of alfalfa and struck the road leading past Max's house. They hadn't meant to come this way. But Max found his footsteps pulling him along. He wanted to see his house. He wanted to see who lived there.

"Into the ditch!" Max hissed. A moment later, a strange car swept by, a mechanical horse and carriage that floated on a field of blue energy. The driver wore a topcoat and top hat, while the passengers inside were hidden by smoky glass.

As the Griffins clambered out of the ditch, Max smiled. "I'd expect something like that in New Victoria. But in Avalon?"

Dear Reader,

Whatever you do, do NOT read the books in my *New York Times* bestselling Secret Series. I know they are full of exciting adventures and puzzling mysteries about evil villains and a secret society—but all these things are strictly confidential—and dangerous! Oh no, have I accidentally tempted you to read them? Well, do so if you must, but remember: You've been warned!

pseudonymous bosch

Book #1

Book #2

Book #3

Book #4

Book #5

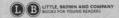